RANDALL SILVIS

INCIDENT ON TEN-RIGHT ROAD

Incident on Ten-Right Road © 2019 Randall Silvis

This is a work of fiction. Names, characters, places, and incidents are products of the author's imagination or are used factiously and are not to be construed as real. Any resemblance to actual events, locations, organizations, or person, living or dead, is entirely coincidental.

All rights reserved. No part of this book may be used or reproduced in any manner whatsoever without written permission, except in the case of brief quotations embodied in articles and reviews.
.
For more information contact:
Riverdale Avenue Books/Dagger Imprint
5676 Riverdale Avenue
Riverdale, NY 10471
www.riverdaleavebooks.com

Design by www.formatting4U.com
Cover photo by Johannes Plenio on Unsplash

Digital ISBN: 9781626015104
Trade ISBN 9781626015111
Hardcover ISBN 9781626015128

The short Story "Snap" originally appeared in the *Ellery Queen Mystery Magazine*.

First edition, June 2019

Praise for Randall Silvis' Work

A LONG WAY DOWN, Sourcebooks Landmark
Ryan DeMarco Mystery series Book #3, forthcoming June 2019

"Silvis is at it again, striving for a blend of crime story and literature, mutilated bodies and lapidary prose."
—*Booklist*

"Words cannot adequately describe this novel and Silvis' beautiful writing. He infuses lush, poetic and evocative descriptions [with] plenty of action and suspense to drive this thriller; however, Silvis has a unique way of reaching down into the soul of his haunted characters... There is darkness, suspense, action, misery, death, violence. Despair and sorrow. But there is also good, beauty, joy, hope, compassion and light. A series not to be missed!"
—*JDC MustReadBooks*

FIRST THE THUNDER, Thomas & Mercer
AN AMAZON TOP TEN BESTSELLER

"Randall Silvis is an author's author. Those who write for a living (or aspire to do so) could hardly do better than to study his significant body of work, which has been critically acclaimed and recognized throughout the world... *First the Thunder* is an impressive work—one of this year's best—

by an author who never disappoints. Set aside a long evening and start reading. You won't want to stop, even as you reach the end of the story."

—*Bookreporter.com*

"Silvis is a self-made master of fiction. His writing elicits visceral imagery, palpable conflict, and a core understanding of the human condition. *First the Thunder* is no different. A redemptive story of heartbreaking brilliance, *First the Thunder* is a must-have on your library shelves."

—Bestselling author Susan Wingate, host of *Dialogue: Between the Lines* radio podcast

ONLY THE RAIN, Thomas & Mercer
AN AMAZON FIRST READS SELECTION
AN AMAZON #1 BESTSELLER

"A gifted storyteller, a master of complicated human souls, Randall Silvis brings readers…a remarkable heartrending blend of literary, drama, mystery, suspense, and psychological thriller. Most importantly, as with all Randall Silvis books, *Only the Rain* is thought-provoking and insightful. The author's lyrical prose is spellbinding, drawing you into the raw and emotional world of his characters."

—*LibraryThing.com*

"*Only The Rain* is noir at its best—dark and tender, beautiful and brutal. A classic crime novel for the modern age."

—Rebecca Drake, best-selling author of *Just Between Us*

WALKING THE BONES, Sourcebooks Landmark
A BEST BOOK OF 2018: JDC MUST READ BOOKS

"Silvis' deeply satisfying sequel to *Two Days Gone* (is) filled with the psychological language of memory and

dreams (and) heart-pounding moments of suspense.... Silvis smoothly blends moments of exquisite beauty into a sea of darker emotion to create a moving story heavy with the theme of the 'past is never past.'"
—*Publisher's Weekly* starred review

"*Walking the Bones* is a tour de force. I read this novel in one long, breathless gasp. Outstanding!"
—Karen Dionne, international bestselling author of *The Marsh King's Daughter*

TWO DAYS GONE, Sourcebooks Landmark
FINALIST FOR THE HAMMETT PRIZE FOR LITERARY EXCELLENCE IN CRIME WRITING

"A gripping new literary thriller... The fact that this book will be marketed as genre fiction is misleading; it's more than that. It's literature posing as a mystery...one of the best reading investments you will make this year."
—*BookPage*

"...a suspenseful, literary thriller that will resonate with readers long after the book is finished. A terrific choice for Dennis Lehane fans."
—*Library Journal* starred review

"(In this) chilly suspense novel...Silvis tells his parallel stories... with finely tuned sensitivity."
—*New York Times Book Review*

THE BOY WHO SHOOTS CROWS, Penguin/Berkley
A BARNES & NOBLE BOOKSELLER'S PICK
EDITOR'S PICK JANUARY MAGAZINE

"(A) stunning, elegiac tale of love and loss...."
—*Minneapolis Star Tribune*

"A masterpiece... a work of genius, a novel so filled with such immense imagery and strength as to make you catch your breath.... I cannot recommend this book more strongly."
—*Over My Dead Body* Magazine

"Poetically written, finely-wrought, richly imagined... a literary thriller of the first order. Randall Silvis gets to the hearts and souls of his characters like few other, if any, novelists...."
—*New York Times* bestselling author John Lescroart

IN A TOWN CALLED MUNDOMUERTO, Omnidawn
EDITOR'S CHOICE TOP TEN BEST BOOKS OF 2007, SFSITE.COM

"This beautiful, melancholy novel from Silvis unfolds as a timeless Central American seaside fable... A masterful storyteller, Silvis doesn't waste a word in this tale about 'the tart nectar of memory's flower.'"
—*Publishers Weekly* starred review

HEART SO HUNGRY, Knopf Canada, Vintage Canada
A TORONTO GLOBE & MAIL
BEST BOOK OF THE YEAR
REPUBLISHED AS *NORTH OF UNKNOWN*
BY THE LYONS PRESS

"Through Silvis' masterful research, empathetic sensitivity, and skilled storytelling, readers are treated to a tantalizing adventure that celebrates one woman's steadfast love and uncommon courage."
—*Booklist*

"Vivid, comprehensive, and compelling.... *Heart So Hungry* is a notable addition to the literature of northern exploration."
— *The Globe and Mail*

DISQUIET HEART, Thomas Dunne Books
  EDITOR'S PICK *JANUARY MAGAZINE*
  RE-RELEASED BY SOURCEBOOKS LANDMARK 2017

"There have been, in the past five or six years, several books written with Edgar Allan Poe as a protagonist. None has brought the man so clearly to life as Mr. Silvis has done."
—*The Blue Iris Review*

"Atmospheric and cleverly researched, (*Disquiet Heart*) races to a sparkling denouement."
—*Publishers Weekly*

"Moody, emotionally tortured, and convincingly atmospheric, (*Disquiet Heart* provides) a graphically described descent into Poe's opiate addictions."
—*Kirkus Reviews*

ON NIGHT'S SHORE, Thomas Dunne Books
  NEW YORK TIMES
  RECOMMENDED READING LIST
  RE-RELEASED BY SOURCEBOOKS LANDMARK 2017

"A riveting tale of murder and betrayal.... *On Night's Shore* drips with descriptive power."
—*The New York Post*

MYSTICUS, Wolfhawk Books

"*Mysticus* is that rarest of rare books, the one that stays in the brain long after the hands have put it down, the book that heaves the heart as much as it haunts the head, the book for the longest of the long runs that yet remain."
—Lee K. Abbott, author of *Living after Midnight*

"Lyrical and parodic, philosophical and stylish and elegant. A tour de force. *Mysticus* is Silvis's most important novel to date…a book that washes away genre like passing steps on wet sand; a book where literature and thought are the heroes."
—*Collages & Bricolages,*
An International Literary Magazine

DEAD MAN FALLING, Carroll & Graf

"A superbly written and eminently readable crime novel."
—*Booklist*

"Randall Silvis's voice moves with a subtle depth and compassion that entrances the reader, drawing one deep within this absorbing narrative. Very highly recommended."
—*WordWeaving,com*

UNDER THE RAINBOW, Permanent Press

"A funny, engaging journey toward some pretty sweet truths."
—*The New York Times Book Review*

"One of the funniest books of the year. It is about human resiliency as much as human oddness, and its message is ultimately upbeat. Highly recommended."
—*Library Journal*

AN OCCASIONAL HELL
PERMANENT PRESS, BALLANTINE BOOKS
FINALIST FOR THE HAMMETT PRIZE FOR LITERARY EXCELLENCE IN CRIME WRITING

"The storyline is riveting—complex, convoluted, and compelling; Silvis engages the reader from first word to last. I couldn't put this novel down."
—*Los Angeles Reader*

"*An Occasional Hell* is a first-rate novel, a fast-paced, highly suspenseful murder mystery so very well written that it brings new literary distinction to the genre. A stunning performance by a writer of exceptional talent."
—John W. Aldridge, author of
Talents and Technicians

EXCELSIOR, Henry Holt

"A funny and touching fable (transformed by) the author's gift for tart comic dialogue and screwball invention. A ruefully comic, entertaining and ultimately impressive first novel."
—*Publishers Weekly*

"Splendidly funny scenes. (The main character) is ingratiating and despicable; he has a complex appeal to the best and worst in human nature."
—*Pittsburgh Press*

THE LUCKIEST MAN IN THE WORLD
UNIVERSITY OF PITTSBURGH PRESS, AVON BOOKS
WINNER OF THE DRUE HEINZ LITERATURE PRIZE

"Silvis is an engaging storyteller... seductively entertaining. (His) ear for natural speech and eye for the ways individuals accommodate themselves to their perceived reality is combined with the dark humor that has the pulse of life."
—*Publishers Weekly*

"Wonderful stories. Randall Silvis is a masterful storyteller."
—*New York Times Book Review*

*For my sons, Bret and Nathan
heart of my soul
soul of my heart*

Table of Contents

Incident on Ten-Right Road	1
Watch and Listen	118
A Little Rest	136
Snap	141
On the Verge	173
And Sometimes the Abyss Winks at You	219

Author's Note

This collection of crime stories includes scenes, images, and language that might be considered graphic and unsettling, and is not suitable for immature readers. The title novella is a prequel to my Ryan DeMarco Mystery Series; its action takes place eight years prior to the action of the first novel in that series, *Two Days Gone*.

The story "Snap" originally appeared in the *Ellery Queen Mystery Magazine*.

If you enjoy these stories, please let others know about them.

An Amazon review would be greatly appreciated.

Incident on Ten-Right Road

Case # 20-N-09AC-20-2009/08/12
Victim: Meghan Malinda Fletcher, 19, Caucasian

Investigator: Sgt. Ryan DeMarco, Pennsylvania State Police Troop D, Mercer County PA

The following case notes and interview transcripts (with additional notes recorded immediately post-interview, or sometimes post my transcription of the interview) have been prepared for my own personal reference. Pertinent pauses and sounds have been indicated in the transcript. No other use of this document is authorized without my written consent.

On the afternoon of August 13th, after conducting an initial investigation into the incident occurring in the early morning hours of August 12th at 201 Ten-Right Road in French Creek Township, Mercer County, Pennsylvania, French Creek Township Chief of Police Lloyd Melvin contacted the State Police to request assistance from their evidence recovery team. Not long afterward, he indicated to Troop D Station Commander Lukovich that a full homicide investigation was not something his three-man department could handle effectively. Commander Lukovich assigned the case to me. The following narrative was reconstructed from a verbal summary provided to me by Chief Melvin.

On the evening of August 11th, from approximately 7:20 p.m.-12:40 a.m., Meghan Fletcher (19) and Tad (Theodore) Blyler (25), both residents of Mercer County, were observed by several individuals at the Taco King Grille on Route 22 one half-mile south of Hubbard, Ohio. They had dinner in a booth in the restaurant section, then moved to the barroom where they danced and played pool until leaving for home.

According to bartender Shirley Eppinger (48), Fletcher consumed two cans of Diet 7-Up while in the barroom area; Blyler consumed eight shots of Jack Daniels. The restaurant receipt shows an additional soft drink for Ms. Fletcher, two draft beers for Blyler. Blyler later denied to Chief Melvin that he had shared any of his whiskey with Fletcher, but admitted that "she might have sneaked a sip or two" when he wasn't looking.

Two other customers (Laitshaw and Pizzuti, on separate Individuals Questioned Contact list) stated that Fletcher and Blyler argued prior to leaving the establishment for the evening. The argument started in the pool table area, but was continued outside after first Fletcher, then Blyler exited the building. The argument apparently concerned Fletcher conversing with her former boyfriend, Alex Gessler (21). Gessler and Fletcher ended their relationship shortly after his graduation from West Middlesex High School; Fletcher and Blyler started dating that same summer. However, according to Melissa (Missy) Cochran (19), who identified herself to Chief Melvin as Fletcher's best friend, Fletcher continued to "hook up with" Gessler on the sly whenever he was home from Denison College,

Incident on Ten-Right Road

which was approximately once a month and over school holidays.

At the time of her death, Ms. Fletcher was a part-time student at Mercer County Community College, and worked approximately 25 hours per week at the local 7-Eleven convenience store.

Cochran also stated that Blyler was "jealous as hell" and "would have dropped Alex on the spot" had he known about the continuing relationship between Gessler and Fletcher. Blyler is a former Amish, having left the community after rumspringa; he has lived on his own for the past three years. He is employed as a carpenter with Bryce Construction.

Eppinger stated, and was corroborated by Laitshaw and Pizzuti, that after the argument outside the establishment, which lasted for approximately 10 minutes, Blyler returned to pay the bar tab. He and Fletcher then drove away in his pickup truck. The time was approximately 12:40 a.m. Eppinger stated that Blyler did not appear drunk but "he did look mad enough at somebody to do some damage."

At approximately 1:11 a.m., Blyler's truck was seen pulling into the driveway at 201 Ten-Right Road by Richard Mark Hickman (63), resident of 100 Ten-Right Road, the only neighbor of Meghan Fletcher and her mother Junie (36). The houses face each other across opposite sides of the road. Ten-Right Road is a gravel lane approximately 100 yards off old Route 68 in French Creek Township; it dead-ends at a small gravel parking lot at the entrance to State Game Lands #42.

Hickman is a retired science teacher at French Creek Area High School, from which Fletcher and Cochran graduated. He stated to Chief Melvin that he was in his side yard watching the Perseid meteor shower through a pair of astronomical binoculars mounted on a tripod when Blyler dropped Fletcher off at her home, and that she climbed out of his truck "in a hurry," then ran up onto the porch, appeared to fish a key out of a hanging basket containing a spider plant, unlocked the front door, returned the key to the basket, and entered the house. Blyler's pickup truck then "tore off with a godawful squeal of tires." The time was "precisely 1:11," according to Hickman. Shortly after that, he said, the lights went out in the Fletcher home. He continued to watch for meteors for another half-hour or so, then went inside to bed. He heard no other anomalous or suspicious sounds that night, and slept until approximately 8:00 a.m. the following morning.

Junie Fletcher, mother of the victim, later stated to Chief Melvin that she was in bed but awake when her daughter arrived home. She did not rise out of bed or speak to her daughter but took note of the time, which corroborates her neighbor's statement: 1:11 a.m.

Junie Fletcher stated that she rose from bed at 5:05 that morning, washed and dressed for the morning shift at the Belmont Diner on route 19, a brisk 20-minute walk from her home. At approximately 5:25 she scribbled a note for her daughter and left it under the saltshaker on the kitchen counter: *Meg—I'm running late and its raining so I'm taken the truck. Besides your grounded. One day for every minute late just like I said would happen. C u around 2. Love you!!!* According to Chief Melvin, the rain started at approximately 4:00 a.m. that morning and "kept drizzling" until approximately 6:30 a.m.

At approximately 11:20 that same morning,

Incident on Ten-Right Road

Missy Cochran, after placing several unanswered calls and texts to Meghan Fletcher, drove to the Fletcher residence. Aware of Junie's work schedule, Cochran was not surprised when her knocks on the front door went unanswered. She then retrieved the door key from the hanging basket, unlocked the door, returned the key to the basket, and went inside.

When questioned by Chief Melvin as to why she went to the Fletcher home that morning, Cochran stated that she was eager "and a little worried" to find out how Fletcher's date had gone, and that Fletcher had not responded to Cochran's texts and calls earlier that morning. She suggested that Fletcher had been drinking the previous night, an assumption based on "the way she sounded" when she telephoned Cochran "a half-hour or so after midnight" and asked if Cochran could come to Taco King and pick her up. "But I could hear him (Blyler) telling her no, damn it, that he was taking her home. And pretty soon she told me to forget about it and hung up."

As noted above, Cochran entered the Fletcher home at approximately 11:20 a.m. Saturday morning. When Meghan did not respond to her friend's calls, Cochran proceeded to Meghan's bedroom and opened the door. She found the deceased lying on her stomach, wearing only a pair of black thong panties, her left leg hanging off the bed between the bed and the wall. Her throat had been slit from just below her left ear to the jawbone below her right ear, which, along with the blood pattern as observed by Chief Melvin and the evidence recovery team, suggests that the assailant approached from Meghan's left as she was sleeping on her back, and that upon awakening she attempted to roll away to her right, which caused the knife to sever the left carotid artery but to exit prior to completing a full arc.

Cochran's telephone call to 911 was logged in at 11:37 that morning. When asked by Chief Melvin why she allowed 17 minutes to pass before placing the call, Cochran responded, "I think I passed out for a little bit."

No weapon was found on the premises. No sign of forced entry. Junie Fletcher reported that nothing appeared to be missing or out of place in her daughter's bedroom.

Awaiting forensics reports on Blyler's truck and the Fletcher home. Follow-up interviews to proceed immediately. August 13, 5:54 p.m.

Notes:

- That key in the hanging basket is concerning. How many people knew it was there?
- Start the interviews with Missy, who might be the person who best knew the victim and her other associates. Why did Missy wait so long to call 9-1-1?
- Record all interviews. And make sure ambient noise, especially wind, is minimal or else the recording will be worthless.
- Add Meghan's boss and coworkers at 7-Eleven to list of potential interview subjects.

Interview with Melissa Cochran

DeMarco: This interview with Melissa Cochran, also known as Missy, is taking place on August 13th, 7:03 p.m., in the dining room of the Cochran home at 316 East Venango Street. Missy's mother, Mrs. Cochran—

Patti Cochran: Please. I'm Patti.

DeMarco: Missy's mother, Patti Cochran, is also present, though she will not be taking part in this interview. If an interview with Mrs. Cochran is needed, it will be conducted separately.

Patti: There's nothing I can tell you about what happened except what Missy told me. What I can say is that she was home here all night long. She never once left the house.

DeMarco: Thank you. We'll, uh—

Patti: I will swear on a stack of bibles that she never left the house.

DeMarco: That won't be necessary. If we could keep it to just your daughter and me from here on in?

Patti: Absolutely. Can I get you some coffee or anything?

DeMarco: I'm good. Thank you.

Patti: Okay then. Do you mind if I get some?

DeMarco: That's fine. But if you could just…not talk during the interview?

Patti: Not another word. I just wanted to make that one thing clear. She was home. All night.

DeMarco: Thank you. *(short pause)* How are you, Missy?

Missy Cochran: I'm all right, I guess. Considering that my best friend has been butchered.

(long pause)

DeMarco: Let's start with the phone call you received from Meghan Friday night. When she called you from the Taco King.

Missy: Okay. What do you want to know?

DeMarco: What was the purpose of the call?

Missy: She asked me to come pick her up. She said Tad was being an asshole again.

DeMarco: In what way?

Missy: Same as always. He gets loud and crude. I guess he told her she needed a good punch in the face. I wouldn't have wanted him to take me home after that either.

DeMarco: Yet she ended up going home with him after all.

Missy: Unfortunately.

DeMarco: Did she explain to you why he was upset with her that night?

Missy: All she said was that Alex was there, which I knew he was going to be, except that he was being a pussy and wouldn't stand up for her. Two losers, she called them. But then I could hear Tad telling her to hang up and go get in the truck.

DeMarco: Did you hear anything else?

Missy: It kind of sounded like maybe he grabbed the phone out of her hand.

DeMarco: You heard the sounds of a struggle?

Incident on Ten-Right Road

Missy: Yeah but it didn't last long. I called her back right away but it went to voicemail. And then a couple minutes later she sent me a text saying she was fine.

Patti Cochran: Show him the text, why don't you.

Missy: You want to see it?

DeMarco: I was going to ask.

Missy: Sure, no problem.

(pause)

DeMarco: Thank you. Would you mind reading it out loud for the recording?

Missy: The text says, 'I'm fine, don't worry. Headed home with loser #1. Ttyl.'

DeMarco: Loser #1 being...?

Missy: Tad, I assumed. She'd never called Alex a loser before. Not to me anyway.

(pause)

DeMarco: So the next morning, you called and texted her several times?

Missy: Well yeah, I wanted to find out what all had happened that night. But she wouldn't pick up. Eventually I started getting worried about her and went over to her place.

DeMarco: According to Chief Melvin, you let yourself into the house?

Missy: Yep. With the key in the hanging basket.

DeMarco: You had used that key before?

Missy: Lots of times. I mean, sometimes I would get there a few minutes before Meggie got home from class or work, and I'd just let myself in. Her and Junie knew about it, of course. They didn't care.

(pause)

DeMarco: I would like to talk now about your initial discovery of the body. Are you okay with that?

Missy: I don't like it, but I can do it, I guess. If it helps you catch the guy.

DeMarco: You let yourself into the house, then opened the bedroom door and—

Missy: I called out once or twice from the living room first.

DeMarco: But when she didn't respond, you went to her bedroom.

Missy: Her door was closed, which was unusual. It was almost never closed that I know of. Both her and Junie sleep with their bedroom doors open. Always have.

DeMarco: So you opened the door and...

Missy: I saw her on the bed. And I saw the blood everywhere.

DeMarco: Can you tell me more specifically what you saw?

Missy: She was laying facedown on her bed, wearing nothing but her panties. And there was blood all underneath her and even up against the wall.

DeMarco: Did you see this from the threshold, or were you inside the room at that time?

Missy: I might have taken a couple steps inside. I'm not all that sure. Everything went sort of weird when I saw her like that.

DeMarco: Weird in what way?

Missy: All dreamy like, I guess. Like a nightmare.

DeMarco: But you did eventually approach the bed.

Missy: It was like, that's not even real. I mean, the blood was darker than I thought it should have been. I figured she was playing some kind of sick joke

Incident on Ten-Right Road

on me. But the smell was… Do you know how blood smells? All thick and funny?

DeMarco: Like a handful of old copper pennies.

Missy: Exactly!

DeMarco: And then what did you do?

Missy: Yeah…well…I guess I touched her. Felt how cold and still she was. Like I said to the other guy, it's all pretty blurry.

DeMarco: You said that to Chief Melvin?

Missy: Yeah, the first guy. The sheriff or whatever he is.

DeMarco: And when did you call 911?

Missy: It felt like right away. But apparently there's 17 minutes missing somewhere. All I can figure is I must have passed out.

Patti Cochran: She hates the sight of blood. Always has.

DeMarco: Did you try to roll her over, take a closer look?

Missy: I just told you I passed out, didn't I?

Patti Cochran: Just answer the man's questions, Missy!

Missy: Sorry.

DeMarco: When you passed out, how, and where, did you fall?

Missy: Now how would I know that if I was passed out?

Patti: Missy!

Missy: Well how would I? This is gruesome! I don't even like talking about this. What do you think it was like being there?

DeMarco: Where were you when you regained consciousness?

Missy: On the floor beside the bed.

DeMarco: And then what did you do?

Missy: I got up onto my knees and looked at her again.

DeMarco: Looked at her how?

Missy: Just looked at her. Like I still couldn't believe what I was seeing.

DeMarco: Did you touch her in any way?

Missy: No. I don't think so. I really don't know, but I don't think I did.

DeMarco: And then what?

Missy: You know how it gets when something happens that you just totally don't believe could happen? How it gets all slow and heavy-like?

DeMarco: I do.

Missy: So, second by second? I don't know what I did. I do remember taking out my phone and dialing 911. And then just kind of sitting down on the floor again until the sirens started. I guess that's when I got up and went out and stood on the porch.

DeMarco: You don't remember how you got the blood on your hands and on your T-shirt?

Patti: She probably fell onto the bed when she passed out.

DeMarco: Mrs. Cochran. Please.

Patti: But it makes sense, though, doesn't it? She saw the blood, got all woozy and fell on top of Meghan, felt herself sliding off the bed and tried to grab hold of something to stop herself, and that's how she got the blood on her.

Missy: That sounds exactly like what happened. Besides, there wasn't that much of it on me. That Melvin guy told me the blood was dried solid under

Meggie, and that's how he knew I hadn't done it. He said it looked to him like I got a little on my hands and then wiped my hands on my shirt.

Patti: He made her take off the shirt so he could have it. Gave her one of Meggie's to put on. Which kind of freaked her out, of course, having to put on her dead friend's T-shirt like that.

DeMarco: Mrs. Cochran, if you would just allow me to conduct the interview without interruptions....

Patti: Well I know my daughter, and you couldn't pay her a million dollars to hurt anybody, let alone her best friend!

DeMarco: Mrs. Cochran. I have agreed to let you to sit here with us as a courtesy. But your daughter is over 18. I am not required to have a parent present. So I'm going to ask you to move to the kitchen or to the living room so that we can get through this interview without any more interruptions.

Patti: You're going to chase me out of my own dining room?

DeMarco: My other option is to escort Missy to the barracks and question her there.

Missy: Just leave, Mom. I'm a big girl. I don't need you watching over me.

Patti: I can't believe I'm being ordered around in my own house.

Scraping sounds. A couple of banging noises from the kitchen.

DeMarco: Let's go back to you regaining consciousness in the bedroom, Missy. Can you remember seeing anything unusual or out of place?

Missy: Other than my best friend's dead body, you mean?

DeMarco: Yes, other than that.

Missy: Like what, for instance?

DeMarco: Anything out of the ordinary.

Missy: Give me a hint. What am I supposed to have seen? *(pause)* Oh, I get it. The knife. No, I did not see a knife.

DeMarco: You're certain of that?

Missy: I know what a knife looks like. There wasn't one there. Period.

DeMarco: When did you become aware of the blood on your hands and shirt?

Missy *(after a long pause)*: When the paramedic guy asked if I was cut somewhere.

DeMarco: And then what did you do?

Missy: I was shocked to see it, I guess. I think I probably tried to clean my hands on my shirt. Or because my hands felt sticky, I don't really know.

DeMarco: Is there anything else at all that you remember about your time in the bedroom? Anything else you did while you were in there?

Missy: I have no idea what that would be. I came to, I saw her, I called 911. I heard the sirens and went out onto the porch. Didn't somebody tell you that's where I was when they showed up?

Several seconds of silence.

Patti *(from the kitchen)*: Are you finished in there?

DeMarco: Missy, what can you tell me about Tad Blyler?

Missy: He's an asshole. What else do you want to know?

DeMarco: Could you be a little more specific?

Missy: He's loud and vulgar mostly. Uses the c-word all the time, which I despise.

Incident on Ten-Right Road

DeMarco: And yet Meghan was dating him.

Missy: People hook up, you know? I mean, who she really loved was Alex. Always did, ever since 10th grade. And a part of her always hoped they would end up together.

DeMarco: Why weren't they together?

Missy: Because he was going off to college and she still had her senior year to do. And she knew she was never going to be able to go to college, not to Denison anyway. Not with her grades or her mother's income. So where would that put them? Him with a degree or two, her with nothing. It just seemed the right thing to do to cut him loose.

DeMarco: So it was her idea?

Missy: She figured if she didn't do it then, he'd do it later.

DeMarco: Yet they kept seeing each other.

Missy: Like I said, she never stopped loving him.

DeMarco: So how does Tad Blyler fit into all this?

Missy: Meg knew that Alex was having his fun at college. And she was okay with that. But she had needs too. I don't know why people think boys have a right to play around and girls don't.

DeMarco: So she was just playing around with Tad? Did he know that?

Missy: Tad Blyler isn't….

DeMarco: Isn't what, Missy?

Missy: I mean he's not bad to look at, I'll give him that. He's big and strong, even handsome in a rough kind of way. Plus, according to Meg he has all the right equipment and knows how to use it.

Patti *(from the kitchen)*: Missy! For God's sake!

Missy: Grow up, mother! But anyway, yeah, truth to tell, Tad's got a vacancy or two upstairs.

DeMarco: Meaning what?

Missy: He's got a hair-trigger temper, for one thing. And he's moody as shit. He misses the Amish way, he hates the Amish way, they're all a bunch of hypocrites, *we're* all a bunch of heathens…. Day to day you never know what it is he believes.

DeMarco: That doesn't explain to me why Meghan was involved with him. Just the opposite, in fact.

Missy *(after a pause):* I think her father was a lot like Tad is. Moody, you know? Unpredictable. Except that his problem wasn't with the Amish, it was with booze and fentanyl.

DeMarco: He was an addict?

Missy: You'd have to ask Junie about that. He took off whenever Meg was little. Personally, I think there might have been some other nasty stuff behind it all. The way he disappeared, I mean.

DeMarco: Nasty how?

Missy: With him and Meghan.

DeMarco: Sexual abuse?

Missy: All I'm saying is, she thought it might have happened. Thought she had a kind of memory of it. I mean, one day he's there, next day he's gone. And anytime she'd ask her mother about it, Junie would say, 'He's dead to us. Don't ever mention him again.'

DeMarco: So…if I'm understanding you correctly, you're saying that Meghan was attracted to Tad Blyler because he reminded her of her father.

Missy: She knew Tad was an asshole, make no mistake about that. She felt drawn to him, but at the

Incident on Ten-Right Road

same time she wanted rid of him. Personally I think that's why she took him to Taco King Friday night.

DeMarco: I need for you to explain that to me.

Missy: It's why she took him to Taco King when she knew Alex was going to be there.

DeMarco: She was engineering a confrontation?

Missy: Seems that way to me.

DeMarco: Did you discuss that with her?

Missy: Not in so many words. We were best friends and all, but still. It just wasn't like her to spill her guts to anybody. You always kinda had to read between the lines with her.

DeMarco: Can you remember what *was* said on the subject?

Missy: I said something like, 'Aren't you afraid of what will happen when the two of them run into each other?' And she just laughed and said, 'Whatever happens, happens.'

DeMarco: In your opinion, what did she want to happen?

Missy: Taco King isn't the kind of place Tad would normally take her. I mean it's not the Hilton or anything, but it's still a couple of steps above the kind of place he usually goes. I think she wanted him to feel out of place, surrounded by people he didn't know. And maybe, just maybe, she wanted somebody to beat the shit out of him when he started bad-mouthing people the way he always does. It would give her a reason to dump him finally.

DeMarco: Somebody like Alex?

Silence for three seconds.

DeMarco: The tape recorder can't hear nods, Missy.

Missy: Yes, somebody like Alex. I think she wanted to force him to stand up for her. To show whether he really cared about her or not.

DeMarco: Interesting relationship.

Half a minute of silence.

Missy: Are we done then?

DeMarco: What kind of relationship did Meghan and her mother have with their neighbor?

Missy: With Mr. Dick?

DeMarco: Mr. Hickman. I'm not familiar with a Mr. Dick.

Missy: They're the same guy. That's what we called him in high school. Behind his back, of course.

DeMarco: Because his first name is Richard?

Missy: If you say so.

DeMarco: Is there another reason?

Missy: Why else would you call somebody Mr. Dick?

DeMarco: Okay. So what I need from you, Missy, is to explain things. It's not my job to guess or speculate. It's my job, right now, to record everything you know that might be relevant to the death of your best friend.

Missy: You think that Mr. Dick, I mean Mr. Hickman, is relevant?

DeMarco: Based on what we know right now, he might have been the last person to see Meghan alive.

Missy: Geez, I never thought about that. (*pause*) We called him Mr. Dick because he was always, you know, trying to get students into his little room. Girl students.

DeMarco: What do you mean by 'little room'?"

Missy: It was this little room in the back of the lab.

Incident on Ten-Right Road

Patti *(from the kitchen)*: It used to be a darkroom! Back before digital cameras.

Missy: Yeah, and after that it was used mostly for storage. Stuff for the lab.

DeMarco: And Mr. Hickman would take female students in there alone?

Missy: Of course alone.

DeMarco: During class?

Missy: No, he wasn't that obvious about it. During study periods, after school, whenever he wasn't teaching a class.

DeMarco: And these were the rumors you heard?

Missy: It was common knowledge more than rumors.

DeMarco: He would take them in there for sex?

Missy: For screwing? I never heard that he screwed anybody in there. But I heard he got a lot of hand jobs. Maybe even blowjobs, for all I know.

DeMarco: Female students went in there willingly?

Missy: I can think of three that I know personally who did. Including Meghan.

DeMarco: She told you this?

Missy: More than once.

DeMarco: What exactly did she tell you?

Missy: That she gave him a hand job.

DeMarco: Why would she do that?

Missy: Why did any of them do it? For money or grades. With her it was grades.

Silence.

Missy: Look, she had this idea that if she could get on the Principal's list, she could get a scholarship somewhere. Maybe even where Alex was going. But that idea only lasted a couple of months. She was getting a D in Algebra and nothing higher than a C+ in most everything else. Chemistry and Art were the only A's she got that semester. An A-, actually. You couldn't get an A in chemistry unless you blew him.

DeMarco: Apparently the administration had no idea this was going on?

Patti *(from kitchen):* Everybody knew it! He'd been doing it for years!

A long silence.

Missy: *Now* are we done?

DeMarco: For the time being, yes. For tonight anyway, we're done.

Missy: Oh, wait a minute. You know about his retirement, right? Why he stopped teaching?

DeMarco: Tell me.

Missy: So, as the story goes, some ninth grader's mother got wind of what was going on. She told Hickman to quit his job or she was calling the police on him. And after that, he never came back to school.

DeMarco: Do you know who this mother is?

Missy: No idea.

DeMarco: How about you, Mrs. Cochran?

Patti *(from the kitchen)*: Wish like hell I did! I'd pin a medal on her.

Missy: I doubt if it stopped him, though. I know for a fact it didn't stop him from watching Meghan get undressed. He lives right across from her, you know.

DeMarco: Do you have any more details than that?

Missy: He's got this telescopy thing he watches her with. I mean watched, I guess. He takes it outside almost every night, even in the winter.

Incident on Ten-Right Road

DeMarco: This is according to Meghan?

Missy: I saw it happen! We'd spend nights at each other's place sometimes. A lot, in fact. You could see when those black thingies, the things you look through, I can't think of what you call them.

DeMarco: Lenses?

Missy: Right. You could see a reflection in the lenses sometimes when he turned them toward her house. She used to tease him by undressing in front of him. I mean she'd keep the sheer curtains closed, but with the light on in the room so he'd still get an eyeful.

Patti *(from the kitchen)*: You both did it, and you know it!

Missy: I always kept my panties on, though. She'd strip right down to nothing. Then we'd put the music on and dance in front of the curtain.

Patti: You girls got as much of a thrill out of it as he did!

Missy: That's not true! It's not. It was funny is all. Thinking about him over there whacking off when all he could see of us was the silhouettes.

DeMarco *(after a pause)*: I believe I have enough for tonight. Thank you for your cooperation.

Patti *(from kitchen)*: Now don't *you* go home thinking about young girls. You can come out here and have some coffee with me, if you want.

Missy: Mother, for God's sake!

End of interview.

Notes:
- I was still sufficiently troubled by Missy's time lapse between finding Meghan and calling 911 that I asked for a DNA sample. Plus the lab will

need to know who was in Meghan's bedroom and who wasn't. Missy readily agreed to the sampling. At the insistence of Patti Cochran, a sample was collected from her as well.
- Missy seemed a little too eager to paint Tad Blyler as a jerk. Could she have been jealous of him? Or…could she have been interested in him romantically, and jealous of Meghan?
- It might be productive to interview the two other female students whom Missy alleges to have had sexual contact with Mr. Hickman, if Missy will impart that information. But I will first try to corroborate the allegations from a more mature source.

Interview with Regis Madura

DeMarco: This interview with Mr. Regis Madura, principal of French Creek Area High School, is taking place in his office in the high school building on August 14th at 9:14 a.m. Thank you for meeting with me this morning, sir.

Madura: Call me Rege, please. I'm always happy to accommodate law enforcement. I'm assuming this has something to do with our former student, Ms. Fletcher? I pulled her records, just in case you want to see them.

DeMarco: I'll take a look before I go, thank you.

Madura: I'm appalled by the possibility that somebody from our community might be responsible for this tragedy.

DeMarco: It affects everybody, I'm sure.

Madura: And especially in a place like this. We're a very rural school district, as you know. Mostly lower, lower middle-class. People in the city, I imagine they become inured of this kind of thing. But this is a shock for us. It's going to send ripples through our community for a long, long time. *(pause)* So what can I tell you about her? I remember Meghan as a very likable young woman. And a pretty good athlete.

DeMarco: Actually I wanted to ask you about Mr. Hickman, your science teacher.

Randall Silvis

Madura: Oh God. No. You are not here to tell me that he had something to do with this. Please say you're not.

DeMarco: Were you aware of the rumors that he was…being intimate with students in exchange for grades and/or money?

Long silence.

Madura: The thing about French Creek is, people around here take care of each other. I mean if something happens, something real, people are very quick to jump in and do what they can to help out. But at the same time, when there's no actual proof of any wrongdoing, we do our best to give the benefit of the doubt. Rural people are tough and self-reliant. Very private folk. To them there are two Golden Rules: Treat other people the way you want to be treated yourself. And two: Don't stick your nose where it doesn't belong.

DeMarco: So what I'm hearing you say is, you knew about it, but you didn't do anything.

Madura: That is not correct. Absolutely not correct. I questioned him about it, and more than once.

DeMarco: You directly asked Mr. Hickman if he was taking liberties with his students?

Madura: Twice that I can clearly recall. Right here in this office.

DeMarco: And how did you become aware of those allegations?

Madura: One of the teachers during lunch hour overheard a couple of the kids talking. She later questioned the children—the students, I mean—who later claimed they were just making it up. Plus there were things written on the stalls in the girls' restroom.

Incident on Ten-Right Road

DeMarco: What kind of things?

Madura: I really don't care to repeat that kind of language.

DeMarco: Even if it might help identify Meghan's killer?

Madura: I can't for a moment believe that Mr. Hickman could have had anything to do with that.

DeMarco: So you are refusing to tell me what was written on the bathroom stall?

Madura (*after a sigh*): Suck Mr. Dick for an A. That's what it said.

DeMarco: And this message appeared more than once? I'm assuming you had it cleaned off each time.

Madura: Of course we did. It appeared maybe three or four times in total. All during the same school year. Two years ago.

DeMarco: And you say you questioned Mr. Hickman about this?

Madura: He wasn't well-liked by some students. He was a tough grader. Demanded excellence. Which many of our students just aren't equipped, temperamentally or intellectually, to provide.

DeMarco: So you're saying—

Madura: There are always rumors about teachers. Always. I remember when I was in school, we were all dead certain that the gym teacher and the English teacher were having an affair. We believed they were having sex in the faculty lounge. And then we come to find out that the English teacher is a lesbian! We couldn't believe it. We couldn't believe that we had been so wrong.

DeMarco: I'm not sure I'm following you. Are you saying that the stories about Mr. Hickman were fabricated by students who didn't like him, or that they are a product of youthful imaginations?

Madura: Both, I suppose. I'm saying that I questioned him, on two separate occasions, and he vehemently denied the rumors. And nobody came forth to refute his denials. I ended each of those conversations with a very, very stern admonition regarding the consequences of such behavior, were any teacher to engage in it. What else was I supposed to do? Interrogate the entire student body?

DeMarco: My understanding is that he retired very abruptly. In the middle of a semester.

Madura: He called me over Thanksgiving break last year, said he wouldn't be returning. Doctor's orders. He had to go to Cleveland for emergency heart surgery. Left town that same day. And that's the last anybody heard from him for seven, eight weeks. We couldn't even file the paperwork until he came back home again, all patched up apparently.

DeMarco: So there's no truth to the rumor that a mother threatened him with statutory rape of her ninth grade daughter if he didn't retire immediately?

Madura *(after a pause):* Sir, I...I can't offer any comment on that one way or the other. A high school administrator is forever neck-deep in rumors, 95 percent of which prove untrue.

DeMarco: So you were aware of that particular rumor?

Madura: I was.

DeMarco: And how did you come by that information?

Madura: Sir, you put me in a difficult position. Rumors usually reach me as a last resort. A student tells

Incident on Ten-Right Road

a student who tells another student, and that student tells a teacher, and that teacher tells another teacher…

DeMarco: You're at the end of the grapevine.

Madura: Precisely. And the success or failure of my position here depends on trust. I can't maintain that trust if I'm tossing out names without any foundation of evidence to back up the accusations.

DeMarco: Fair enough.

Madura: But I promise you this: If I am ever convinced that that particular rumor belongs in the five percent rather than in the 95 percent, I will notify you immediately.

DeMarco: Thank you for your time, sir.

Madura: I trust that this conversation will remain confidential?

DeMarco: All interviews are subject to review by law enforcement. And that includes the D.A.

Madura: Gosh. I wish you had told me that before we started.

DeMarco: And why would that be, sir?

Madura: No, no, you're right. The truth is the truth. And like the Good Book says, "The truth will out."

DeMarco: Actually, that quote is from Shakespeare's *The Merchant of Venice*: "Truth will come to light; murder cannot be hid long…at the length truth will out."

Madura: I'm impressed. You're not looking for a job teaching English, are you?

DeMarco: Not at the moment. Thank you again for your time. You say you have Meghan's file for me?

Madura: Just stop at the front desk and ask Debbie for it.

End of interview.

Randall Silvis

Notes:
- According to Meghan Fletcher's academic records, she received an A- from Mr. Hickman in both her junior and senior years. Her overall GPA for those terms, with those grades factored in, were 2.44 and 2.56 respectively on a 4.0 scale. Her only other A grades were for Physical Education, the electives Family and Consumer Science (Home Ec) and Visual and Performing Arts (Senior Choir and Basic Still Life Drawing).
- Is Madura in denial, or just covering his own butt? Or maybe I'm not giving him enough credit. He told me what he could without compromising his principles. Tough job he has, riding herd on students *and* teachers, and trying to treat all of them, plus the kids' parents, fairly. All while keeping his own butt covered. I'm glad it's not me walking that tightrope.
- Call Cleveland Clinic to substantiate Hickman's bypass surgery. Can't wait to hear how he explains his retirement.

Interview with Richard Hickman

DeMarco: This interview with Mr. Richard Hickman is taking place in his residence at 100 Ten-Right Road, French Creek Township, Mercer County, Pennsylvania. Today is August 14th and the time is 11:46 a.m. We are seated in his living room, from whose front window we can look directly across the road at the home of the deceased, Meghan Fletcher. You are a retired science teacher from the French Creek Area School District, is that correct, sir?

Hickman: That is correct. Why did you say that you can see Meghan's house from here?

DeMarco: So that I can resituate myself, so to speak, when I listen to the interview later on. It helps me to remember anything I might forget between now and then.

Hickman: I understand. It just sounded like maybe you were implying something.

DeMarco: What would I be implying?

Hickman: That's what I was asking myself.

DeMarco: It is important, though, that you have such a clear view across the road. The information you provided to Chief Melvin about your whereabouts on the night of Meghan's death, about you seeing Tad Blyler pull up and drop her off, all of that is very useful to us. We're very grateful for your cooperation.

Hickman: I'm happy to tell you what I know. Though I did that once already.

DeMarco: And thanks to that I have Chief Melvin's notes to draw upon. So instead of repeating everything you told him...unless you want to make some corrections or clarifications to it?

Hickman: No, I'm good.

DeMarco: Tad's truck pulled in at.... What time did you say it was?

Hickman: 1:11 a.m. Meghan jumped out and ran up onto the porch and let herself into the house. Then he drove away. That's it in a nutshell.

DeMarco: And exactly how did Meghan let herself into the house?

Hickman: There's a hanging basket off to the side of the front porch steps, has a spider plant in it. She reached into the basket, took something out, and opened the door. It seems logical to assume the something she took out was a key.

DeMarco: Was this the first time you saw her take a key from the basket?

Hickman: Obviously I couldn't tell that it was a key, but no, I've seen her or Junie do it a number of times.

DeMarco *(after a pause)*: Approximately how long did she remain sitting in the truck after it pulled into the driveway?

Hickman: Do you want it in nanoseconds? Because that's how long. Single digit.

DeMarco: As far as you know, did Tad call out to her through an open window, or did she say anything as she was getting out of the truck?

Hickman: I would have heard if they did.

Incident on Ten-Right Road

DeMarco: How far away would you say you were from the truck when Meghan jumped out?

Hickman: I was just off the corner of my house, more or less.

DeMarco: The front corner or the rear corner?

Hickman: The front. But out in the yard a ways. So I could look at the stars above the house, of course.

DeMarco: Above your house or Meghan's?

Hickman: Both, actually.

DeMarco: You mind if I pull your curtains back a bit more?

Hickman: Help yourself.

DeMarco: So then…considering the position of your house, Perseus would be out to the northeast there about, what, 45, well, almost 60 degrees to the right of the Fletcher house?

Hickman: I see you know your constellations.

DeMarco: Only a couple of them. But in that direction…you wouldn't need to see overtop of your house. Or over the Fletcher's either. Am I right?

Hickman: Not for the Alpha Persei Cluster, no—

DeMarco: Nor for the Swift-Tuttle cloud, I think.

Hickman: No, that's right, you're perfectly right. But you see a dozen meteors, you've seen them all, you know what I mean? I'm kind of a restless stargazer. There's a lot to look at up there.

DeMarco: That's for sure. Friday night, though, if I recall correctly, there was a fairly heavy cloud cover.

Hickman: Yeah, at times, I suppose. Lots of breaks in the clouds, though. Still lots of opportunities.

DeMarco: Weather records show only an average 28 percent layer transparency across the whole county most of the night. Plus the rain a few hours later.

Hickman *(after a pause)*: Well... like I said, there were breaks from time to time. Just have to be patient and take what you get.

DeMarco: Not easy for a restless stargazer, I bet.

Hickman: It's a routine, that's all. Some people are afraid of the dark; I prefer it. There can be a real serenity to it. That's why I live out here, away from other houses. Darkness has a way of smoothing out all of life's imperfections. Everything looks better in the dark.

DeMarco: Life is imperfect, I can't argue with that.

Hickman: The meteor shower won't peak till tomorrow night. I'm still hoping for at least one night of clear skies.

DeMarco: We could all use a lot more clarity.

Hickman: That sounds like a metaphor, Sergeant.

DeMarco: Just talking in general. Life in general. *(pause)* So let's get back to what you saw, didn't see, heard, didn't hear that night. Meghan goes into her house, and Tad pulls away with...I believe you called it "a godawful squeal of tires."

Hickman: That's exactly what I called it.

DeMarco: And did the manner of his exit suggest anything to you?

Hickman: Well, first there was the truck door being slammed shut. People don't close a door that way unless they're seriously ticked off about something. And then there was the way she went up to the house.

DeMarco: According to Chief Melvin, you said she ran up onto the porch.

Hickman: I might have used that word, but now that I'm seeing it all again in my mind's eye, I would describe it differently. It was more like a brisk, angry

Incident on Ten-Right Road

walk. Her arms were pumping like pistons. And I'm fairly certain she had her fists clenched.

DeMarco: You could see all that?

Hickman: Well, you know, the headlights were right on her most of the time.

DeMarco: Right. I forgot about the headlights. Was the porch light on?

Hickman: That too. Her mother always leaves the porch light on when Meghan is out late at night.

DeMarco: This is really good information, sir. We're lucky you have such a fine memory. And are so observant. So what about the house lights? Any lights on inside?

Hickman: Before Meghan went in? I think maybe the kitchen light was on. But it went out after a couple of minutes. Then her bedroom light upstairs went on. And maybe three, four minutes later, it went out too.

DeMarco: And you know it was her bedroom light that went on...how?

Hickman. Just a logical assumption. I guess her mother might have turned on her light. But it's just human nature, isn't it? You come home at night, turn on your room light, do what you need to do, turn it off and go to bed.

DeMarco: Sure sounds logical to me. *(pause)* So you didn't hear any kind of verbal exchange between Meghan and her mother that night?

Hickman: I can't say there wasn't one. But if there'd been anything loud, their voices would have carried this far.

DeMarco: Especially at that time of night, when everything else is so quiet.

Hickman: I would have heard.

DeMarco: How late did you stay out that night?

Hickman: Best guess? Another hour or so at most. Like you said, the cloud cover was getting heavier by the minute.

DeMarco: And then you returned to your house?

Hickman: Straight to bed. Swallowed a couple of melatonins, took a leak, and hit the sack.

DeMarco: Remind me what time you awoke in the morning.

Hickman: I'd say 8:00-ish, maybe a little later.

DeMarco: So from 2:00, 2:30 to a little after 8:00, you were sound asleep?

Hickman: At my age there's no such thing as 'sound asleep.' I slept for a while, got up and took another leak, and went back to bed. I keep a little tablet computer on the bed so I can listen to meditation music. It helps me fall back to sleep after I get up in the middle of the night.

DeMarco: And you turned on the music that night?

Hickman: I'm almost sure I did. I do every night. But I keep the volume very low. Otherwise I wouldn't be able to fall asleep again. So if you're wondering if it might have kept me from hearing anything going on across the road, I'd have to say no, it wouldn't.

DeMarco: And did you hear anything from across the road?

Hickman: Not a peep.

DeMarco: Straight through till 8:00 or a little later?

Hickman: Straight through. And I can't say for sure I got up only once to take a pee. Sometimes it's two, sometimes it's three times a night. But whatever

Incident on Ten-Right Road

it was, I didn't hear a thing except maybe the truck pulling out when Junie headed off to work.

DeMarco: And how did you know that Junie drove to work that morning? She usually walks, doesn't she?

Hickman: Well...there were the sirens, you know. The ambulance and police arriving. And maybe 20 minutes after that, Junie comes roaring down the road in the pickup. I could see when she climbed out that she was still wearing her blue Belmont shirt. So, you know, two plus two equals four.

DeMarco: On which side of the house is your bedroom located?

Hickman: This side. It's the room adjacent to this one. Contiguous, you might say.

DeMarco: So when Junie pulled out in the truck that morning, her headlights would have shone straight into your bedroom window, correct?

Hickman: Which is why I have the blackout curtains in there. I'm a night owl. Definitely not a morning person. Didn't realize that until after I stopped teaching. In fact I'll have a little nap around 2:00 or 3:00 every afternoon. That's why I require only four or five hours total at night. It's called polyphasic sleeping. Da Vinci, Edison, Tesla, they were all polyphasic sleepers too.

DeMarco (*after a pause*): Meghan took some of your classes, is that right?

Hickman: Chemistry and Phys Sci 1. She would have had Mrs. Ramsey for Biology and Earth Sciences.

DeMarco: Was she a good student?

Hickman: She was an earnest student. She did her best.

Randall Silvis

DeMarco: Would you happen to remember what grades she received?

Hickman: Not off the top of my head, no. I know she passed. Unfortunately I've had to lower my academic standards over the years—the entire school has—so what's average now probably wouldn't have passed muster in our day.

DeMarco: So she didn't really stand out in any way?

Hickman: When you deal with over 100 students a year for as long as I did, you tend to remember only the stars and the complete wastes of your time. The rest just all blur together.

DeMarco: Even when they live across the road from you?

Hickman: Well, you're not talking about grades now. I only said I don't remember her grades.

DeMarco: I just thought she might have lingered in your memory longer than the other average students, seeing as how she and her mother are your only neighbors out this way.

Hickman: The truth is, when I left teaching, I just emptied out all the clutter. Threw away all the old grade rosters, the reams and reams of leftover handouts and lesson plans.... I burned it all. And I guess I did the same thing with some of my memories. I recognize students' faces now, but their names and histories? That's pretty much a blank.

DeMarco: So you don't remember having any of those special teacher-student moments with her? I thought every teacher has those.

Hickman: But not with every student. Most of them just disappear in the crowd.

Incident on Ten-Right Road

DeMarco: You and the Fletchers have been neighbors for how long?

Hickman: Since my divorce. And that was 10…10 years and five months ago.

DeMarco: So you've known Meghan since she was a girl.

Hickman: I wish I could say that's true. Fact is, there has never been much interaction between me and the Fletchers. I got the lawn mower started for Junie one time, after she flooded the engine by leaving the choke open. And let's see…Junie asked me to take care of a groundhog once that was living under her back porch. I set up a trap, caught the critter, took it out to the game lands and let it go. Other than that…. It's a sad commentary on our society, isn't it? How little we know each other.

Silence.

DeMarco: Okay. We're just about done here. Thank you for being so patient with me. How's your heart, by the way? I heard you had bypass surgery last year.

Hickman: All is well, thank you. I'm doing just fine.

DeMarco: Those people at the Cleveland Clinic, they know their stuff, don't they?

Hickman: Thank God they do.

DeMarco: That's where you had it done, right? Somebody I talked to mentioned Cleveland, so I'm just assuming….

Hickman: No, that's right. The Cleveland Clinic. Dr. Abdus Salam. How come all the best surgeons these days are from India?

DeMarco: Was your heart condition the reason for your retirement?

Hickman: Yes. Yes, it was.

DeMarco: Doctor's orders? To avoid the stress, and all that?

Hickman: No... As you can see, there's no physical reason to not return to the classroom. And I still might someday, who knows? But you lie there in bed, you know, with stitches in your chest, after some complete stranger has been mucking around with your heart, I don't know, it gives a man pause.

DeMarco: Intimations of mortality.

Hickman: Well said. Makes you think about how you want to spend the rest of your time. And trust me: grading quizzes every night isn't going to be on anybody's bucket list.

DeMarco: I'm just glad to hear everything worked out. You've been a big help to me today, thank you.

Hickman: I suppose you'll probably head over to talk to Junie now?

DeMarco: She appears to have company at the moment. Two cars in her driveway.

Hickman: Very nice woman. Very pleasant.

DeMarco: You ever have the western scramble at the diner where she works? First they brown and season the home fries, ham, bell peppers and onions, then they pour in the egg mixture. I get mine with some chopped jalapenos. Great way to get the motor running.

Hickman: I don't, uh...I cook for myself most of the time. I'm not much for dining out.

DeMarco: You're a practical man. I can appreciate that. *(pause)* So now all I need is a DNA sample.

Incident on Ten-Right Road

Hickman: Which requires a warrant, am I right?
DeMarco: Unless you volunteer to provide one. Is there any reason you wouldn't?
Hickman: None whatsoever. I already jumped through that hoop with the school district. Every teacher does these days. Just wanted to let you know that I am aware of my rights.
DeMarco: I'll get the kit from the car.

End of interview.

Notes:
- DNA sample collected from Richard Hickman. I left my phone recorder running without his knowledge, but after I came back with the kit, he was far less talkative. Nothing more of relevance was recorded.
- Conclusion: According to weather maps, there was nothing to see in the sky the night of Meghan's death but dark clouds. Obviously his interests were of a more terrestrial nature. On the other hand, I have to be wary of my own feelings; would I distrust him half as much if I hadn't been told about his behavior with students?
- Options:
    1. The rumors about his actions with female students are untrue. I deem this option unlikely based on previous interviews with Junie Fletcher, Missy and Patti Cochran, and superintendent Madura. Therefore:
    2. He had a relationship of a sexual nature with Meghan Fletcher, but it ended when she graduated from high school. Or,

3. It continued after high school up to the time of her death. But if this were the case, why would he kill her? Because he was jealous of Blyler and wanted her for himself? Possible, but my gut tells me no. So then,
4. On a cloudy, starless night, he is standing in his yard at one in the morning, looking through his high-power binoculars. At what? At the Fletcher house. Waiting for a glimpse of who? Meghan Fletcher. Why? Because he was obsessed with her. (But doesn't this contradict my previous option? Except that when I write it out like this, it makes more sense. So okay, he was obsessed with her.) But how obsessed? Enough to follow her into her own home after she went to bed? And then do what? Demand sex? Threaten her with a knife? Maybe he never intended to harm her, but she panicked and jerked away. Could he do all this without waking Junie Fletcher? See next interview.
5. Or maybe all he wanted that night, and all he did, was to spy on her through his binoculars, get his jollies, whack off, and go to bed. The truth will out.

- I wish I had asked to see his astronomical binoculars. Lots of astronomers hook up cameras or laptops so as to capture video of what they're viewing. He might have years of Peeping Tom material on his hard drive.
- We need to search his house. Unfortunately, my gut feelings won't get us a search warrant. I need to find something that will.

- Interview Junie Fletcher, then contact Cleveland Clinic to verify/refute Hickman's heart surgery story.

Interview with Junie Fletcher

DeMarco: I'm sorry to disturb you, Ms. Fletcher. I'm—

Fletcher: Don't start calling me Ms. Fletcher now. Western scramble with jalapenos, link sausage, whole wheat toast, coffee black. How many times have I served you?

DeMarco: I've eaten more sausage there than I should, that's for sure.

Fletcher: I thought all you guys did was to pull over cars on the interstate.

DeMarco: We do our share of investigations too. I've taken over your daughter's case from Chief Melvin, and I—

Fletcher: Why? Doesn't he want to handle it?

DeMarco: It isn't that he doesn't want to. He has a very small staff, and the State Police have access to more resources than he does.

Fletcher: Oh. Okay. So…?

DeMarco: I see that you have company today, and I wasn't going to interrupt, but then I thought that as long as I'm here, I could maybe schedule a time more convenient for us to—

Fletcher: What did he have to say?

DeMarco: Chief Melvin?

Incident on Ten-Right Road

Fletcher: My neighbor. Your car's been over there for most of an hour.

DeMarco: I can't discuss that with you. I'm sorry. I know what a difficult time this must be.

Fletcher: Do you?

DeMarco: I lost a son. He was just a baby, but still….

Fletcher: I knew there was something sad about you. Always have breakfast by yourself. Sit and stare out the window. Never look at your phone, never bring a book or paper to keep you company. You're a good tipper but never once have you tried to hit on me. *(pause)* How did he die?

DeMarco: Car accident.

Fletcher: You were driving, weren't you?

DeMarco: I was. A guy ran a red light. Slammed into us.

Fletcher: Was it recent?

DeMarco: About four years ago. If you would like to—

Fletcher: And you've never gotten over it. I can see it in your eyes.

DeMarco: Ms. Fletcher, I…I just came by to set up a time—

Fletcher: You're still wearing your wedding ring, so I guess the marriage survived. Why doesn't your wife come to breakfast with you?

DeMarco: How about if I go grab a sandwich or something, come back in an hour or so, and we can sit down then and talk.

Fletcher: Relax. It's not like you're interrupting anything. We've just been setting in there crying, that's all.

DeMarco: Your friends?

Fletcher: Peggy Wolfe and Erica Gathers. We do spinning together three nights a week. Meggie used to join us too sometimes. Peggy has the black card, which means she can bring a guest.

DeMarco: How does a person have the energy for spinning when she's been on her feet all day?

Fletcher: Sounds crazy, doesn't it? Actually, it's very relaxing. They gave me the membership for my birthday last fall. Must have noticed that I was eating too much sausage too.

DeMarco: I have just a few questions, but we can—

Fletcher: Oh God, I forgot to call him.

DeMarco: You forgot to call who?

Fletcher: I was going to call Chief Melvin and tell him what was missing. I just noticed it this morning. But then the girls showed up and I completely lost track of what I was doing.

DeMarco: There's something missing from the house? My information is that there was nothing missing.

Fletcher: I was numb when I told him that. I couldn't even see straight. I'm still pretty much the same, except that I was looking at her things this morning…just wanted to touch them and smell them, you know?

DeMarco: Of course.

Fletcher: She had this old photo from high school of her and Alex. The two of them in that play about some little town in New England or somewhere. She played Emily and he played George. They got married in the play.

Incident on Ten-Right Road

DeMarco: *Our Town*. That's the name of the play.

Fletcher: She never would have been able to take that part if he hadn't helped her memorize the lines. She was never very good at reading.

DeMarco: And the photo is missing now?

Fletcher: That and a little jewelry box. It was about the size of, I don't know, the box a set of bank checks come in. It was made of that real light, spongy kind of wood. I think she bought it at the Dollar General.

DeMarco: Was there anything inside the box?

Fletcher: Over $1,000. I'm not sure of the exact total but I know it was up there. She called it her dowry. She started saving in 10th grade.

DeMarco: Where in the room were those two items placed?

Fletcher: Top drawer of her dresser. Underneath her bras and panties. I never saw her take one out without taking the other one out. I can't tell you how many times I'd find her sitting on her bed with that photo on one side of her, the box and the money on the other side.

DeMarco: And now they're both missing?

Fletcher: I can't find them anywhere.

DeMarco: Nothing else?

Fletcher: Not that I can tell. But somebody was in that drawer. Everything was a mess. Not neat, the way she always kept it. Bras on one side, panties on the other. *(pause)* Why would somebody take just those two things? Why didn't they take her laptop or the TV or whatever? The money I can understand but… I don't know. Why would they take the photo?

DeMarco *(after a pause)*: Junie, why don't I come back later today, or even tomorrow, and we can—

Fletcher: What—you don't like to see a woman cry?

DeMarco: I never like to see a woman cry.

Fletcher: It's a damn shame all men aren't that way. *(sniffing sounds)* Screw it, let's get this over with. But not in here. You mind meeting me out back? I need a smoke.

DeMarco: See you there.

Pause in recording.

Fletcher: You take that glider and I'll set downwind of you. You don't smoke?

DeMarco: Never took it up.

Fletcher: One of the stupidest things a person can do. Not *the* stupidest, but it's one of them. Trust me; I've done them all. *(pause)* We're weak, you know. Addicts. We can't quit because we're all so freaking weak. My only defense is that it's not meth or heroin. Not yet anyway. *(pause)* I don't get this thing about calling addiction a disease, do you?

DeMarco: I'm not sure I know what you mean.

Fletcher: You tell somebody they have a disease, it's like you're telling them they aren't responsible, they're a victim. Like when you're a victim of cancer, or a victim of baldness, or whatever.

DeMarco: And you don't agree with that?

Fletcher: It's not true. It's a flat-out lie. I *chose* to smoke my first cigarette. People *choose* to drink 10 beers every night or to snort crack or shoot heroin. If that's a disease, it's because they gave it to themselves. And they should be held responsible for their stupidity.

Incident on Ten-Right Road

Not treated like they're innocent victims. The people they hurt, those are the victims. Those are the ones who didn't have a choice.

DeMarco *(after a pause)*: Do you mind if I record our conversation? Actually it's running right now. I forgot to shut it off when I left Mr. Hickman. But I can erase all that if you want me to.

Fletcher: What difference does it make?

DeMarco: It's for my own use, just so I don't forget anything important. Easier to maintain clarity that way.

Fletcher: Go ahead and let it run. I'm all for clarity. I notice you don't have the expensive one. I bet you're a frugal man.

DeMarco: Just a basic android, yeah. It does everything I need.

Fletcher: Meggie just had to have the iPhone. And how do you tell a teenager no? When she means all the world to you? When am I going to get it back, by the way?

DeMarco: We're making a record of the relevant calls and texts. Should be finished soon.

Fletcher: Are you able to listen in on the phone conversations somehow? The ones she made that night?

DeMarco: Unfortunately, no. Phone companies only keep the metadata. Time, number, length of call. *(a pause)* I'll just...there's this thing I say to identify every interview....

Fletcher: Do what you have to do. That's why we're here, isn't it?

DeMarco: This interview with Ms. Junie Fletcher is taking place on the back porch of her residence at

201 Ten-Right Road, French Creek Township, Mercer County, Pennsylvania. Today is August 14th and the time is 12:57 p.m.

Fletcher: Who else have you talked to before coming to me? Besides Richard, I mean?

DeMarco: I started out the morning with the high school principal.

Fletcher: I bet he gave you an earful.

DeMarco: He had nothing but kind words for Meghan.

Fletcher: I bet he did. *(pause)* He didn't tell you about all the times he sent her to detention?

DeMarco: Never mentioned it.

Fletcher: It wasn't like she was bad or anything. Took after me is all.

DeMarco: In what way?

Fletcher: We just don't know when to keep our mouths shut. Plus she's got this sarcastic sense of humor. Some people take it the wrong way.

DeMarco: People like teachers?

Fletcher: I think it must be part of their training. They have their sense of humor removed. *(pause)* School wasn't easy for Meggie. The studying part, I mean. She would read stuff and just couldn't understand it half the time. I had her tested for dyslexia, but they said she didn't have it. But I don't know. She always seemed so smart to me. Some of the teachers even said so. Others said she needed to pay closer attention, that she just wasn't applying herself. My feeling is that half of those teachers don't know what the hell they're doing. It's not like we get the cream of the crop around here.

DeMarco: How was she doing at the community college?

Incident on Ten-Right Road

Fletcher: Better. It was still hard for her. But one of her nursing instructors was helping her out. There are *some* good people in this world, thank God. *(pause)* My baby wasn't a bad girl. If anybody ever tells you she was, they're lying to you. She had an independent spirit, that's all. I encouraged it. Always told her it was her life and she should live it however she wanted. Anybody didn't like it, that was their problem, not hers.

DeMarco: She seemed to be handling her job okay.

Fletcher: She was doing fine. Once she got used to the cash register. It was touch and go there for a little while. But she plowed through it. When Meggie wanted something, nobody was going to keep her from getting it.

DeMarco: How did you feel about her relationship with Tad Blyler?

Fletcher: That boy. *(pause)* You know how when you first meet somebody, and you just don't like them but you don't know why?

DeMarco: That's how you felt about Tad?

Fletcher: He never did a single thing wrong to offend me. Always polite, respectful, sweet as can be. But I just had this feeling. Right from day one. It was like there was a shadow over him, you know?

DeMarco: What kind of shadow?

Fletcher: Those Amish are a bunch of hypocrites; you know that, right? I don't see how a person can live around here and not know that.

DeMarco: Hypocrites in what way?

Fletcher: Take your pick. They're not allowed to own electronics but they sure don't mind using everybody else's, or even buying their own and keeping them hid. And Amish craftsmanship? What a load of bull that is. *(pause)* You know how many Amish girls get raped by their fathers and uncles and brothers and such? They do it with animals too, I've heard. You've probably come across that kind of stuff.

DeMarco: We've dealt with the incest a couple of times. The other, no, not to my knowledge.

Fletcher: Horses and cows and goats can't complain, that's why.

DeMarco: Did you have some suspicions about Tad Blyler?

Fletcher: I just think you can't grow up in a culture like that, full of that kind of evil stuff, and not be affected by it, whether you do any of it yourself or not. I don't know; maybe that's why he left them. Because he couldn't take it either.

DeMarco: Was this something you or Meghan discussed with him?

Fletcher: I discussed it with her.

DeMarco: And…what was her response?

Fletcher: She never intended anything long term with him. He was a lot more serious than she ever was.

DeMarco: Because of her feelings for Alex Gessner?

Fletcher: Missy told me you talked to her yesterday. We were the only two knew about Meggie and Alex.

DeMarco: And how did you feel about that relationship?

Fletcher: All I cared about was, I didn't want her getting hurt. She figured Alex would sow his wild oats and come back around to her eventually.

Incident on Ten-Right Road

DeMarco: I get the feeling you didn't believe that would happen.

Fletcher: I was young once too, you know. You learn things along the way.

DeMarco: And what did you learn?

Fletcher: Apparently nothing useful. *(pause)* What did Missy tell you about her dad?

DeMarco: She didn't talk at all about her father.

Fletcher: About Meggie's dad. What all did she say about him? I know she told you that she thought Meggie was attracted to Tad because he reminded her of her father. She told me she told you that. But what else?

DeMarco: You know I can't discuss somebody else's interview. You wouldn't want me discussing yours, would you?

Fletcher: He had that shadow too. And I just ignored it. For a while I did. And then I threw his ass out.

DeMarco: Meghan's father.

Fletcher: Probably.

DeMarco: Excuse me?

Fletcher: He probably was her father. I wish now I'd told her that. Other than that one thing, I never once lied to her. *(pause)* Do you think it's true about the sins of the fathers coming back onto their children? Because if it is, it's got to apply to a mother's sins too.

DeMarco: No. I don't believe that.

Fletcher: Yeah, right. You blame yourself same as I do.

DeMarco: It's what parents do, I guess. *(pause)* How long has it been since she's seen her father?

Fletcher: Since the day I threw him out.

DeMarco: And when was that?

Fletcher: Ten years ago. She was nine.

DeMarco: Phone calls, birthday cards, things like that?

Fletcher: Nothing. Total silence. Exactly the way I wanted it.

DeMarco: And why did you want it that way?

Fletcher: Because I wanted him gone. Out of our lives forever. Healthier for everybody concerned.

DeMarco: But why no involvement with his own daughter?

Fletcher: Maybe his own daughter.

DeMarco: Did you tell him that?

Fletcher: I might have let it slip.

DeMarco: Exactly why did you want him out of your lives so completely?

Fletcher: You mean other than the drinking and the drugs and the punching and slapping and lying and cheating and making me feel like a worthless piece of shit every minute of my life?

DeMarco: Was he abusive with Meghan too?

Fletcher: No. If he'd ever laid a finger on her, I would've…. He treated her like a princess. She could do no wrong.

DeMarco: Did that bother you?

Fletcher: Why would it bother me? *(pause)* What bothered me was that I had to do all the parenting. If I told her she was grounded for something, 10 minutes later he'd go into her bedroom and take her out for ice cream. This one time, I put a lock on her bike, told her she couldn't ride into town to see her friends, and while I was at work, he went out and bought her another bike. *(pause)* Do you have any idea what it's like to be the only adult in the family? I had a daughter to raise, and I was good at it. Firm but fair. I loved being a mother. But I sure as hell wasn't going to raise a 38 year-old man too.

DeMarco: At any time while you were together, did you feel that his relationship with Meghan crossed the line into…inappropriate behavior?

Fletcher: Did he mess with her—is that what you're asking?

DeMarco: That's what I'm asking.

Fletcher*:* Ha. Was it Missy told you that?

DeMarco: Did you have any reason to suspect it might be happening?

Fletcher *(after a pause)*: About a year or so after he left, I noticed she stopped being such a tomboy. Wanted to wear my make-up, skirts instead of jeans, stuff like that. I just figured she was growing up. But then I also noticed that she was paying a lot more attention to men than she used to. Not boys, but men. And not the right kind of men. The kind with their pants halfway down their butts, their ball caps turned sideways or backwards. The kind all tatted up and with a cigarette dangling out the corner of their mouth.

DeMarco: Is that a description of your husband?

Fletcher *(nods):* Meggie and me were in the Dollar General once, picking up a couple of things. This was back when she was 10, no, 11 years old. And I turn around and she's gone. I ran up and down the aisles looking for her, but she wasn't there. I finally found her out in the parking lot talking to some loser who was 40 if he was a day. I mentioned it to one of my friends, and she said it sounded like the way a victim of child sexual abuse behaves. So I asked

Meggie about it. Did your father ever touch you in your private places? And thank God, she said no. But then she said, I don't think so. *(pause)* I was in a panic. I, like, couldn't breathe.

DeMarco: What did you do?

Fletcher: I threw her into the car and we drove to the doctor's office. I barged right in where he was listening to some old man's ticker and I told him you got to look at my little girl *now*.

DeMarco: He examined her?

Fletcher: He said she was fine. Absolutely no sign of any kind of sexual contact. *(pause)* I think she might have held onto that question, though. That possibility. Maybe even, in a strange kind of childish way… I don't know. I blame myself for sort of planting that idea in her mind. Kids are just so impressionable. You have to watch everything you say.

DeMarco: Did she receive counseling of any kind? To help her adjust to her father's absence?

Fletcher: She missed him, that's all it was. And we talked, we talked a lot, about why he was bad for us. Why he wasn't a good person. Why we were better off without him. *(pause)* I still believe I did the right thing in making him leave. Guys like him, they don't change. My guess is he either OD'd or he's in prison somewhere. I'm hoping he's been dead a good long time.

Silence.

Fletcher: Look, I'm not trying to tell you your business or anything. But where is all this getting us in terms of who hurt my baby girl? *(pause)* It happened right here under my nose! What kind of a person would do that to my baby?

Incident on Ten-Right Road

DeMarco: You can't blame yourself. In all likelihood, you had already left for work.

Fletcher: Between 5:00 and 7:00 a.m., I know. That means it might have happened right before I woke up. Or while I was in the bathroom.

DeMarco: It probably didn't.

Fletcher: Fuck probably.

DeMarco *(after a pause)*: Okay, let's talk for a minute about the timeline. You went to bed right after Meghan returned home that night?

Fletcher: I was already in bed. Couldn't sleep, though, you know, waiting up for her. She was supposed to be home no later than 1:00.

DeMarco: Did you speak to her that night?

Fletcher: I didn't want to yell at her, and I was pissed. But I also remembered what *I* was like at that age. I wouldn't wish me on any mother.

DeMarco: How soon did you fall asleep after she came home?

Fletcher: How long does it take Ambien to work?

DeMarco: So you got up to take a sleep aid?

Fletcher: I didn't have to get up. *(pause)* I'm not hooked or anything, I don't take it every night. But if I'm up after midnight, and have to be awake by 5:00 for work? Yeah, I'm going to take one. Plus a wine chaser. Fortunately I keep both of them close at hand. And now you're going to tell me how stupid it is to mix wine with a sleeping pill.

DeMarco *(after a pause)*: Besides you and Meghan and Missy, who else would have known about the door key in the hanging basket?

Fletcher: Not in your job description, huh? Pointing out the folly of our ways?

DeMarco: More like the pot having no right to call the kettle black.

Fletcher: Really? And you sitting there looking so starched and put together. My, my, my.

DeMarco: If we could return to the door key in the hanging basket?

Fletcher: You think I haven't thought about that? Anybody who ever saw either one of us using the key, that's who knew where it was.

DeMarco: And who would that include?

Fletcher: I might as well have just let the freaking door wide open. Her friends, my friends…. Anybody we ever brought home with us would know the key was there.

DeMarco: Then let's talk about who might have been angry enough, or frustrated enough, or, I don't know, demented enough to hurt Meghan that way. Have you thought about that?

Fletcher: Of course I have. And it all comes down to one of the boys. Tad or Alex. Tad has the temper. And like I said, he's got that shadow around him. But Alex, I don't know. I can't imagine *why* he would do it. He never struck me as the type to get physical. Even so….

DeMarco: Did Tad get physical with her?

Fletcher: I never saw that side of him. According to Meggie, though, he'd get up in her face all the time. A lot of yelling, swearing, maybe grabbing her by the arm, stuff like that. She swore to me he never hit her. I'd have called the cops on him if he did.

DeMarco *(after a pause)*: Let's go back to your 'even so' for a minute.

Fletcher: Back to my what?

Incident on Ten-Right Road

DeMarco: You said that Alex never struck you as the type to get physical. Even so....

Fletcher: Boy, you don't miss a beat, do you?

DeMarco: Do you have suspicions about him? What he might be capable of?

Fletcher: Sometimes people just seem too good to be true, you know?

DeMarco: That's how you feel about Alex?

Fletcher: But on the other hand, my mind keeps telling me that's just stupid. He's a spoiled college kid trying to get all the pussy he can, that's all there is to him. He had no reason to want to hurt her. She would've dropped everything for him.

DeMarco: How did he and Meghan meet, seeing as how they went to different schools?

Fletcher: Meggie ran track. The 100 meters and the 4x200 relay. He was at a meet in West Middlesex when she was in 10th grade. That Saturday, he was at my front door.

DeMarco: And they were together until...?

Fletcher: Officially together? Till the August before her senior year. Two days before he left for college. *(pause)* It was clear to her way before then that she wouldn't be going to college. Not out-of-state anyway. I don't even want to tell you what a server at the Belmont makes.

DeMarco: There's no shame in not going to college. I never went.

Fletcher: Tell that to the rest of the world. *(pause)* Anyway, she'd seen enough of his family and he'd seen enough of hers to know there was no future for them. He plans to get an MBA and work on Wall Street, and her just praying to squeak through high school?

DeMarco: And yet they never really broke up.

DeMarco: Teenage hormones. You remember those, don't you?

DeMarco *(after a pause):* What's your relationship with Mr. Hickman?

Fletcher: What do you mean, my relationship?

DeMarco: There has been some speculation...I don't know if you've heard the rumors or not....

Fletcher: That he likes young girls? Everybody knows that. *(pause)* You don't need to look so shocked. I told you that me and Meggie had no secrets. None. Other than that thing about her father, I mean.

DeMarco: So you knew about Mr. Hickman and, uh, his room at the back of the lab?

Fletcher: You want to hear my philosophy on sex?

DeMarco: Sure.

Fletcher: God gave us the equipment to use it. To have fun with it. To give and receive pleasure. Because if He didn't, He's the most sadistic sonofabitch there's ever been. Tell me one thing in this life, one other physical pleasure, that feels half as good.

DeMarco: So in terms of Mr. Hickman and Meghan....

Fletcher: You're avoiding the question. What else feels as good? What else in this hard, nasty, painful, ugly existence of ours makes you even consider for half a second that there maybe is a God in heaven?

DeMarco: I don't know.

Fletcher: The hell you don't. *(long pause)* My cigarette's done. And I feel like I haven't even smoked one.

Incident on Ten-Right Road

DeMarco: I don't want to belabor this point, but...I do think it might be relevant.

Fletcher: She was going to flunk chemistry. Three weeks into the course and she was hopelessly lost. He made them memorize the freaking Periodic Table of Elements! What good does that ever do anybody?

DeMarco: Was he making overtures toward her?

Fletcher: She asked me what she should do. She was 17. Already having sex with Alex. I told her that a woman in this world is entitled to use whatever gifts God gave her, same as men do. Just not to let it go too far. And she didn't. She might not have had the book smarts she wanted to have, but she was smart and strong in lots of other ways. She got herself through high school just fine. And she got herself into community college too. Now what *you* need to do is to quit setting there judging us and go find that rotten, slimy bastard who sneaked into my house *right under my nose* and killed my baby girl!

(At this point, I stood to leave.)

Fletcher: Wait a minute, I'm sorry. I shouldn't have taken that tone with you. None of this is your fault.

DeMarco: I will do everything I can, Ms. Fletcher. I promise you that.

Fletcher: I'm sorry I barked at you. You're the only person I've met who might have some idea of what I'm going through right now.

DeMarco: I do. And I give you my word—

Fletcher: Stop, stop, stop. I know you're going to do everything you can. You're a good man, I know that. I also know that you know it's not going to change anything, is it? *(pause)* What happened to the man who crashed into your car four years ago?

DeMarco: He spent 18 months in jail. Two years probation.

Fletcher: You'd like to kill him, wouldn't you?

DeMarco: No.

Fletcher: Liar.

(long pause)

DeMarco: I would keep him alive. Keep him chained in my basement. Give him just enough food and water to keep him from dying. And I would beat him. Every morning and every night.

Fletcher: And twice every afternoon.

DeMarco: Yes, ma'am.

Fletcher: Is that how you cope, then? Is that what keeps you going?

DeMarco: I guess so, if that's what I'm doing. Coping.

Fletcher: You have any other survival tips you could share with me?

DeMarco (*after a pause*): Don't follow my example. That's probably the best advice I could give anybody.

Fletcher: Your example being what, exactly?

DeMarco: Keep your friends close. Don't shut them out. And don't think that passing out every night is any kind of remedy. It's not. *(pause)* I'm sorry, I, uh…I need to get going here.

Fletcher: Mister, you need to give yourself a break.

DeMarco: Call the barracks if you think of anything new, okay? I'll keep you apprised of our progress. Thank you for your time.

Incident on Ten-Right Road

Fletcher: Hey, just hold on a minute. Hey! What was your baby's name?

End of interview.

Notes:
- It is interesting that Junie Fletcher suspects Alex as much (or more than?) she suspects Tad, though she has no concrete reason to do so. She seems to have good instincts and insights into human nature, but obviously doesn't let those skills guide her life.
- I need to find out exactly what went on at the Taco King. Did Meghan humiliate Alex somehow? Could he have assumed that she would be meeting him there alone?
- Identify any other interesting parties at the bar.
- And what about the people she knew at the community college and from work? Track down those contacts if necessary.
- Hickman said he moved to Ten-Right Road 10 years ago: Junie Fletcher said she threw her husband out 10 years ago. Coincidence?
- Note to self: Do not let your sympathies for the subject of an interview allow the subject to control the interview. I need to watch that.
- Do your job and follow the law, but do not judge. The complexities of the heart make their own laws, and these must also be respected.

Summary of cell phone records: Meghan Fletcher

The iPhone belonging to Meghan Fletcher, victim, was recovered from her bedroom upon discovery of her body by Chief Melvin of the French Creek Township Police Department on August 12. The phone was offered for police examination by the victim's mother, Junie Fletcher, who also provided the password to access voice messages. A compilation of the incoming and outgoing calls and texts on the phone logs for August 7-12 was compiled by Trooper Carmichael, Pennsylvania State Police Troop D, Mercer County, Pennsylvania.

What follows is a summary of the data deemed relevant to this investigation. Junie Fletcher expressed to Chief Melvin a willingness to provide copies of the phone company's full records upon request. However, based on the sheer number of texts and calls listed in Trooper Carmichael's full compilation, it does not appear that any texts or calls had been deleted from Meghan's phone.

August 11
 Text exchanges between M. Fletcher and A. Gessler:
  4:32 p.m. to Gessler: What u doin tomorrow nite? U free?

Incident on Ten-Right Road

4:33 p.m. from Gessler: Maybe. What's up?
4:33 p.m. Missing u. Thinking of coming over.
4:34 p.m. In that case I'm free. Where when?
4:35 p.m. Haven't shot any pool for months. Losing my touch. I hear Taco King has tables. (smiley face)
4:35 p.m. Not sure about Taco King. A little too public.
4:35 p.m. U ashamed of me?
4:36 p.m. You know better than that.
4:37 p.m. Then C U there. 8:30-9ish.
4:37 p.m. You're going to be the death of me.
4:38 p.m. Exacly my plan. (kissy face)
4:41 p.m. to M. Cochran: Guess who Im seeing tomorro nite?
4:41: p.m. from M. Cochran: !!! thought u had a date with T?
4:42 p.m. I do. (smiley face)
4:43 p.m. Call received from M. Cochran. Call terminated 5:19 p.m.

August 12

Text exchanges between M. Fletcher and T. Blyler:

1:14 p.m. to Blyler: Not feeling like a movie tonight. U any good at pool?
1:15 p.m. from Blyler: Good enough to beat you.
1:15 p.m. Doubt it. Pick me up at 8.
1:16 p.m. Where we headed?
1:17 p.m. Taco King Hubbard. Three pool tables.
1:17 p.m. Cool. Been there once or twice. Winner gets whatever he wants.
1:18 p.m. Whatever she wants. (kissy face)

Randall Silvis

August 13:
All texts and calls:
12:28 a.m. Text to Alex Gessler: Can you give me a ride home?
12:29 a.m. Text from Gessler: What the hell was that all about!? Are you trying to get me killed?
12:30 a.m. Text to Gessler: I need a ride home! Unlock your car so I can hide in it.
12:30 a.m. Text from Gessler: Why didn't you tell me he was coming with you? What made you think that was a good idea?
12:31 a.m. Text to Gessler: Are you taking me home or not?
12:33 a.m. Text from Gessler: Don't make matters worse. I'll call you tomorrow.
12:34 Text to Gessler: Ur an even bigger pussy than I thot. Btw I'm pregnant. And guess whose the only guy I let go bareback.
12:35 a.m. Call to Missy Cochran. Call terminated 12:42 a.m.
12:43 a.m. Call from Missy Cochran; went to voicemail; no message left.
12:44 a.m. Text from Meghan to Missy: I'm fine, don't worry. Headed home with loser #1. Ttyl.
1:19 a.m. Text to Alex Gessler: So what are you going to do BMOC? Going to man up or not?
1:36 a.m. Text to Gessler: Coward.
9:25 a.m. Call from Tad Blyler. Went to voicemail. Message recorded: Hey. You still sleeping? That's okay. Anyway, I just called to say I'm sorry about getting so pissed last night. You know the way I get when I see you talking to other guys. And him especially. I know I gotta

Incident on Ten-Right Road

work on that, and I will, I promise. Give me a call when you get up, okay? Love you.

10: 07 a.m. Text from Cochran: What happened last nite?

10: 51 a.m. Text from Cochran: You ok? Call me!

10:56 a.m. Call from Cochran. Went to voicemail. Message recorded: What the hell are you doing, Meghan? You need to talk to me. I just need to know you're okay. Call me! Please!

11:00 a.m. Call from Cochran. Went to voicemail. No message recorded.

11:03 a.m. Call from Cochran. Went to voicemail. No message recorded.

11:06 a.m. Call from Cochran. Went to voicemail. No message recorded.

Notes:
- Missy Cochran when interviewed made no mention of Meghan's alleged pregnancy. Nor did Junie Fletcher. They didn't know? Inquire of medical examiner.
- Telephone call placed to the Cleveland Clinic: Clinic has no record of admitting Richard Hickman for bypass surgery or any other procedure. There is no Dr. Abdus Salam on staff. Online search identified only one Abdus Salam, a theoretical physicist who was co-winner of the Nobel Prize in 1979 for something called the electroweak unification theory. He was the first Muslim to win a Nobel Prize for science.
- Update: The medical examiner has confirmed that Meghan Fletcher was *not* pregnant at the time of her death. Could Meghan have

mistakenly believed that she was pregnant? Or told Gessler she was so as to force the desired outcome?

Interview with Theodore Blyler

This interview with Theodore Blyler (25), also known as Tad Blyler, is taking place inside my vehicle at a work site along route 173, Sandy Lake Road, Mercer County, Pennsylvania. Mr. Blyler is employed as a carpenter with Bryce Construction. Today is August 14th, and the time is 3:21 p.m.

DeMarco: According to what you told Chief Melvin, you and Meghan spent approximately a little over five hours at the Taco King Grille last Friday night.

Blyler: Sounds about right. You mind if I light up?

DeMarco: Yes I do. This shouldn't take long. Just need to verify some information.

Blyler: I can stand outside the car and talk, makes no difference to me.

DeMarco: I need you to focus here, Tad. It's nice and cool with the air conditioner running, you have that big field of corn to look at. Let's just get through this and you can get back to work.

Blyler: Yeah but I'd like to grab a smoke before I climb back up on that roof.

DeMarco: Here, take this. The bottle's never been opened.

Randall Silvis

Blyler: Feels warm.

DeMarco: Warm water is better than lung cancer, isn't it?

Blyler: I guess I'll find out.

DeMarco: Does Bryce always work you fellas on a Sunday?

Blyler: The rain don't care what day it is. We need to button up that roof by nightfall. There's supposed to be a cell out over Cleveland right now.

DeMarco: I'll be as quick as I can. Though I think the rain is going to miss us this time. Last I looked, it was heading north.

Blyler: Still got to play it safe.

DeMarco: *(after a pause)* So how did you and Meghan spend your time at the Taco King?

Blyler: Had some dinner. That took an hour or so. Then we went into the bar and waited for a pool table to open up. We played a couple games of eight-ball, sat around, talked, listened to the music, played a little more pool. That's about all there was to do.

DeMarco: Did you go there frequently with Meghan?

Blyler: That was the first time with her. I'd been there once or twice in my younger days, back when it was just a shot and beer bar called The Majestic, of all things.

DeMarco: Whose idea was it to go there last Friday night?

Blyler: Hers.

DeMarco: What made her want to go there?

Blyler: What makes a woman want to do anything? Some idea pops into her head, and that's that. This time it was playing pool.

Incident on Ten-Right Road

DeMarco: You didn't mind driving to Ohio just to shoot some pool?

Blyler: It's 20 miles, no big deal. Besides, I only had a quarter of a tank in my truck, so I figured I'd save six or seven dollars and fill up over there before coming home.

DeMarco: And did you?

Blyler: Yeah, at that Love's station back toward town. Gas is 40 cents cheaper a gallon there than it is here.

DeMarco: Approximately what time was it when Alex Gessler arrived at the bar?

Blyler: So you know about that, huh? *(pause)* I wasn't paying much attention to the time, but I'd say... We'd just started shooting pool, so a little after 9:00 maybe?

DeMarco: Were you aware that he would be there that night?

Blyler: Hell no.

DeMarco: But you were aware that he lived over that way, right?

Blyler: Yeah, but as far as I knew, he was away at college.

DeMarco: In August?

Blyler: I guess I didn't think about that. I mean, Meggie was taking classes. I figured it was normal to go to school in the summer. Truth is, he never entered my mind. He was in her past.

DeMarco: You knew that he and Meghan had dated in high school?

Blyler: She told me all about that back when we first got together.

DeMarco: Did you recognize him when he came into the bar?

Blyler: Nope. Never saw him before.

DeMarco: How did you find out who he was?

Blyler: I asked her.

DeMarco: Just out of the blue? You said who's that guy at the bar?

Blyler: She kept looking over at him and smiling, and he kept looking back. So after a while I asked her what was going on.

DeMarco: What made you think something was going on?

Blyler: It was like she was...performing for him, you know? Dancing and singing and always looking his way.

DeMarco: And how was he reacting to all this?

Blyler: Honestly, he looked confused. I caught him holding out his hands one time like, you know, what the fuck, girl? That's when I asked her if she knew him.

DeMarco: And she said what?

Blyler: She said, I know him very well. We dated all through high school.

DeMarco: How did you feel about that?

Blyler: How do you think I felt?

DeMarco: Tell me.

Blyler: Kinda sick. Kinda mad.

DeMarco: And then what happened?

Blyler: I said that's Gessler? And she said yeah, handsome, isn't he?

DeMarco: Did that make you see red?

Blyler: I was already seeing red. I told her to keep her eyes on the pool table or on me. Those were her only two choices.

DeMarco: Did she listen?

Incident on Ten-Right Road

Blyler: Not long enough. *(pause)* We finished our game, and there were other people waiting for the table, so we headed back to our booth. At least I did. I got there and turned around, and she was talking to him up at the bar.

DeMarco: And what did you do?

Blyler: I went up and told him to keep his fucking eyes to himself if he knew what was good for him.

DeMarco: And?

Blyler: He said some smartass thing like, it's a free country, he could look anywhere he wanted to look. So I got up in his face a little bit and told him to look at her again and see what happened.

DeMarco: Keep going. Take me through this.

Blyler: That's about all there was too it. He turned around and smiled at her, she kinda laughed a little, so I took her by the arm and I…escorted her back to the booth.

DeMarco: Would you say you escorted her forcibly?

Blyler: She didn't fight me, if that's what you're saying.

DeMarco: So you sat in the booth a while longer. Did you argue?

Blyler: Hell yes, we argued. *(pause)* And okay, maybe I said some things I wish I hadn't. Called her a name or two I shouldn't have. So then she said she'd find herself another way home, got up and went outside and called her friend Missy.

DeMarco: How do you know it was Missy she called?

Blyler: Cause I went out after a while and that's who she was talking to.

DeMarco: What do you mean by 'after a while'?

Blyler: I don't know. Five minutes or so.

71

DeMarco: You weren't worried about her being outside alone?

Blyler: I figured I'd give her a little time to cool off.

DeMarco: Had you cooled off?

Blyler: Not hardly. I was thinking about going up to the bar and ripping that guy a new asshole.

DeMarco: But you didn't.

Blyler: He was setting there with his back turned, hunched over the bar. So I finally got up and went outside to get her.

DeMarco: You didn't know that the two of them were texting back and forth?

Blyler: When?

DeMarco: While she was outside.

Blyler: That's bullshit.

DeMarco: I read the texts.

Blyler: You serious?

DeMarco: One hundred percent.

Blyler: What did they say?

DeMarco: I can't tell you that.

Blyler: Why the hell not? I have a right to know, don't I?

DeMarco: Actually, you don't.

Silence. Then the sound of the car door popping open.

DeMarco: Hold on a minute, Tad. You said you filled your tank up that night? Was that before or after you went to Taco King?

Blyler: What did the texts say?

DeMarco: Calm down for a minute. We're almost done here. Do me a favor and pull the door shut; you're letting all the cool air out.

Incident on Ten-Right Road

Blyler: I know you think it was me did that to her. It wasn't. I loved that girl.

DeMarco: Just tell me when you filled up your tank—before or after the Taco King?

Blyler: What's that have to do with anything?

DeMarco: I'm putting together a timeline. Pull the door shut and let's figure this out together, okay?

The sound of car door shutting.

Blyler: It was after.

DeMarco: So you have an angry young woman in your truck, you're angry, and you still take the time to get gas?

Blyler: What did you expect me to do—run out halfway home? You can get gas and still talk, you know. Ever hear of a window?

DeMarco: So what did you talk about?

Blyler: What did she say in those texts you claim she wrote?

DeMarco: No deal.

Blyler: Then fuck your questions. I need to get back to work.

DeMarco: So you weren't aware that ever since they broke up after high school, they were still hooking up every month or so?

Silence.

Blyler: Is it legal for you to make shit up like that? Just to see if I lose my temper or not?

DeMarco: That's not what I'm doing.

Blyler: You're feeding me a lot of bullshit, I know that much.

DeMarco: You never suspected there was still something going on between them?

Blyler: I still don't.

DeMarco: Then why were you so angry when you saw her talking to Gessler?

Blyler: Because it wasn't respectful, that's why. People in a relationship need to have respect for each other.

DeMarco: On the ride back home in your truck, did she happen to say that she was through with you?

Blyler: No.

DeMarco: That she wanted to be with Alex instead?

Blyler: Hell no! We argued about her talking to him, that's all. Couples argue all the time. It's no big deal. *(pause)* She's the kind that likes to push people's buttons, you know? I mean Jesus, she even argued with the guy at the truck stop. She was an argumentative person.

DeMarco: What was the argument at the truck stop about?

Blyler: I'm not even sure. She went in while I was getting gas because she said she was hungry. By the time I got inside, she was bitching out the guy behind the counter. Something about the pizza oven and hot food tables all being closed. Not even a hot dog left to buy.

DeMarco: She made a scene over a hot dog?

Blyler: More or less. And after I'd already bought her a nice dinner she hardly touched.

DeMarco: And the truck stop guy was angry too?

Blyler: Oh, he was giving it right back at her. Some gay guy. It was like watching a couple of alley cats spitting and hissing.

DeMarco: Can you think of anybody else she might have ticked off in the recent past? Somebody she made seriously angry?

Incident on Ten-Right Road

Blyler: I don't know. Just that shit-for-brains ex-boyfriend of hers. Plus she was scared to death her mother would be waiting up for her when she got home.

DeMarco: Scared how? What did she think her mother would do?

Blyler: Hide the truck keys. Ground her. She'd done that before.

DeMarco: Was she afraid of violence?

Blyler: From her mother? You mean like hitting and punching? Not that I know of. Junie isn't like that.

DeMarco: Did Meghan ever talk to you about her neighbor?

Blyler: Who? Mr. Dick?

DeMarco: So you heard the rumors too?

Blyler: They weren't no rumors, man. The guy's a pervert.

DeMarco: You didn't attend that school, right? So how would you know?

Blyler: Why would I not believe her?

DeMarco: So you heard about it from Meghan. What exactly did she tell you about him?

Blyler: Just what I said, he's a pervert. Got hand jobs and blowjobs from some of the girls. She knew several who'd done it.

DeMarco: Did that surprise you?

Blyler: That girls like sex too? You been living under a rock all your life?

DeMarco: Did you ever suspect that Meghan and Mr. Hickman were involved in some way?

Blyler: Why would you even ask something like that? That's sick.

DeMarco: She never told you she was one of those girls in the closet with him?

Blyler: Man, if you didn't have that uniform on, I would punch you right in the mouth.

DeMarco: Sometimes we don't know people as well as we think we do.

Blyler: Well I know this. She wasn't outside the bar trading texts with Gessler. She wasn't hooking up with him. And she thought Hickman was a joke. You can take all that to the bank.

DeMarco *(after a pause):* Here's what I keep getting hung up on. After leaving Taco King, you were alone with her in the truck for over 30 minutes. If none of what I told you is true, why were you both still so angry when you dropped her off?

Blyler: I never said we were.

DeMarco: Others said it.

Blyler: You telling me people were watching us at a quarter after one in the morning? That's another laugh. Don't think you're going to trick me into saying I did something I didn't.

DeMarco: After you left her off at the house that night, you were so angry that you burned rubber 20 feet down the highway.

Blyler: If it's illegal to burn rubber, arrest me. Otherwise....

DeMarco: Are you sure Meghan didn't say something on the ride home that made you lose your temper?

Blyler: What if she did? You already said you know I dropped her off and left. And that's the last I seen of her.

DeMarco: How did Meghan gain entry into her house? Did she carry a key?

Blyler: Now you want to talk about a fucking key? After what you said about her?

Incident on Ten-Right Road

DeMarco: Did you stay long enough to watch her go inside the house?

Blyler: I don't know, I probably did. I always did every other time.

DeMarco: Was the door unlocked, or did she have to unlock it? Or did her mother open it for her?

Blyler: They had a key hid in that plant hanging from the rafter.

DeMarco: So you saw her reach in and get it?

Blyler: That night? I don't know for sure. Maybe I did, but maybe I was peeling out by then.

DeMarco: But you knew where the key was?

Blyler: How could I tell you it was there if I didn't know it was there? It was always there.

DeMarco *(after a pause)*: How would you have reacted if Meghan had told you she was pregnant?

Blyler *(chuckling):* I would've laughed.

DeMarco: And why is that?

Blyler: Because I always wore a raincoat, that's why. She wouldn't let me do it otherwise.

DeMarco: So if she *were* pregnant….

Blyler: Oh fuck this bullshit. I don't know what you're trying to pull on me, man, but I'm done with it. Fuck you and the horse you rode in on.

Sound of car door popping open, then slamming shut.

End of interview.

Notes:
- The water bottle from which Blyler drank was left behind by him in the car, and was turned in to the lab for DNA sampling. I made the decision

not to ask him for a voluntary sample, sensing that he would become uncooperative and terminate the interview, which he did anyway.
- Question: What did Meghan tell Blyler in the truck on the ride home from Taco King? If she told him the truth about her relationship with Gessler, all bets are off. If she told him she was pregnant by Gessler, all bets are off. However, his surprise when I told him about her relationship with Gessler seemed genuine. On the other hand, even telling Blyler only that she did not want to see him anymore, and leaving Gessler out of it, would probably have been enough to set him off.
- What *was* her intention in bringing Gessler and Blyler together in the bar? Did she hope to incite Gessler to make their relationship permanent? Did she hope Blyler would beat him up? Did she simply want to make a side-by-side comparison of the two for her own benefit? Or did she just like to cause trouble?
- Would the coroner be able to differentiate between bruises made a few hours apart? I'm thinking about when Blyler "escorted" Meghan back to the booth. Did he leave any bruises on her arm? Were there any older bruises visible on her body? It's worth asking the coroner to take another look.
- Add Love's gas station attendant to list of potential witnesses. He might have observed some interaction between Blyler and Meghan.
- This much is certain: Blyler is known for having a short temper. Blyler knew the layout of the Fletcher home. Blyler knew the location of the

Incident on Ten-Right Road

house key. Blyler's Amish upbringing and attitude toward women would have flown in the face of Meghan's more liberated attitude. Apparently she feared his response had she admitted to being in the closet with Mr. Hickman, and so kept that information to herself. But then why would she have brought her two boyfriends face-to-face?

- I have to ask myself why a girl like Meghan would ever allow herself to get involved with a guy like Blyler. To tick off Gessler? Or does it all come back to her father, just as Missy suggested? I do not know. Though wasting time on that question is a zero-sum game if ever there was one. Sixty-two women in this state alone dead of domestic violence this year. A lot of bad choices are being made out there. A lot of reasons that nobody will ever know.
- Time to track down Boyfriend #2.

Interview with Alex Gessler

DeMarco: This interview with Alex Gessler is taking place in the living room of the Gessler family home at 34 Oak Tree Court, West Middlesex, Pennsylvania. Mr. Gessler is a student at Denison College—do you start your senior year this fall?

Gessler: Yes sir, in a couple of weeks. On the 27th of this month.

DeMarco: Mr. Gessler is a senior at Denison College. Today is August 14th, and the time is 5:10 p.m.

Gessler: It's Denison University, actually.

DeMarco: Okay, thanks. Are you employed somewhere this summer, Alex?

Gessler: No, Dad wanted me to spend the summer working on my game. I play golf at school.

DeMarco: What fairway are we looking at out there?

Gessler: That's number 14. It's a 493 yard par five, dogleg right.

DeMarco: Do a lot of balls find their way into your back yard?

Gessler: Not as many as you'd think. We're at just over 300 yards here, so most guys hit short, then pop an iron over the water.

Incident on Ten-Right Road

DeMarco: You must have quite a game to play on the college team.

Gessler: I'm fairly steady in the high 60s, low 70s.

DeMarco: Do you plan to play professionally?

Gessler: I'm not good enough for that. But it's a good game to play, and play well, in the business world.

DeMarco: That's what you're studying?

Gessler: Security and risk management. That's where the big money is.

DeMarco: Sounds like you have it all figured out.

Gessler: I hope so.

DeMarco: It's a beautiful house you have here. You said your mom and dad are away for the weekend?

Gessler: We have a place at Put-in Bay. They go out almost every weekend. Should be home later tonight.

DeMarco: I'm sorry I missed meeting them. You have any brothers or sisters?

Gessler: One sister. Jenna. She's six years older than me. She's in pediatrics in Chicago.

DeMarco: She's a nurse?

Gessler: Doctor of Pediatric Medicine.

DeMarco: That's impressive. *(pause)* Meghan was studying to be a nurse, wasn't she?

Gessler: Yeah, I think that's right.

DeMarco: You're not sure?

Gessler: No, I am. It's the, uh, associate's in applied science degree. Sorry; I'm just nervous, I guess.

DeMarco: There's no need to be nervous, Alex.

I'm just trying to fill in the gaps, you know? I appreciate you agreeing to meet with me.

Gessler: I'm glad to help.

DeMarco: What makes this so difficult is, by all accounts Meghan was very well-liked. No enemies whatsoever. You, of course, must have been very fond of her.

Gessler: I was, yeah. Yeah. I was.

DeMarco: How long did the two of you date?

Gessler: She was in 10th grade when we started, I think. I was 11th. So two years.

DeMarco: You broke up the summer after you graduated?

Gessler: Yeah, we just, uh…. We agreed it would be the best thing for both of us, seeing as how I'd be away most of the year.

DeMarco: How far is Denison from here? We're basically sitting on the state line right now, so it's got to be what, three hours?

Gessler: A little less on a good day. But she's another…her house is another 20 minutes east.

DeMarco: You're right, though; it's true. Long distance relationships seldom work. Especially at that age.

Gessler: That's sort of what we figured.

DeMarco: And after that, she started dating Tad Blyler. And how about you? Do you have a girlfriend?

Gessler: I've just sort of been, you know, playing the field.

DeMarco: But after three years of college? There's nobody special in your life?

Gessler: Not really.

DeMarco: Well, that's your business, not mine.

Incident on Ten-Right Road

Let's go back to Tad for a minute. Did you know him at all?

Gessler: Only through what she told me about him.

DeMarco: And what did she tell you?

Gessler: I know he's a good bit older than her. Mid-20s, I think. Used to be Amish. Works as a carpenter. Just general things like that.

DeMarco: She never said anything about their relationship? How serious it was? How he treated her? You ever talk about anything like that?

Gessler: She did say he has a bad temper. Tends to blow up over little things.

DeMarco: So you and Meghan must have kept in touch after you broke up. Is that correct?

Gessler: Yeah, we, uh, you know, stayed in touch by text. Talked on the phone now and then.

DeMarco: Never got together face-to-face?

Silence.

DeMarco: Is that a difficult question to answer, Alex? *(pause)* Alex?

Gessler: Who all have you talked to so far?

DeMarco: All that matters is that I'm talking to you right now. Since you and Meghan broke up, you've never gotten together to reminisce about old times?

Gessler *(after a pause)*: So how much do you know?

DeMarco: What I *need* to know is everything. Everything you know. If you want to help me find out who did this terrible thing to Meghan—and you do, right?

Gessler: Of course I do.

DeMarco: I know you do. So listen. I'm not here to judge anybody. My only job right now is to find out who killed Meghan and why. I'm sure you would like to know that too.

Gessler: Yeah, but I don't see what our friendship has to do with any of that. She must have been involved in stuff I never knew about.

DeMarco: What kind of stuff?

Gessler: I don't know, maybe drugs? Her father was into drugs, using them and selling them, I remember her telling me that. Maybe he came back or something. Nobody seems to know what happened to him after he left.

DeMarco: Did she ever give you any indication that she was in touch with her father?

Gessler: No, I'm just saying…I don't know. Maybe it's a possibility.

DeMarco *(after a pause)*: So here's the thing, Alex. I am aware that you and Meghan never stopped seeing each other. I know you saw her at the Taco King on Friday night. And I know she texted you that same night.

Gessler: I didn't get any texts from her!

DeMarco: This isn't going to go well for you if you lie to me, Alex.

Gessler: I swear! I don't have any texts from her on my phone!

DeMarco: May I take a look at your phone?

Gessler: I, uh…I'm not sure I, uh….

DeMarco: You were holding it in your hand when you answered the door. Is that it in your pocket?

Gessler: Yeah, yeah I guess it is.

DeMarco: Do you mind letting me have a look?

Incident on Ten-Right Road

(pause) You can either say sure, why not, or I can dig into your phone records. Your choice.

Gessler *(taking cell phone from his side pocket)*: There are no texts from her, I swear. Nothing all week, actually.

(He handed me the phone, and I checked the text message log. Last text exchange with Meghan was ten days earlier. Back-and-forth joking about a 7-Eleven customer she thought looked like Steven Tyler with a dead cat for a hairpiece.)

Gessler: There, you see? Nothing from her at all.

DeMarco: Nothing from anybody that night except your mom. Does that strike you as unusual? Because it strikes me as unusual.

Gessler: I don't know what you mean.

DeMarco: You're a popular guy. Dozens and dozens of texts on every day except last Friday. And your contact list is a mile long.

Gessler: Why are you looking at my contact list? Can I have my phone back, please?

DeMarco: Here you go. *(pause)* So do you have an explanation as to why Meghan's phone shows several texts to you on Friday night, and yours shows none? *(pause)* Alex?

Gessler: I didn't have anything to do with what happened to her. I swear to God I didn't!

DeMarco: Is that why you deleted the texts? Because you were afraid they implicated you somehow?

Gessler: They didn't implicate me in anything. I just didn't want anybody thinking I was involved.

DeMarco: Why would they think that if the texts didn't suggest it?

Randall Silvis

Gessler: I don't know! But you're thinking it. I can hear it in your voice.

DeMarco: Have I even once insinuated that I suspect you of being involved? If I did, I apologize. I came here hoping to get some help from you, that's all. Because I know you two were close. I know you cared deeply about each other. What I don't understand, though, is why you deleted her texts.

Gessler: I don't know, I wish I hadn't. I just got scared when you called me. I'm sorry. I'm sorry I did it.

DeMarco: Who's your carrier?

Gessler: What?

DeMarco: Your phone carrier. ATT, Verizon, T-Mobile—which one?

Gessler: Verizon.

DeMarco: Then we're in luck. Verizon retains the contents of all text messages for several days. I can have a printout of them by tomorrow.

Gessler: Don't you need a warrant or a subpoena or something like that?

DeMarco: A phone call, Alex; that's all it takes. We do it all the time. But you know what? I already have Meghan's phone. She didn't delete any texts. So all I would be looking for on your phone are texts and calls to somebody else. *(pause)* You okay? *(pause)* You doing okay there?

Gessler: I don't think I can talk anymore tonight. I'm not feeling well.

DeMarco: To be honest with you, you don't look well. I hope you're not coming down with something. We haven't even gotten into what happened at the bar that night. Why you were there, why she was there, who said what to whom, all that kind of stuff.

Incident on Ten-Right Road

Gessler: I'm sorry, I can't do anymore tonight. Maybe we better wait till my mom and dad get back.

DeMarco: Tomorrow's good. How's tomorrow afternoon work for you and your folks? That will give me time to get the warrant and look over your texts.

Gessler: I didn't do anything! I don't know why you should be allowed to look at my texts. They're supposed to be private.

DeMarco: Sit down for a minute, Alex. Come on, just a minute. I know you're not feeling well, and I apologize for that. It was not my intention to upset you. But you need to know something. Innocent people cooperate with the police. People who have something to hide, they don't. *(pause)* If there is any information in your deleted texts that I can use, then those texts are evidence. And you know what it's called when people hide evidence, right?

No verbal response from Gessler; he nodded.

DeMarco: All right then. You let me have your phone for a day, we recover the texts without having to get a warrant, and I bring the phone back to you tomorrow. How does that sound?

Gessler: What do you mean you recover them without a warrant?

DeMarco: There's an app we use. Most times it works great, sometimes we can only recover part of the material. But either way, with or without a warrant, we will recover every single text you deleted. It takes the bull's eye off you if you hand the phone over voluntarily.

Gessler: Are you going to look all through it? At the pictures and everything?

DeMarco: I'm not here as a porn cop, Alex. I'm not here as a drug cop. How about if we agree that only information pertinent to this case can be accessed? There's no kiddie porn on there, right?

Gessler: God, no.

DeMarco: Then you have nothing to worry about. Just say this for the recording: I am voluntarily giving you my cell phone so that information pertinent to the death of Meghan Fletcher can be accessed.

Gessler *(after a pause):* I am voluntarily giving you my cell phone so that information pertinent to the death of Meghan Fletcher can be accessed.

DeMarco: Excellent. Thank you. You have no idea what a wise choice you've made. I'll call you tomorrow, okay? To set up a time to return the phone to you.

No verbal response from Gessler; he nodded.

DeMarco: Very good. By the way, I'm going to need a sample of your DNA before I go.

Gessler: Do I have to?

DeMarco: Do you want to clear yourself of suspicion or not? It's just a mouth swab, that's all. Walk out to the car with me. It will take you five seconds max.

Gessler: What if the neighbors see?

DeMarco: I could have come in full uniform in a patrol car. And if you don't agree to the sample voluntarily, that's what I'll have to do tomorrow. Come on, you can sit in the car for a few seconds. I have tinted windows.

The sound of walking.

Gessler: What am I supposed to tell my mom and dad?

DeMarco: I'd go with the truth if I were you.

End of interview.

Notes:
- My guess is he deleted the texts because of Meghan's claim that she was pregnant to him. I bet he needed a diaper change after reading that. However, he doesn't strike me as a kid who could slice somebody's throat. But could he call a buddy afterward? Make a business arrangement? In all likelihood he knew about the key in the hanging basket. Did he pass that information on to somebody who could do what he himself isn't capable of doing? But why not just man up and take responsibility (even though the claim, unbeknownst to him, was bogus.) Wait a minute; she wanted him to man up. Maybe that's why she engineered the vis-à-vis with Blyler at Taco King. Because she wanted Gessler to man up, quit playing around and be with her. She must have believed that seeing her with Blyler would make Alex come to his senses. When it didn't, she played the pregnancy card. Unfortunately, that didn't do the trick either. And why not? Because she's been focused on her emotions, whereas Gessler has been focused on his future. "Security and risk management," he said. "That's where the big money is." I am so looking forward to reading that phone data.

Data recovery info

Several of the texts recovered from Alex Gessler's cell phone by Trooper Carmichael of Pennsylvania State Police Troop D, Mercer County, duplicate texts found on the cell phone belonging to the victim. The following additional texts were all sent and/or received by Gessler between 1:41-2:02 a.m.

August 12.

Gessler to Liz: I need to tell you something.

Liz to Gessler: Thanks for waking me up.

Gessler: I might have a problem.

Liz: I'm not driving anywhere tonight. You want to come here, okay. He's away for the weekend.

Gessler: I just need to tell you something. This is really bad.

Liz: What is?

Gessler: I saw Meghan tonight.

Liz: Asshole!?

Gessler: Just talked. Went to Taco King for a beer. She was there with her boyfriend.

Liz: What a nice coincidence.

Gessler: It was weird. I think she wanted us to get into a fight.

Liz: Didn't I tell you she's nothing but trouble? You need her out of your life.

Incident on Ten-Right Road

Gessler: I know. I'm going to tell her we're done.
Liz: Get ready for her to go ballistic.
Gessler: She'll have to get over it eventually.
Liz: You hope. She seems dangerous to me.
Gessler: Dangerous how? You don't even know her.
Liz: I know the type. A woman scorned is a dangerous thing. Pretty soon you'll need to tell all your little playthings goodbye. One more year and that's it.
Gessler: I need to tell you something else.
Liz: Hurry up. I need my beauty sleep.
Gessler: She promised me she was on the pill.
Liz: OMG!!! Did you get that bitch pregnant?
Gessler: I don't know what to do. What if she won't have an abortion?
Liz: You'll be paying child support for the next 20 years. And if that's the case I'm staying put right where I am.
Gessler: I just feel like taking off somewhere. Mexico maybe. Been there a couple of times.
Liz: You've been to resorts. You think Mommy and Daddy will finance a dead-beat babydaddy in Cozumel? You know what your mother is like. You really screwed yourself this time, Alex.
Gessler: What can I do?
Liz: Short of killing her? Can you pay her off?
Gessler: I don't know. Probably not.
Liz: How much money can you pull together?
Gessler: Four or five thousand of my own. But I'm supposed to use that for books and food at school this year.
Liz: You see what I mean about the way your mother is? She'll make you marry her.
Gessler: WHAT SHOULD I DO?

Liz: Any chance you could scare her into getting rid of it?

Gessler: How?

Liz: Tell her you have some kind of genetic disease that the baby will get.

Gessler: She can have that tested though, right?

Liz: Then really scare her. Scare the life out of her.

Gessler: And how do I do that?

Liz: You tell her she either gets rid of the kid, or she tells her bf it's his, or—How does she know it isn't his?

Gessler: She made him use a condom.

Liz: And she told you she was on the pill? Couldn't you figure out she was lying to you?

Gessler: I didn't know till tonight that she made him use a condom.

Liz: She WANTED you to knock her up. You have to get rid of that kid one way or the other.

Gessler: Maybe I should just go ahead and marry her. That would make everybody but me happy.

Liz: Everybody but you, asshole?

Gessler: We could still keep seeing each other. You stay married and we just keep going on like nothing ever happened.

Liz: And I keep letting him stick his dick in me? That doesn't bother you anymore?

Gessler: It does but I don't know what else to do.

Liz: You're such a child. One crisis in your life and you wimp out.

Gessler: I don't want to be a father yet! We'll end up living in a trailer somewhere!!

Liz: I already told you what you need to do.

Gessler: You don't know her. She doesn't scare that easily.

Incident on Ten-Right Road

Liz: You're worthless, you know that?
Gessler: I'm sorry.

Text exchange at 6:29 a.m.
  August 12,
   Liz to Gessler: You owe me BIG TIME.
   8:19 a.m., **Gessler to Liz**: Just woke up. Owe you why?
   8:24 a.m., **Liz to Gessler**: I must've been sleep-texting. Don't even remember writing that.
   End of text exchanges.

Notes:
- The individual named "Liz" has since been identified as Elizabeth Tenney née Foltz (23) of 6809 Chestnut Ridge Road, Hubbard Township, Hubbard, Ohio. Married, no children. Mrs. Tenney is employed as the loan officer of the Hubbard Huntington Bank.
- Where was Tenney between 2:02 and 6:29 a.m. on August 12? Need tower ping info.
- Question: Blyler said Meghan made him use a condom. She told Gessler she was on the pill. Was she really on the pill, or trying all this time to get pregnant by Gessler? Junie Fletcher might be able to answer the pill question, but.... Is that information worth causing her more grief? Chief Melvin collected Meghan's cell phone at the scene of the murder, which means that Junie never read the texts and doesn't know that her daughter told Gessler she was pregnant. Tricky situation. I'm going to consider it a moot point at least for now. Tenney is up to bat.

Summary of forensics reports

Tad Blyler's truck: Trace amounts of blood on the steering wheel of Blyler's pickup truck tested positive for Blyler's DNA. No other matches. Hair samples collected from the passenger seat match the victim's DNA. Other hair and skin cell samples indicate at least two additional individuals: currently unknown.

Meghan Fletcher's bedroom: Blood samples collected from various places throughout Meghan Fletcher's bedroom show positive matches for Meghan Fletcher only. No other individuals identifiable. Hair and skin cell samples match the victim, plus Missy Cochran, Theodore Blyler, and the victim's mother, Junie Fletcher. The identity of the two other samples remains unknown. Awaiting DNA results for Alex Gessler. Must obtain DNA sample from Elizabeth Tenney ASAP.

Summary report of my examination of PA State Game Lands #42 entrance area

Having weighed the probability for each of the persons of interest in the death of Meghan Fletcher (Missy Cochran, Richard Hickman, Tad Blyler, and Alex Gessler), I considered the possibility that the true assailant is an individual as-yet unknown. Neither Junie Fletcher nor Richard Hickman reported hearing or seeing a vehicle on Ten-Right Road in the early morning hours of August 12 (though Hickman reports being asleep, and Junie Fletcher was busy getting ready for work.) The two functioning security cameras nearest Ten-Right Road (the 7-Eleven store and the Ace Hardware store, both on old route 68), are nearly four miles from the intersection of Ten-Right Road and route 68; all vehicles captured in that footage have been identified and their drivers/passengers cleared. Therefore, the assailant who entered the Fletcher home on the morning of August 12th must have approached the house from another direction. Only two possibilities exist.

At approximately 6:30 a.m. on the morning of August 15th, I drove down Ten-Right Road to explore the possibility that Meghan Fletcher's assailant might have entered Ten-Right Road via one of the two intersecting trails. According to Trooper Morgan, an avid hunter, a seasonal road borders the eastern perimeter of State Game Lands #42 not far from where Ten-Right Road dead-ends at the entrance to the Game Lands. The unpaved, grassy road is said to intersect with old Route 68 near the West Middlesex Conservancy building. The only other ingress or egress from Ten-Right Road is an ATV trail that branches off the State Game Lands trail 20 yards beyond the trailhead; its terminus is currently unknown to this investigator, but is assumed to be the nearest farm to the north of the Game Lands. Both trails show signs of recent use. The ATV trail, however, is too narrow and deeply rutted in places to allow passage of a full-size vehicle.

The other road is wide enough to accommodate any standard vehicle, though heavy brush and small trees closely flank both sides of the road. A vehicle equipped with 4-wheel drive could negotiate the Game Lands road without difficulty. I noted that several small branches had been broken from the recent passage of a vehicle. Tire ruts were deep and well-defined, suggesting that a vehicle had used that road when the ground was soft from rain, but not so early during the last rainfall (on the morning of August 12th) that the subsequent rain would have washed the tread marks away. I used my cell phone to take several photos of those tread marks.

After assessing the proximity and sightline from the Game Lands entrance to the Fletcher home, I ascertained that a vehicle might approach the game lands from the Conservancy, drive to within 20 yards of the Game Lands #42 sign, and remain invisible from Ten-Right Road. Had the driver of said vehicle

Incident on Ten-Right Road

then walked another 50 yards or so in the direction of the Fletcher and Hickman homes, heavy brush and trees alongside the road would have provided excellent concealment. From that point on or closer, the Fletcher home could easily be watched with a pair of inexpensive binoculars. More powerful binoculars, such as those owned by Richard Hickman, would of course permit surveillance of the house from an even greater distance.

By crossing the road and approaching the Fletcher house from the woods behind it, an assailant would be nearly impossible to see. If this were done between 5:30 a.m., by which time Junie Fletcher had left for work, and 8:00 a.m., at which time Hickman claims to have awakened for the day, it is likely that no one would have seen the assailant. Mail delivery to Ten-Right Road does not take place until late morning. Sunrise on August 12 was at 6:25 a.m., but at that time the cloud cover was still thick; during that hour between Junie's departure from the house and sunrise, the assailant could have followed the gravel road from the Game Lands entrance to the Fletcher house with a minimal chance of being seen by anyone.

The rain on the morning of August 12th might or might not have obliterated any shallow foot tracks between the Game Lands trail and the gravel lot. But even if the rain had stopped before the assailant entered the house, the assailant's feet and cuffs, possibly up to the knees or higher depending on the path taken, would have been soaked by rain and, if the assailant ventured off the road, by wet weeds and grass. The fact that neither Junie Fletcher, Missy Cochran, the EMTs nor the ERT or other law enforcement personnel noticed any signs of anomalous moisture inside the house suggests that the assailant entered the house after Junie Fetcher's departure that morning, and well before Missy Cochran arrived at 11:40 a.m., by which time the moisture would have evaporated. It is also possible that any anomalous moisture went unnoticed by those individuals because of the moisture they brought onto the porch and into the house. Less probable is the possibility that the assailant left his/her wet clothes at the door.

Having made this determination, I then walked up Ten-Right Road as far as the Fletcher house, remaining a few feet within the tree/brush line. I did pass three separate places where either a large animal or a human had exited the tree/brush line, but found no other evidence to conclude more than that. I then crossed to the Hickman side of the road and walked back toward the Game Lands parking lot.

Approximately 40 yards from that lot, I spotted a disposable e-cigarette in the weeds. I returned to the car for a camera and evidence bags, then documented the position of the e-cigarette before bagging it. An area approximately five feet from the e-cigarette appeared to be trampled down more than the surrounding area. Photographs were taken, and later turned over with the e-cigarette to the ERT for cataloging and forwarding to the lab.

Conclusion: On the day of the incident, the ERT found no signs of forced entry to the Fletcher home. Did Meghan get out of bed to let somebody inside? Then return to bed, only to have her throat cut? Unlikely. The most probable scenario is that the individual, dressed in dark clothing, followed the

Incident on Ten-Right Road

gravel road from the Game Lands entrance to the Fletcher home sometime between 5:30-6:30 a.m., left his wet shoes at or just inside the door, proceeded to the victim's bedroom, and assaulted the victim. There is no reason to believe that robbery was the motive. It is more likely that the missing money was happened upon by chance, and that the photograph was taken as a trophy. My gut tells me that the assailant knew Meghan Fletcher, knew the location of the door key, had some knowledge of the area, and was familiar with the layout of the house.

Notes:
- How many other people knew about the key? Missy Cochran, Tad Blyler, Alex Gessler, and Hickman for sure. Meghan's father? Other Fletcher acquaintances?
- How many of those individuals informed others of the key's placement? Could be dozens.

Second interview with Alex Gessler

Because of the information about Elizabeth Tenney recovered from Alex Gessler's phone, and the implication of some of those texts, I decided that Gessler would be more receptive to further questioning if alone with me and not accompanied by his parents in the comfort of their home. I telephoned him at 8:00 a.m., and, fortunately, he was not eager to be questioned in front of his parents, and agreed to meet me a few miles from his home.

DeMarco: The following interview with Alex Gessler is taking place in my vehicle in the West Middlesex Dairy Queen parking lot. Today is August 15th and the time is 9:11 a.m. *(pause)* So, Alex, thank you for the use of your phone. Turns out we have a little more to talk about, don't we? Do you want a coffee or cold drink before we get started?

Gessler: You got all the texts?

DeMarco: We did. So you know what I'm going to ask now, right?

Gessler: You want to know about Liz.

DeMarco: Elizabeth Tenney, to be exact. Age 23. The loan office at the Huntington Bank in Hubbard. That's the Liz we're talking about here, correct?

Gessler: Same one.

Incident on Ten-Right Road

DeMarco: How long have you had a relationship with her?

Gessler: I met her during orientation at college. First day. She was one of the orientation leaders.

DeMarco: And that's when you started dating?

Gessler: I wouldn't call it dating. She was already engaged. We started fooling around.

DeMarco: Having sex? *(pause)* I need a verbal answer, please.

Gessler: Yes, having sex.

DeMarco: And eventually it became something more serious?

Gessler: I guess so. I mean… After she got married it was like…she didn't want to be with him anymore. She started finding all these things wrong with him. And that's when she said she wanted to be with me. That we'd be good for each other.

DeMarco: You were still seeing Meghan during this time?

Gessler: Not as often, though.

DeMarco: And Liz knew about this?

Gessler: She was cool with it at first. Then after she started getting annoyed with everything her husband did, she wanted me to stop. But I said as long as you're having sex with him, I should be able to do the same with Meghan.

DeMarco: She was planning to divorce her husband?

Gessler: She was going to file around the first of the year sometime. So we'd be free and clear by the time I graduated.

DeMarco: Was her husband aware that she was going to ask for a divorce?

Gessler: Still isn't, as far as I know.

DeMarco: So you were okay with the idea of eventually marrying Liz?

Gessler: Well, like she always said, we'd be good for each other.

DeMarco: Good how?

Gessler: Professionally. She had a degree and a good job, she was intelligent and spoke well, dressed nice, knew how to act around people.

DeMarco: And Meghan didn't?

Gessler: We moved in different circles. She wouldn't have fit in.

DeMarco: This is what you thought or what Liz thought?

Gessler: She's the one who said it first but...I always knew it was true. Ever since high school. So did Meghan. *(pause)* It turned out that Liz's father and mine knew each other. Even played golf together a couple of times. Her dad works for Wells Fargo Advisors out of Youngstown. He has lots of good connections.

DeMarco: Which bode well for your future career.

Gessler: I guess you could say that.

DeMarco: And that's why you panicked when Meghan told you she was pregnant.

Gessler: I didn't hurt her! I had nothing to do with what happened to her.

DeMarco: Why was your DNA found in her bedroom?

Gessler: What?

DeMarco: Do you need for me to repeat the question?

Gessler: We had sex there. Lots of times. In her bedroom and in the living room. And out back in the yard. Her mother was gone every day until 2:00 or so.

Incident on Ten-Right Road

DeMarco *(after a pause):* What exactly did you think Liz meant when she suggested, in reference to Meghan, that you "scare the life out of her?"

Gessler: I don't know what I thought. Threaten her, I guess.

DeMarco: Threaten her with what? Threaten her life?

Gessler: I never could have done that. I just figured she wanted me to hit her or something. But I never would have done that either.

DeMarco: Could Liz do something like that? Does she have it in her?

Long pause.

Gessler: Maybe. Probably so.

DeMarco: She sounds like a very ambitious woman. Is she more ambitious than you?

Gessler: My parents don't think I'm ambitious at all. Dad calls me a coaster. Says I just coast along through life.

DeMarco: Is he right?

Gessler *(after a pause)*: I guess so.

DeMarco: What kind of vehicle does Liz drive?

Gessler: A Jeep Wrangler. Why?

DeMarco: What model?

Gessler: The Sport. Soft top.

DeMarco: Year and color?

Gessler: Inca Gold. The idea of being surrounded by gold appealed to her. She bought it new two years ago when she got the job at the bank.

DeMarco: Four-wheel drive?

Gessler: Yes sir. Why does that matter?

DeMarco: Does she do much off-roading with it?

Gessler: That's sort of why she bought it. I guess her husband's into that kind of thing big-time.

DeMarco: Any chance you might have told her Meghan's address?

Gessler (*after a pause*): No.

DeMarco: But she knew Meghan's last name, right? And where she went to high school?

Gessler: Actually….

DeMarco: Spit it out, Alex. This is not the time for secrets.

Gessler: She made me drive by her house one time.

DeMarco: Liz made you drive by Meghan's house?

Gessler: She wanted to see where she lived. I guess because I was always defending Meghan to her, telling her how poor she was, how rough she had it. But I wish I hadn't done that. Liz just made even more fun of her after she saw her house. Called her my redneck girlfriend, my hillbilly honey, stuff like that.

DeMarco: Did you tell her where the front door key was hidden?

Gessler: God, no. Why would I tell her that?

DeMarco *(after a pause):* What kind of vapor cigarette does Liz smoke?

Gessler: How do you even know she smokes them?

DeMarco: What kind?

Gessler: She hardly ever does it. Not around me anyway. She knows I don't like it.

DeMarco: What kind, Alex?

Gessler: It's one of those disposable minis that come two to a pack. Vanilla. Why are you asking me all this?

DeMarco: So the time you drove past her house. You just drove past? And then what?

Incident on Ten-Right Road

Gessler: We went down to the end of the road, turned around, and drove back to my place.

DeMarco: That's all you did?

Gessler: That's all.

DeMarco: All those times back in high school when you visited Meghan at her house, did the two of you ever go down to the Game Lands?

Gessler: Lots of times, yeah. She loved walking down there.

DeMarco: On the Game Lands trail?

Gessler: Yeah, it's a nice quiet place to walk.

DeMarco: Did you ever go all the way to the Conservancy?

Gessler: A couple of times. It's almost five miles roundtrip, so not that often. She used to practice on it when she was running track.

DeMarco: Did you ever take Liz back that trail?

Gessler: Never.

DeMarco: Neither walking nor driving?

Gessler: No sir. My car's not made to go off-road.

DeMarco: How about in Liz's Jeep?

Gessler: She didn't like me riding in her Jeep. She was always afraid somebody would see us together and tell her husband.

DeMarco: I want you to think back on the time you drove Liz past Meghan's house. You went down to the end of the road, which is the Game Land's trailhead, and you turned around. But did you sit there for a while and talk?

Gessler: I guess that's possible.

DeMarco: Did you or she happen to mention the trail?

Gessler: I suppose one of us might have. I really can't remember what we talked about. I mean, why is any of that important?

DeMarco *(after a pause)*: We're done for now. But you need to avoid all contact with Liz until I tell you otherwise. Do you understand?

Gessler: What if she contacts me?

DeMarco: You don't respond. Period.

Gessler: Okay.

DeMarco: No texts, no phone calls, no face-to-face. No direct or indirect contact of any kind whatsoever. You don't give anybody else a message to convey to her. If I find out you've done otherwise, there will be consequences. Are we clear on this?

Gessler: Yes sir. We're clear. Am I, uh…so I'm not in any trouble then?

DeMarco: We'll see how it goes.

End of interview.

Notes:
- He's still holding back. Who is he afraid of? Me? His parents? Liz Tenney? Prison? Yep; all of the above. But he's my ace in the hole. I need just a little more pressure in the hose, and then I'm going to flush him clean.

Narrative of August 15th activity

Based on the results of my examination of the Game Lands #42 area, and the texts exchanged between Alex Gessler and Liz Tenney a few hours prior to the murder of Meghan Fletcher, and the information gleaned from my most recent conversation with Gessler, I thought it prudent to take a preliminary look at Mrs. Tenney's vehicle asap. At approximately 10:40 on the morning of August 15th, I found it parked in the Hubbard, Ohio Huntington Bank parking lot. I drove my personal vehicle and was dressed in plainclothes.

The vehicle appeared to have been washed and waxed recently. However, the left front fender of the vehicle bore scratches that might have been incurred by driving the vehicle down a narrow lane lined with trees and bushes. Clumps of dried mud and grass could be observed packed into the undercarriage. The tread pattern on her tires appeared to match the tread marks I photographed on the Game Lands road.

At this point I contacted Station Commander Lukovitch by telephone and apprised him of the situation. With his approval I contacted Hubbard Chief of Police Ron Jeffries and informed him of the texts, the tread marks, the e-cigarette, and Gessler's confirmation that Liz Tenney smokes e-cigarettes identical to the one I recovered, and I requested that the vehicle be seized.

He agreed to do so. He dispatched Deputy Simpson to the scene.

Deputy Simpson arrived on the scene a few minutes before the tow truck. I informed him of the situation. He proceeded to photograph the vehicle and its visible contents. He also collected samples of the mud and grass lodged in the undercarriage.

Mrs. Tenney emerged from the bank as the tow-truck was being moved into position. She first approached Deputy Simpson and demanded to know what was going on. He referred her to me. As Ohio is a one-party consent state, and as I feared that Mrs. Tenney would not agree to be questioned if she knew I was recording the conversation, I chose not to inform her of that fact. The following is a transcript of that recording:

> **Tenney**: What are you doing with my car?
> **DeMarco**: Is your name Elizabeth Tenney?
> **Tenney**: Who are you?
> **DeMarco** *(here I showed her my badge)*: I'm Sergeant Ryan DeMarco of the Pennsylvania State Police. That man by your vehicle is Deputy Simpson of the Hubbard Police.
> **Tenney**: This isn't Pennsylvania, you know.
> **DeMarco**: That's why the deputy is here.
> **Tenney**: Then maybe I should ask him what the hell you're doing with my car.
> **DeMarco**: So you are the owner of this vehicle?
> **Tenney:** How many times have I said 'my car' already? Why is it being hooked up to that truck?
> **DeMarco**: I'm investigating a crime that took place in Pennsylvania a few days ago. A vehicle matching your Jeep's description was seen in the area around that time.

Incident on Ten-Right Road

Tenney: Do you know how many Jeep Wrangler's look just like mine?

DeMarco: Where were you between 5:00 and 8:00 a.m. last Saturday morning?

Tenney: I was in bed, where I should have been.

DeMarco: Can your husband corroborate that?

Tenney: He was at a weekend golf outing.

DeMarco: And where did this outing take place?

Tenney: Quail Hollow.

DeMarco: In North Carolina?

Tenney: The one in Painesville. Why are you asking me these questions?

DeMarco: So you were alone that morning?

Tenney: I just told you I was alone all weekend.

DeMarco: And you were not in French Creek Township, Pennsylvania?

Tenney: I don't even know where that is.

DeMarco: Do you know Meghan Fletcher?

Tenney: Who? I don't know anybody named Fletcher.

DeMarco: Do you know Alex Gessler?

Tenney: He's, uh…yeah, his father and mine are business associates. I've seen him a couple of times.

DeMarco: So you wouldn't call him a friend?

Tenney: Why? Has he done something wrong?

DeMarco: Would you call him a friend?

Tenney: I don't know him well enough to call him a friend. Where are they taking my Jeep? And how am I supposed to get home today?

DeMarco: So you do not have a sexual relationship with Alex Gessler?

Tenney: What? Why would you even ask such a question? I'm married. So no. I do not have a sexual relationship with Alex Gessler or anybody else other than my husband. Don't you need a search warrant to take my Jeep?

DeMarco: We can seize it without a warrant. A warrant will be obtained in order to search it.

Tenney: Why would you search it? What are you expecting to find in there?

DeMarco: Would you mind if I have a look at your cell phone?

Tenney: Hell yes, I mind. Look, I have to get back to work. I need to know where my Jeep will be at 5:00 tonight so that I can pick it up. I assume you will be bringing it back here for me.

DeMarco: I'm afraid it won't be available to you tonight. Have you ever been to Meghan Fletcher's home?

Tenney: Who the hell is Meghan Fletcher?

DeMarco: So you deny knowing Meghan Fletcher, and having a relationship with Alex Gessler?

Tenney: This is bull. This is illegal. You can't stand here at my place of employment and talk to me like this. I'm calling my lawyer.

At this point Ms. Tenney returned to the bank.

Notes:
- On the basis of the several falsehoods stated by Ms. Tenney, I requested that Deputy Simpson obtain search warrants for the Jeep Wrangler, the Tenney home, and for a DNA swab from Ms. Tenney. I apprised him of the items of interest to look for, namely the knife involved in the assault, an e-cigarette mini, the missing photo of Meghan and Alex, the missing jewelry box containing

Incident on Ten-Right Road

$1000 or more, and any shoes or articles of clothing that showed traces of blood. I turned over to him the e-cigarette recovered near the Game Lands, and sent to his phone my photos of the tread marks made in the Game Lands trail. I then returned to Mercer County to await the results of the requested searches.

Third Interview with Alex Gessler

DeMarco: This interview with Alex Gessler is taking place in the Troop D Pennsylvania State Police barracks in Mercer, Pennsylvania. In addition to myself and Mr. Gessler, his attorney, David Ardmore Esq., is also present. Today is August 16th, and the time is 9:04 a.m.

As with my previous interviews with Mr. Gessler, my cell phone is recording this conversation. The session is also being videotaped.

DeMarco: First of all, Alex, thank you for coming here this morning.

Gessler: I didn't really have a choice, did I?

DeMarco: The coffee okay? Either of you need a refill?

Ardmore: We're good.

DeMarco: So you're aware, I assume, that earlier this morning, Mrs. Tenney was arrested and taken into custody.

Ardmore: We have been so informed.

Gessler: I can't believe she did it. I just can't get my head around it.

DeMarco: There's just one last bit of information I need from you.

Gessler: If I have it, I'll give it to you.

DeMarco: Somehow Mrs. Tenney knew how to let herself into Meghan's house. I need you to explain that to me.

Incident on Ten-Right Road

Gessler: I really don't know.

DeMarco: Mr. Ardmore, would you care to remind your client of the benefits of being forthright with me?

Here the videotape will show Ardmore whispering to Gessler.

Gessler: I would've told you before but, it's just.... I'm embarrassed by what we did. I'm ashamed of myself.

DeMarco: Let's start with the "we" in that statement. To whom are you referring?

Gessler: Me and Liz.

DeMarco: And what did you and Liz do?

Gessler: We went inside.

DeMarco: Just for clarity's sake: Are you saying that you and Liz Tenney went inside Meghan Fletcher's house?

Gessler: Yes sir. That day I told you she made me drive past the house so she could see it. She said she wished she could go inside and see how people like Meghan live.

DeMarco: And you took her inside?

Gessler: I knew Junie was at work. I knew Meghan was at the 7-Eleven. So I got the key out of the basket and let us in.

DeMarco: You weren't worried about being seen by Mr. Hickman or anybody else?

Gessler: He'd seen my car in the driveway before. Ever since high school I'd been going there.

DeMarco: And what did you do when you were inside?

Gessler: Basically I just followed Liz from room to room. She had a stupid comment about everything. The furniture, the linoleum in the kitchen, even the

113

shower curtain with seahorses on it. She thought it was incredible that people could live with just one bathroom in the house.

DeMarco: Is that it? You just walked around in there? *(pause)* What else did you do, Alex?

Gessler: It was Liz's idea.

DeMarco: I'm sure it was. But be specific, please.

The video will show Ardmore whispering to Alex.

Gessler: We had sex on her bed.

DeMarco: You and Liz had sex on Meghan's bed.

Gessler: Like I said, it was her idea.

DeMarco: And you never told Meghan about this?

Gessler: God, no. She would've castrated me.

Long pause.

DeMarco: One of the last texts Liz sent to you. She wrote, 'You owe me big time.' Do you remember that?

Gessler: I never asked her to do a single thing! I never expected her too!

Gessler sobbing.

DeMarco: Do you feel that you owe her something for what she did on your behalf?

Ardmore: That's uncalled for, Sergeant. Totally inappropriate.

DeMarco: Thank you both for your time. We're finished now.

I stood up here, followed by Ardmore. Then Gessler stood.

Gessler: So I'm in the clear?

DeMarco: We'll see how that goes.

End of interview.

August 17

Results from the DNA sample taken from Elizabeth Tenney show a positive match with those on the e-cigarette recovered from the Game Lands area, and with the DNA from the previously unknown individual recovered from Meghan Fletcher's bedroom. There was also a match from the bedroom with Alex Gessler's DNA.

The tread pattern on the tires of Elizabeth Tenney's Jeep Wrangler Sport match the tread marks left in the mud on the Game Lands road.

A security camera mounted on the West Middlesex Conservancy building shows a gold Jeep Wrangler Sport entering the Game Lands road at 5:07 a.m. on the morning of August 12. The same vehicle exited the Game Lands road at the Conservancy building one hour and nine minutes later.

The wooden jewelry box taken from Meghan Fletcher's bedroom was found in a bag of garbage in a can outside the Tenney home.

The photo of Alex Gessler and Meghan Fletcher taken from Meghan Fletcher's home was found in a drawer in Elizabeth Tenney's bedroom dresser.

The missing money has not been recovered, nor has the murder weapon.

Trace evidence found on the gearshift of Elizabeth Tenney's Jeep tested positive for human blood; unfortunately the evidence was contaminated by cleaning solvents; no DNA could be extracted.

A half-empty two-pack of e-cigarette minis, vanilla, was discovered in the glove box of Elizabeth Tenney's Jeep; the remaining e-cigarette was an exact match with the e-cigarette recovered at the Game Lands.

Alex Gessler has agreed to testify for the prosecution. According to information supplied by Gessler through his lawyer, Elizabeth Tenney has a history of violence against other females. As a junior in high school, she was expelled for two weeks for assaulting another student in an altercation involving a prom dress. As a freshman in college, and again as a sophomore, she was charged with battery for assaulting an individual she considered a rival for a male student's affection. Both assaults took place off campus and were not reported to the university; the charges were subsequently dropped. Elizabeth Tenney's, (then Foltz) high school record and Hubbard police records verify Gessler's statements, though no records exist to verify Gessler's claim that the latter charges were dropped with the help of "her daddy's money." The source of this information, he said, was Elizabeth Tenney.

Mrs. Tenney is currently in the Hubbard County jail awaiting arraignment.

Recommendations/follow-up

Make Chief Melvin aware of Richard Hickman's alleged history, including the fact that his alleged heart surgery cannot be verified.

- Inform Hubbard Chief of Taco King's lax attitude toward minors in bar/pool room.
- Tactfully suggest to Junie Fletcher that she find a different place to hide the door key, if she hasn't done so already. But be careful lest you imply that her placement of the key is somehow responsible for her daughter's death. Do not add to her sense of guilt.
- Try to hook Junie Fletcher up with a local survivor's support group and some free counseling.
- Try to stop being so ticked that Gessler is walking away scot-free. Accept what you cannot change.
- Also, always take a book to read when you have breakfast at the Belmont. You haven't read *A Moveable Feast* in a while. Lay that one out for tomorrow.
- You need to get some sleep, DeMarco. Maybe then you won't need to write everything down before you forget it.
- And try to remember Junie's assertion that "There are *some* good people in this world, thank God."

Watch and Listen

All this I am about to tell you happened a long time ago. Looong time ago. And you, young man, you are the first person to ever hear a word of it. I swear to God.

"So why are you telling it to me?"

Couple of reasons. One, because everybody else in this story is dead now. And two, because you're 15, and by all appearances not getting any smarter. By all appearances, on the road to doing something very stupid, same as I did. Something likely to ruin your life, same as I ruined mine.

"Your life doesn't look so ruined to me."

You see, that's what I mean about being stupid. Basing your judgments on only what you think you know. What your eyes know. When what you *don't* know is what you need to be paying attention to. What you do know is tiny, but what you don't know is immense.

"That doesn't make any sense. How can you know what you don't know?"

You know what? Grandson or no grandson, you keep talking like that, and I'm likely to just go away and let you sink in your own stink.

"I'm just trying to understand what you're saying. How is it possible to know what you don't know?"

Did I say you have to *know* it? I said you have to

Incident on Ten-Right Road

pay attention to it. Be aware of it. Have some sense of the immensity of your ignorance.

"Okay."

Okay what?

"Okay, I know I don't know everything."

You don't know *anything*. Nada. Zip. Zero. You're getting a third-rate education, and still have over two years of that to go. You have no marketable skills. No discernible talents. You are wholly and completely dependent upon others for your existence. Tell me if any of this is untrue.

"I can do stuff."

You can do stuff like what? Shoplift? Get into fights? Piss off your teachers and your parents with your sass? Go take a look at the classifieds, see how many job openings there are in that line of work.

"I could get a job in construction if I wanted to."

I'll take that bet. A thousand dollars. I'll give you a full week to do it. Here, let's shake on it.

"_____"

That's what I thought. Now here's something else you probably don't know. The reason you don't yet know anything worth knowing. It's because your gray matter won't be fully mature for another eight or nine years. You make bad decisions and think they're good ones, because that's what you're undeveloped brain tells you. You got to learn not to listen to it.

"Isn't that impossible? If my brain tells me one thing, what am I supposed to use to tell my brain it's wrong?"

Did I say this is easy? Did I say growing up is a cakewalk? You have to develop the capacity for self-analysis. For example, when you brain tells you, *Nice*

119

watch. Slip it into your pocket, nobody will know. You hear a thought like that, first thing you should do is to take a step back. Just step back away from it for a second. And ask yourself, 'should I listen to that thought or not?' And the answer is almost always going to be no. But then there's likely to be an argument between those two parts of your brain. One part saying *Do it, do it, do it,* and the other part saying, *Slow down, numbnuts. There's a lot more bad than good coming your way if you pick up that watch.*

"Is that what your story's about? Me stealing something?"

I haven't even started the story yet. I'm still trying to get your attention. You keep doing what you're doing, you're likely to get yourself kicked out of the nest. And believe me, you're close to that right now. And if you do get kicked out of the nest, don't expect to go flying off to another nest somewhere. Expect to dive headfirst into the concrete. So give a little thought to just how hard it's going to be to get airborne from that position.

"I honestly don't understand half of what you're saying."

My point exactly. You finally admitted the truth. That's the first step. Recognize your total ignorance. Second step, swear on your soul you will never repeat this story to anybody. And I do mean anybody. At least until I'm in the ground.

"Swear on my soul?"

You don't believe in such a thing, do you? Neither did I. Not until I drove a bus through it. Youthful cynicism. That's a synonym for ignorance. You know what a synonym is?

Incident on Ten-Right Road

"It's a word that sounds like another word."
Tell you what. Just shut up and listen.

* * *

Why he picked me to be his friend, I have no idea. Though if I'm being honest about it, I'd guess it was because I was the weakest of the three. Not weakest in terms of physical strength, because I was fine in that department, probably even better than the other two. But weak in terms of being easier to manipulate. To bend to his will.

"Who's will? Who's this 'he' you're talking about?"

He called himself JT. Wouldn't ever say what that stood for, or what his real name was. He was one of these loose-limbed, lanky kind of guys always had a little smirk on his lips. Always held his head cocked to the side a little, and with his chin down a little farther than normal. The only time he stood up straight and looked you square in the eye was when he wanted to look down on you and make you squirm. He was at least six-two when he stood up straight, which put him two inches taller than Eddie, four over me, and five over Rich.

"How tall are you?"

Doesn't matter how tall I am now. It's what I was then, at 16 years old.

"You're at least six feet tall, aren't you?"

Let's just forget about height. I'm sorry I brought it up. We're talking about JT now. For some reason, it was me he got buddy-buddy with that first night. I don't see how he could have known that Rich and

Eddie had been best friends since first grade, and therefore would have been tough to separate, to divide and conquer, you know? Just sensed it, I guess. Right from the start, he zeroed in on me as the odd man out.

"Right from the start of what?"

The start of knowing us. He watched us shooting pool for about 20 minutes—

"Shooting pool where?"

The where of it has nothing to do with this. It's irrelevant.

"You can't just have a pool table in the middle of nowhere. You say you were shooting pool, and I'm thinking, there's no place around here to do that."

There's your ignorance popping up again. This was long before you were even a thought, junior. Even long before your daddy was.

"So you're saying there used to be a place to play pool around here? Where was it exactly?"

You don't have an easy time holding a focus, do you?

"If you're not going to tell me, I don't know why I'm even standing here listening to—"

Sit your butt down in that chair! Sit down! You leave this room before I say you can, I reach for my phone and call the police.

"You're not going to have your own grandson arrested."

You stopped being my grandson the moment you walked into this room, picked a $4,000 watch off my desk, and slipped it into your pocket. Sit down!

All right then. I'm not your mother, you need to keep that in mind. You think I'm going to give you a break just because you're her child? I don't give punks

Incident on Ten-Right Road

a break. People who get a break from me get it because they've earned it. You haven't earned it yet. I'll let you know if and when you do. Is that clear?

"All I wanted to know was where you used to play pool around here."

This used to be a nice little town. Busy, even. Every building on Main Street was a business of some kind, all of them getting by just fine. The pool hall was called Harley's back then. And not because of the motorcycle. Harley was the name of the woman who owned the place. Harley Sommers.

"Sounds like a stripper."

You just can't help yourself, can you? Mocking that of which you possess nary a scintilla of knowledge. You are an ignorant, narcissistic, incompetent punk. Get that through your head. And the only way you have any hope of altering that condition is to sit there with your mouth shut and your ears open. Do you think you can manage that?

"_____"

Good. Now then. If you can quit pissing me off, I will continue.

Okay. Harley's. It was on the southern end of town. Where that Sheetz is now. Twelve beautiful tables, a cooler full of soft drinks, a display case full of candy bars and snack cakes. No alcohol allowed. The place was full of blue smoke every night, though. A lot of it coming from Harley herself. You had to be 16 to get through the door. Tables were 50 cents a rack.

I started hanging out there the summer before my junior year. The old man was drinking a lot, my mother was bitching and moaning all the time, two sisters and a brother had already gotten out while the getting was good. My first night there, I spent most of my time leaning against the wall, trying to figure out the games. Eight-ball, nine-ball, cutthroat and straight pool, those were the most popular ones. After a while Eddie asked if I wanted to join him and Rich for some cutthroat. That's how I got in with those two. Both of them a year ahead of me in school. And they treated me good most of the time, but like I was their little brother. There was always that distance between us. They were best friends, I was the third wheel.

It wasn't long after that when JT showed up. The middle of December, it was. He was 22, 23, maybe 24 years old. That first night, though, he watched us finish a game, then came over and introduced himself, asked if he could join us. Said he and I would take on Eddie and Rich in a game of straight pool, nickel a ball. I told him I barely had enough jingle to cover my share of the table, he said no worries, we weren't going to lose. And we didn't. We played three times before Eddie and Rich called it quits, and by then I had an extra dollar in my pocket. JT gave me a ride home, and it was like our partnership was cemented.

So, as I've already said, he must have singled me out from the very start. He was sharp like that. Could sum up a person with a glance. And I was ripe for somebody to treat me with a little respect. One game of pool and he knew I was the best tool for the job. Use it and throw it away.

Six nights later, I was standing in a stranger's back yard, shivering without a coat and looking down at three blue-tinted faces being slowly covered up with snow. And me trying to decide whether to get the hell out of there, or go back inside and call the police.

Incident on Ten-Right Road

"What happened? Did you kill them?"

Keep your panties on, I'm getting to that.

There was this old guy in town, pretty much a hermit. Almost never left his house. His name was Silas something or other. I remember it only because it was such an odd name for these parts. Plus he was rumored to be the richest guy around. A millionaire at least. And that was very big money back when I was your age.

So anyway. For the next five nights, JT and I cleaned up at Harley's.

"This was after the three dead guys in the snow?"

Before the three guys in the snow. Right after I met JT. He could do bank shot, double-bank shots, jump shots, massé shots, whatever. He could put some seriously crazy English on the ball.

"What's that mean—English?"

Spin. He could shoot a ball halfway down the table, make it hit a rail or another ball, spin in a half-circle and come back to the tip of his cue stick. It got to be where nobody would play with us. The thing was, he made all those shots wearing a pair of black lambskin driving gloves. He called them his second skin. Said they gave him a more sensitive touch, like they were magical or something. He never took them off. To me, that just made him even cooler. A very special dude.

"Like Michael Jackson with his sequined glove."

If you say so. Anyway, one night JT says to me, *Let's take a ride*. We get into his car and right away he hands me a beer, which, being stupid like you, I thought was also very cool. Ten minutes later we're cruising very slowly past Silas's big, dark house. There's only a couple of lights on inside, and the sky is as dark as tar, and there's snow coming down at a fairly good rate now. The way it falls past the yellow lights in the windows is kind of mesmerizing for me. That and I have a little buzz on from the beer. And what do you think JT wants us to do?

"Rob the old man?"

You see? When you shut up and listen, you can sometimes figure things out. You can see the relationship between things. The causes and effects. So yes, he wanted us to rob the place. Said he knew for a fact that the old man had a safe full of gold coins.

"How would he know that?"

My question exactly. And his answer was, all I needed to know was that there was a fortune in gold coins in a safe in the den. The fact that he even knew the house had a den impressed me. At the time, I had only a foggy notion of what a den is.

"We're in your den now."

No shit, Sherlock. Yes, it was a den much like this one. And according to JT, the safe held at least 200 ounces of gold coins. Back in 1957, when all this happened, gold was at about $35 an ounce. So 200 ounces would be worth close to $20,000. In today's money, that's about a quarter of a million.

"Wow."

JT seemed to know everything about the place. Knew how to pick the lock on the back door, knew where the old man's bedroom was in relation to the den, knew what time the old man went to bed.

"What about security systems?"

This was 1957, or did you forget that already? Most people didn't even lock their doors at night. All we had to do, JT said, was to tiptoe inside after Silas

Incident on Ten-Right Road

was asleep, pick up the safe and carry it out. It was a two-man job, he said. He would stand guard at the bottom of the stairs, I would slide the safe out into the foyer, then we would both pick it up and get the heck out of there. Easy-peasy, right?

"You said there were three bodies in the snow."

Good for you. You ears do work, and so does your memory on occasion. That's a good sign. So, to continue. According to JT, Sunday night was the time to do it. He said old Silas would spend most of that day drinking wine and that he'd be out cold by 10:00. So the plan was, I would slip out of the house around 11:30. He would pick me up down the road, we'd do the job, and I'd be back in my bed by one a.m. Then we could take our good old time breaking open the safe.

"Weren't you scared?"

That's a salient point. I was scared to death. Truth is, I didn't want to do it. But I also didn't want my new friend to know that I was scared. He made me feel wanted. Needed. And I didn't want that feeling to end. And that was a very stupid, immature way of looking at things. It lacked self-analysis. What I should have done was to ask myself, *do you really need a friend who wants you to do something that could land you in prison? Do you really need a*—if that damn cell phone of yours buzzes one more time....

"Sorry, I'm sorry. I'll shut it off. There. So what happened?"

What happened was, come Sunday night—which was as cold as a witch's tit, by the way, and with a fairly steady snow coming down—we parked the car behind the hedgerow, crept up onto the back porch, where JT takes a key out of his pocket and unlocks the door.

"How did he get a key?"

I started to ask him that question but he shushed me. Drew a finger across his lips. Nothing but sign language from there on in.

So into the house we go, and whatever he does, I do. He takes his shoes off and leaves them on the back porch, I do the same. He hands me a revolver, I take it.

"You had a gun?"

What did I just say? I didn't want to take it. Even shook my head no. But then he pushed it into my chest. And I took it. Because I was weak. Because I had placed myself under somebody else's control. Worst mistake a person can make.

"And then what happened?"

We creep in through the mudroom and the kitchen and the dining room, moving a step at a time. He seems to know where he's going, even without a single light on, so I'm following right behind like a good donkey. Finally we get to the foyer, where the staircase comes down. He stops at the bottom of the stairs and points into the room across the foyer. Then he points to me, then back to that room. So in I go, brainless puppet that I was. Into the den.

"Did you find the safe?"

Think before you talk, all right? It's not a talent most people use, but if you learn to do so, it will make you stand out. You want to stand out?

"I guess."

If you're not sure, I'm wasting my time with you.

"I do. I'm sure."

Fine. Yes, I found the safe. By then my eyes had adjusted to the dark, and the safe was in plain view, on the floor beside the bookcase. Just a square black box,

Incident on Ten-Right Road

a couple of feet tall and wide. With a padlock on the door.

"Just like yours?"

Exactly like mine. I tried lifting it but I couldn't get it off the floor. My guess is it weighed the same as mine fully loaded, which is about as much as you weigh, I'd guess.

"I weigh 152."

And most of it's dead weight. There's only three pounds of you that really matter. You know where those three pounds are?

"My brain?"

Good guess. There's a couple of other parts that matter too, but if I say *heart* you're going to think I mean the actual heart, and if I say *electromagnetic field* it's only going to make you more confused than you already are. So let's go with the brain for now. Anyway...where was I?

"You found the safe."

Okay, right. So I stuck the revolver down behind my belt, worked the safe away from the wall, got in behind it and started pushing it across the floor and out toward the foyer. I was about two-thirds of the way there when I heard a pair of feet hit the floor above my head. And before I know it, those feet were pounding down the stairs. There was only one way out of the den, and that was into the foyer. In other words, I was stuck. So I stood up and pulled out the revolver. Do you need a break, or what?

"No. Why?"

First it was your phone, and now you keep looking out the window. Who's in that blue pickup truck? It's gone past the house three times now.

"How would I know who it is?"

I'm going to finish this story, and then you're going to tell me who it is. You understand?

"But I don't have any idea—"

Be quiet. Not another word from you.

So I'm standing there shivering like an idiot, holding onto that revolver JT gave me, waiting for old Silas to come down the stairs and into the den. But he doesn't. He turns the other way. He goes into the living room and then to the kitchen. I figure he must be in there getting a drink or something. So, as quiet as I can, I start creeping toward the foyer, because by now I'm wondering why the hell Silas never noticed JT out there. But then I hear a sound from the kitchen, like somebody rummaging around in a drawer. So now I'm thinking he's getting himself a weapon of some kind, a big knife or a gun. And I'm thinking I'm a goner. I'm going to have to shoot the old man if he comes in and sees me. But that's when all hell breaks loose.

"What does that—sorry."

Go ahead and ask it.

"What do you mean, all hell breaks loose?"

The old man had taken a pistol out of the kitchen drawer. But he didn't head back toward me, he crept toward the back door, which, as you'll remember, JT and I had left partially open, And what does the old man see out there on his porch but a couple of dark figures. Because by then the snow was falling and the sky was pitch black, so all he could make out were the shapes of two men. And the pistol went *pop pop pop pop*. Four times. Then nothing.

"He shot JT?"

Incident on Ten-Right Road

It wasn't JT. Because what JT had done was to position Eddie and Rich out there without telling me he was going to do it.

"And that's who the old man shot?"

Bingo.

"Why wouldn't JT tell you they were out there?"

You know what a patsy is?

"I think I do."

Spit it out.

"A patsy is somebody who takes the blame for something."

Close but no cigar. A patsy is a weak-minded donkey who takes all the risk so that somebody else can get all the profit. But he's so weak-minded that he doesn't even realize he's a donkey. He thinks he's being smart. Thinks he's a genius. That sound familiar to you?

"Maybe. How does this relate to you and Rich and Eddie?"

I didn't figure this out until later, but I'm pretty sure that JT's plan was for me to kill the old man. I don't think he was counting on the old man going to the back door before heading for the den. Then JT would call Rich and Eddie inside, and JT would take the revolver from me and shoot the three of us.

"What? All that because of the safe? Was he going to carry it outside by himself?"

Didn't I tell you to stop thinking and just listen?

"Yeah, but… The old man's still alive, right? Did he come into the den or not?"

I'm still waiting for him to come in. But then I hear a kind of a bang, more of a thump, I guess, out beyond the kitchen somewhere.

"Another gunshot?"

No, it was different. I'll get to that in a minute. First I heard the thump, and then, maybe 15 seconds later, I heard footsteps coming. And I knew the old man was on his way. It was going to be me or him. So when he stepped into the threshold, I pulled the trigger.

"Grandpa. You shot somebody?"

I missed. And it wasn't the old man standing there looking at me, it was JT. He sees me holding that revolver still pointing in his direction, my whole body shaking to beat the band, and off he runs.

"What?"

I must have stood there for a couple of minutes before I pulled myself together and knew I had to beat it out of there or get blamed for everything. So I dropped the gun and ran. Stopped long enough to grab my shoes and jam them on, then jumped off the porch and tripped over the old man face-down in the snow beside Rich and Eddie.

"That was the bang you heard?"

JT had smashed his head in with a cast-iron skillet. And you know what thought hit me at that very moment?

"What?"

Those black lambskin-driving gloves JT was so proud of. I never saw him when he wasn't wearing them. Including that night. Which meant what?

"No fingerprints."

Good thinking for a change. But *my* fingerprints were on that revolver in the den. So back inside I go. I grabbed it and made like the Invisible Man.

"Huh?"

I disappeared. I ran.

Incident on Ten-Right Road

"And they were all dead? Rich and Eddie and the old man?"

I wasn't sure. So first I wiped the revolver on the tail of my shirt, then heaved it down a storm drain. Then on the way home I stopped at a phone booth on the corner and dialed the operator and told her somebody was shooting a gun at the old man's house. She said it had already been called in.

"By JT?"

We'll never know. But I can't think of anybody else who would've heard the shots that far out of town. And that's the end of the story. I hung up and went home, and have regretted that night ever since. Now, you have any questions?

"Well, yeah. I mean…did you or JT get arrested?"

By the time the police got there, everybody in the snow was dead. Now, you have to remember that this was 1957. Police weren't so careful around a crime scene back then. They found two dead boys, shot with the old man's pistol. And they found a skillet with the old man's brain matter on it. They found the safe pulled away from the wall, and figured that Eddie and Rich had been trying to steal it when old Silas caught them in the act. He then chased them outside, where one of them bashed him on the head. Whether he shot them before or after getting bashed didn't really matter. Dead is dead. Case closed.

"What happened to JT?"

Nobody ever saw him again. I think he was probably staying in one of the motels farther out. About a month later, though, a moving van showed up at the old man's house and hauled everything away. Later that week, the newspaper printed a picture of

Silas' heir, his only son. Apparently the two hadn't spoken to each other in 10 or more years. The kid had his mother's last name, so everybody figured the boy was illegitimate. The newspaper said that the picture was several years old, the son's high school photo. But I could see the similarities. And it explained a lot. It explained how JT knew the layout of the house, and how he might have acquired a key. My guess is he might have visited his father on the sly a few times, probably not long before he came to town and seduced me into helping him get the safe, which was never his real goal anyway, which you can figure out if have half the brains you should have.

"JT was the old man's son?"

I want you to think about all the ramifications not only of JT's actions, but of mine. I want you to think about what will happen to me if you ever breathe a word of this story to anyone. And I want you to think about all the bad things that could have come from you stealing my favorite watch.

"I'm sorry I did that, Grandpa. I really am. But I'm kind of hung up on Eddie and Rich being there that night. JT had you to help him, right? You were the patsy. So what did he really need Eddie and Rich for? That part doesn't make any sense to me."

It was a long time ago, I might have an extra person in there somewhere. I get things mixed up sometimes. Anyway, none of that matters. What matters is what you learned from the story. Did you learn anything at all?

"Do you think JT feels bad about how it all turned out? I mean, he did get the gold, right? Plus everything else."

Incident on Ten-Right Road

Tell you what. Put yourself in his position. If you were JT, would you feel bad?

"I mean, yeah. He killed his own father. Plus got two of his friends killed."

I'm betting that JT didn't have any friends back then. He was probably so full of anger and bitterness that he wasn't thinking about anybody but himself. It's likely that his father was a nasty, miserly person, but that doesn't justify what happened. I would like to think that JT realized this, and that he changed his ways. I hope he gave up cheating and lying and made something of himself. He certainly had the means to do so. I hope he spent the rest of his life trying to help other people. Trying to make up, in some small way, for all the harm he caused.

"He must have worried all the time that you were going to rat him out."

Naw, I doubt it. He picked me because he knew I wasn't a rat. That might have been my only redeeming virtue back then. He saw the good and the bad in me, and took advantage of both.

"I really am sorry I took your watch, Grandpa. I'll never do anything like that again."

Good. Apology accepted. Now let's talk about your friends in that blue pickup truck that keeps going past the house. You want to text them and let them know you didn't get the watch? While you're at it, invite them in for a glass of lemonade. I'd love to meet them.

A Little Rest

The decision did not come easily. Years in the making. Then three days of thinking of nothing else before he committed himself to the action. Much of those days was spent lying on the hotel bed with a too-soft mattress and a foam pillow that made his neck hurt. Once or twice each day he took a walk through the conference room downstairs, where he smiled at people he had met at previous conferences in the same city, and lingered long enough to share a few words with them. Now and then he stood at the back of the room for a few minutes during a presentation.

But most of the time was spent in the hotel room. He thought of his wife 800 miles away and of his daughter Alexa. She had been a talented gymnast and had been working hard to qualify for the Junior Olympics. His favorite way to spend a Saturday back then had been to watch her practice her routines. He had never been much of an athlete himself so her grace and agility and self-composure always took his breath away.

He did not deliberately wait until the next to last day of the conference, the Saturday, to commit himself to the decision, but that was when it happened. At first he thought the juxtaposition of the two events was a coincidence, but later he realized it was probably not.

Incident on Ten-Right Road

On that Saturday he spent most of the day in the conference room, then told a couple of people that he wasn't feeling well and would probably skip the dinner that night. Late in the afternoon he went to his hotel room for an hour to calm himself. Around dusk, when the conference dinner began, he went outside to his car and drove away. He left a light on in his room, one that could be seen from outside the window and left the television on loud enough that he could hear it when he stood outside the door. When he drove away he made a left out of the hotel's driveway, continued on through four stoplights, made a right down a side street and stayed on that road until he was nearly out of the city. Then he made another right and merged onto the same street that ran past the hotel, which was soon miles behind him. He parked across from the man's apartment and watched the light in his second floor window.

A little after 8:00, just as the sun was setting below the buildings, the man came out onto the balcony, checked to make sure that his door had locked behind him, then crossed the balcony to the stairs, came down them and went to his car in the parking lot. Alexa's father did not yet know precisely when the action would be completed, whether before the man went to the bar or when he came back out. Whichever circumstance presented the best opportunity. Alexa's father had spent six conference weeks, six years observing the man's habits, every year since the man had been released from prison. But only this year had he not driven his rental car straight from the airport to the hotel. This year he first drove to a part of town he had never visited before, but where, according to the online research he had done years earlier, he could make a necessary purchase. He thought he would be frightened when he made that purchase, but he wasn't. It was easier than he thought it would be, and only after the purchase had been made did he realize that his lack of fear was directly related to his lack of concern about whether or not he would survive the transaction.

And now, out on the street and a couple of car lengths behind the man's car, Alexa's father sped up in his rental car and passed the man's car and was already parked with his lights out when the man pulled into the bar's parking lot. Nobody was standing around outside the bar and the music was so loud inside that Alexa's father could feel the pulsing booms in the pressure on his eardrums, and that's when he told himself, *It's as good a time as any*. He unlatched his door as quietly as possible and sat waiting.

He allowed the man to climb out of his own car and cross in front of the rental car on his way to the bar. Then Alexa's father fully opened his car door and stood and said, "John. Hey. Wait up."

John turned at the sound of his name, paused and smiled and leaned forward a bit trying to see better in the dim light. Alexa's father walked up to him with both hands in his jacket pockets. He stood close and said, "Remember me?"

John leaned even closer. When he exhaled through his mouth, Alexa's father could smell his breath, a mix of mint and beer. "Think hard," Alexa's father said. "Seven years ago."

A few moments passed before John's eyes widened. Alexa's father drew his right hand from the pocket and pressed the tip of the black pistol to John's chest and pulled the trigger. John went down on his

Incident on Ten-Right Road

knees and Alexa's father aimed at the top of his head and pulled the trigger again. All the way back to his car and as he drove he could feel the vibration of those shots in his hand, and he could hear the two quick shots echoing in the silence throughout his car.

Not far from his hotel he found a side street with mostly abandoned buildings and few streetlights. Then he drove up and down that street until in the darkness he could make out an open sewer drain beneath the curb, and he pulled alongside that curb and put his hand out the window and with a flick of his wrist sent the gun down into the drain.

Alexa's father returned to his hotel room and stayed there throughout the night, then was up early and attended all of the conference's Sunday activities. Every time he looked toward the entrance he expected to see a couple of police officers standing there.

That night he called his wife and spoke to her softly and she asked how the conference had gone. He said, "Fine, but mostly boring," and she said, "Didn't you met any interesting people?" He said, "There is no such thing as an interesting dentist," and she laughed but sounded tired. He told her that his flight would get in at 8:47 the next morning. After collecting his bags and returning the rental car, he should be home by 10:30. "Good," she said. "It's too quiet here."

He arrived home at 20 minutes before 11:00 the next morning, still wearing the conference registration badge on a black cord around his neck. When he came into the kitchen after dropping his bags in the living room, his wife looked up from the table where she sat with both hands wrapped around a coffee mug and said, "You forgot to take off your name badge."

He looked down and touched it and said, "I needed it for the free breakfast. Forgot all about it."

She asked if he wanted a cup of coffee and he said, "No, thank you. I should call in and see if they need me in the office today."

She said, "You just got home. Can't you sit with me and rest a while?"

Only then did he realize how tired he was. He said, looking toward the kitchen window that overlooked the back yard, "I'm thinking that might be the last conference for me. Unless they hold it in a different city next time."

"You've been going every year for the last how many? Ten?"

He nodded. "It's always the same people though. The same food. Only the technology changes."

"You need to stay abreast of it, don't you? I've heard you say that yourself."

He kept gazing at the kitchen window, seeing what wasn't there. Then he shrugged. Looked down at his wife. "There are other conventions. I might go somewhere else for a change. If I do, would you go with me again?"

She looked down at the coffee in the bottom of her cup. Then back to him. "I might," she said, "if it's in another city. I won't ever go back to that one again."

He nodded. Pulled out a chair. Said, "Maybe I will stay home with you today." He sat. Laid his hand atop hers. "A little rest won't kill me."

Snap

At first the rain sounded like a distant tapping, like heels running across metal roofs. Then it became a crowd racing toward me. Finally all the light outside the terrace doors went gray, swallowed in a thundering waterfall of dark rain. I thought, *Now I can go to the bookstore and sit with a latte and a Granta and forget about his sad and angry face for a while.*

But it was one of those summer showers that comes in an explosion and is over too soon. Within minutes the sun was blazing again and the sidewalks steaming. I knew Salandro would be waiting for me. If he had not given me the autographed baseball bat and ball two days earlier, I would not have felt obligated to visit him, but the ball was on the bookcase in my living room and the bat leaned against the wall.

Thirty minutes later I walked into Three Rivers Stadium through the press entrance and there was Salandro in a box above the home team bullpen, just sitting there looking tragic and ruined while he stared at the empty diamond. When he spotted me coming out of the tunnel he grinned with that childish light of hope in his eyes, a look that filled me with dread—a look that asked if today I would snap my fingers and somehow turn back the cursed clock.

He was wearing the same clothes as yesterday, the blue rubber shower thongs and old blue gym shorts that were too tight, and a white T-shirt with the sleeves cut off. He sat with his broken left arm in its blue sling resting atop his huge belly, the cast covered with the signatures of all his fellow Pirates, his former teammates.

"Did you get much rain out here?" I asked. I sat one seat away from him.

He shrugged and said, "We're on the road anyway," as if he believed that he was still a part of the team, that his radius bone was going to heal counter to all the diagnoses. I felt a twinge of contempt for his refusal to face the truth but then I immediately felt bad for my contempt. Up until last week he had been my hero, this boy 19 years my junior, this rookie phenomenon. He had given me half a season of pleasure and now I was sitting there resenting him for ruining a few of my afternoons.

I asked, "Any luck with those endorsements?"

He did not smile or even shake his head. His body sagged and his big round shoulders drooped. There were not going to be any endorsements for this athlete, not ever. A week ago he could clock 96 miles per hour whenever he wanted to, and his slider would break hard to the outside two nanoseconds after the batter decided to swing at it, and he had smacked 20 homeruns before the first of July, but except when he was at bat or on the mound he was one of the least photogenic of athletes. He stood 6'4" and weighed 310 pounds and nearly all of that weight was in his buttocks, belly and chest. His limbs were long and gangly and his hands seemed too small for the rest of his body, but they were big enough to swallow a

Incident on Ten-Right Road

baseball. His teeth were uneven and one of his canines was a russet brown.

"What about that profile thing?" he asked. "Any word on that?"

"It's working its way through the suits."

"I'm really counting on that to get things started."

"I should have an answer for you in a week at the latest."

In fact I was the only suit at the station who had even considered giving our "Local Hero" spot to Salandro. To everybody else he was old news. But I had been in the station's box at the game nine days earlier when Salandro made his wind-up and delivery and I had seen that moment when something snapped in his arm and the ball went wide and Salandro went down on his knees on the mound. The radius had snapped and so had his career. At the age of 22 he was out of the game forever. The press had loved him because he was until then a happy bull of a man, a grinning moonfaced boy from some dust smudge in Texas but with a fierce raw talent that kept all the sportswriters thumbing through thesauruses for the most grandiose of superlatives.

I had loved him because I have loved baseball ever since my second Christmas, when my father handed me an 18" Louisville Slugger with a red bow stuck to its sweet spot. For the next 16 years baseball was the one thing my father and I held in common. We watched the games on TV and when the Pirates were out of town we listened to them on the radio, and five or six times a year we went to the ballpark and felt like Roman senators in the general admission seats.

Then I went away to college and my father died.

Randall Silvis

For the next 20 years I entertained myself with politics and theater and existentialism and work, and I scarcely even thought about baseball until late last spring. It was then I became aware of a buzzing in the air, a murmuring of Salandro's name. I went to one game and heard the sweet fatal thud of his fastball smacking the catcher's mitt, and maybe because I missed my father's love or I missed my youth or I missed the ability to lose myself in a few voyeuristic hours of sport, suddenly I felt a longing for the sounds and smells of the stadium. In my father's company at the ballfield I had felt a part of something, a true kinship with another human being. Also I loved the order and rhythm of the game, nine men struggling toward a common goal. In baseball there is a rule for every possibility. Everything about the game is prescribed but nothing is predictable. Baseball contains everything my life did not, a cadence, a symmetry, and for half a season I had viewed the unlikely Salandro as the maestro of that cadence.

What I really wanted, I suppose, was to believe, for a while, at least, that each one of us is not ineluctably alone.

This might seem a peculiar longing to be fulfilled by a mere game, but baseball is the most ritualized of American games, and in a country where few traditions endure, and to an individual whose nightly work is a moil of ephemera and egos... well, suffice it to say that something was missing in my life, and for a while baseball had filled that void.

I felt something break in me the day Salandro went down on his knees on the mound. I felt sucker punched, just as I had the day I lost my father. Once again my tether to the world, this time improbably

Incident on Ten-Right Road

mended by Salandro, had snapped. But I was grateful too for the salubrious days he had given me and I wanted to give him something in return. So I asked if he would let me bring a crew to tape a profile of him for the late night news. He agreed without hesitation but there was something desperate to his eagerness. Within minutes he started demanding payment for the interview. Before I could think of a tactful refusal he launched into a litany of complaint about his doctors and his agent and about the winters in Pittsburgh, and from there he branched out easily to blame most of western Pennsylvania and all of professional baseball for what had happened to him.

It wasn't that I could not understand his bitterness and fear. Next year Salandro would have signed a long-term contract, but now he would be lucky to get a job coaching baseball for the city league. He had become a wholly different creature than the one I had seen command the mound and the batter's box, just another lost soul who reminded me too much of myself.

On this day, my fourth visit, I sat with him for nearly an hour. An hour was all the whining I could stand. "I have to get back home," I told him. "Some people are coming up from DC."

He lifted his head. "They're coming here?"

I hated the hopefulness in his voice. "Just a friend of mine from college," I said. "My old roommate. I haven't seen him in seven, eight years now. He's bringing his fiancée, wants us to meet each other."

Salandro blinked and looked insulted. "I suppose you won't be coming tomorrow."

"I'll try," I said.

* * *

My friend did not show up or even call so I went to work as usual that evening. There was the usual off-camera tumult, the bickering and chaos and last-minute frenzy in the editing room. Then came the relative calm of the news hour. Then a couple hours of meetings and planning for the next day. All I really wanted was to get away from everybody for a while.

I returned home a little after 1:00 a.m. After a quick shower I went upstairs to visit Isabella. She was sleeping when I knocked but she had been expecting me. She came to the door wearing a short white satin robe and matching teddy, and she held the door open with one hand while shielding her eyes from the hallway light.

She gave me her standard greeting. "Hello, baby. You been missin' me?"

I slipped a hand under her robe while she reshot the deadbolt. "Every time I see you in white I think of Dianne Carroll in the TV show *Julia*."

She smiled sleepily. "You want me to be your maid tonight?"

I liked that she did not bother to turn on any lights in the apartment, that we were left with only the clouded moon and the yellow lights outside the windows. She went into the bedroom and let the robe fall to the floor, then slipped off the teddy and stood there brown and sleek and impossible and waiting. When I did not join her right away she lay atop the white satin sheets and crossed her legs at the ankle.

I stood at the bedroom window and looked out. "It's a pretty city at night, isn't it?"

Incident on Ten-Right Road

"Mmm," she said. "The Renaissance City."

"That's a phrase I haven't heard for a while."

"I'm just an old-fashioned girl, I guess." She stretched her leg out and rubbed a foot against my knee.

I reached for the radio alarm clock on the table. "Do you mind if I set the alarm for 7:00?"

"In the morning?" she said.

"I'm trying to change my routine. Keep a more regular life."

"You need more sleep than that. We all do."

"I'll set the volume really low. You won't even hear it."

But later I awoke after a couple of hours and could not sleep. At half-past five I slipped out of bed, shut off the alarm, then dressed in the dark of the living room. I had my trousers on and was buttoning up my shirt when a peculiar thing happened: my mind went completely blank. Suddenly I had no comprehension of where I was or what I was doing there. It lasted for only a few seconds but immediately afterward a weakness came over me, a heaviness so that I had to put a hand out against the back of the sofa, a debilitating sense of futility. Strangely, the words that came into my head then were Camus', the opening lines from *The Stranger*, a book I hadn't read in at least a dozen years: *Mother died today. Or, maybe, yesterday; I can't be sure.*

Finally I went downstairs to my own apartment and undressed and set the alarm for 7:00 and climbed into bed.

The door buzzer awoke me less than a half-hour later. I stumbled to the door and thumbed down the intercom button. "What?" was all I could manage.

"Open the fucking door, you low gray rat."

I buzzed him in, then unlocked the door and stumbled back to the bedroom for a robe. Then back to the living room to turn on a floor lamp. I was standing there thinking I should make a pot of coffee when the door shot open. There stood Brady Thompson grinning and drunk and 20 pounds heavier than the last time I had seen him.

We shook hands and hugged and made the usual remarks about how good we looked and how long it had been. Under Brady's right eye an old bruise had sallowed to yellow. He caught me squinting at it and said, "Racquetball. What'd ya got to drink?"

"There might be a couple of beers," I said.

"I'll take them both. In the bottle. I can't stay."

He followed me into the kitchen. "You can't sit down and drink a beer?"

"I've got a woman in a taxi waiting."

"Your fiancée? Jesus, bring her up. Let me put some coffee on—"

He took the beers from my hands and headed for the door. "She won't come up. Says it's not an appropriate time."

"She's maybe got a point there."

"Drinks later," he said, and turned at the door to face me. "That place in Shadyside we used to go to—is it still there?"

"Bwana Donna's, still there. But it's a kid's place, you know. We were kids when we went there. There's another place just a block down street...."

"Bwana Donna's," Brady said. "Four o'clock sharp. Be there or be square."

"What are you, 19? One of the richest men in Maryland and you still talk like a freshman."

Incident on Ten-Right Road

He threw an arm around my neck and pulled me close and laid a hard kiss on my cheek. "Four o'clock," he said after he pushed away.

"Come on, bring her up. I'll make omelets. I want to meet her."

He smiled crookedly. The bruise on his cheekbone made it seem more a wince than a smile.

"Which reminds me," I said. "You were supposed to be here yesterday."

He shook a finger at me as if I had said something naughty. Then he turned without another word and went out and when I looked after him he was sprinting down the hallway.

* * *

A few minutes before 4:00 that afternoon I arrived at Bwana Donna's and claimed a table behind the front window. A half-hour later Brady had still not shown. By then the room was packed three-deep at the bar with young office workers and college kids. The servers all wore safari shorts, vests and boots and the bartenders wore pith helmets. As a young man I had thought this place exotic and after enough beers I would talk about how I was going to climb Kilimanjaro or run with the bulls and about all kinds of things I would never do except in a beer fantasy. Now all the youthful servers and patrons and the polyester animal skins on the walls made me feel like an old man sitting on the edge of a poorly written skit in which there was no role for anyone over 30.

The clamor and smoke squeezed my skull with an oscillating grip. Five more minutes, I told myself. Five more and then the hell with it. Brady had never been this unreliable in the old days.

At 5:15 I finally pushed back my chair and stood. I took one more look around the room, just in case I had missed him somehow. When I turned to the front window again there was a woman on the sidewalk looking back at me. A tall woman, at least 5'9", with thick chestnut hair that whispered at her shoulders. She was wearing a yellow summer dress and short white gloves. Her eyes, almond-shaped, gave her a slightly Asian look; they were as dark as oil but flecked with brightness. Her legs were poetry, a couplet of long graceful lines that rose from the concrete to the sublime. Her hips and breasts and shoulders, all the right curves and undulations.... I don't know how else to describe them but to say that she wore her body like an ermine coat, something rare and expensive but she was used to it, comfortable in its luxury.

She held up one finger to indicate that I should wait there, don't move. Then she came inside and it was amazing to watch how the crowd parted to let her pass, so that she did not have to twist and turn to get to my table but walked languidly all the way. She flowed like slow water.

"Michael," she said, and laid a gloved hand against my cheek and leaned very close. "I feel like I've known you forever."

Her perfume was something warm and natural, lighter than musk but immediately dizzying. Her breath smelled of cinnamon.

She kissed the corner of my mouth, then drew away only slightly and said, "I'm Brady's fiancée. Michelle."

Incident on Ten-Right Road

"Michelle?" Only then did it occur to me that Brady had never told me her name. "You're kidding."

"You see how strange it is? Michael... Michelle? It's as if we're... connected somehow." She kept one hand on my cheek, the other on my waist.

My legs were weak. "Should we sit down?" Then, remembering, "Where's Brady?"

"He won't be joining us until later. But this is better, don't you think? We can get to know each other now."

My life seemed suddenly distant, a shadow out there somewhere, watching from behind a corner. "I need to be at the station soon. In fact I should have left for work five minutes ago."

"Can we walk?"

"It's eight or nine blocks."

She let her right hand drop to her side and wove her fingers between mine. "Let's walk."

I could not remember the last time I had held hands with a woman. Despite the thin gloves the heat of her hand came through, the energy in it. Her fingers were long and graceful and they held my hand as if they owned it.

"I'm sorry about the mix-up," she said.

"What mix-up is that?"

"Brady told me we were to meet you for drinks at 6:00. Then, at 4:30 or so, he suddenly remembered that it might have been 5:00."

"It was 4:00."

She grimaced and shook her head. "Let me ask you something. Has Brady always been so... unfocused?"

"How do you mean?"

"Well..." she said. Then, a moment later, "Oh, never mind."

I did not feel comfortable talking about him like this in his absence. So I said nothing.

"It's just that, for a man his age, so successful, he sometimes seems, I don't know... scatter-brained? He forgets appointments, ignores other ones, and then he blames somebody else or makes up a silly excuse. And the way he drinks. He drinks an awful lot, Michael."

"How long have you known him?"

"A little over three months. We've been living together for five weeks now."

"He's in love," I said.

She laughed softly and squeezed my hand. "I would hope so."

"What I mean is.... Sure, he was always a rich kid, an only child, so sometimes he tended to be a bit self-absorbed. But to his friends.... I never had a more generous or loyal friend. And punctual. He used to drive me crazy he was so punctual."

"So you think that what's been happening lately is an aberration?"

"My guess is, he can't believe his good fortune in finding someone like you. It would make me nervous too."

She bumped me with her shoulder. "Do I make you nervous, Michael?"

"What I mean is, the luck of it. The miracle of falling in love."

She held my hand closer to her body, against her hip. "It's a fairly common miracle, don't you think?"

My heart was racing and I felt short of breath, though our pace had not been brisk. I found it difficult to look at her without squinting. She filled my field of vision with a brightness, a glare. The rest of the world was dark and blurred around her edges.

Incident on Ten-Right Road

"This is where I work," I told her.

She turned to face me and laid a hand against my chest. "Can you get off later? Join Brady and me for a drink?"

I nodded toward O'Hanlon's across the street. "Nine o'clock. But I won't be able to stay long."

"Pretend we haven't met," she said.

"Excuse me?"

"He's so excited about introducing us to one another. He'll be awfully disappointed if he finds out that we met like this without him."

"Then why did we?"

"For me," she said. "Later will be for him."

I was troubled by the speed of my heart hammering against her hand. "How will you explain this arrangement to meet at O'Hanlon's?"

"I'll tell him you called and left a message at the hotel."

"I'm not sure it's a good idea to trick him like this."

"Really, it's better this way, you'll see." A moment passed; she looked almost sad. "The friendship you two have is so very special. I want us, you and me, to be good friends too."

I should have told her then that Brady and I had spoken by telephone only once or twice in the past several years, and that even when we had been roommates at the Chi House he had never stood so near that I could feel the heat of his body going into mine, he had never made my mouth go dry nor filled my brain with clouds as she was doing, never reduced the world to a blur of shadows.

All I could think to say was, "We've known each other a long time."

She touched a finger to the corner of my mouth. "I envy him," she said.

* * *

For the next three hours I watched the clock tick. I was short-tempered with a petulant Fleming, I flirted brazenly with Allison and even with one of the assistant producers, a mousy girl of 22. Allison, married and with two small children, responded with a bemused look, but the assistant producer giggled and blushed and then kept smiling at me every chance she got. In short, I embarrassed myself. Watching myself was like watching an oafish brother but not knowing how to tell him how foolish he looks.

O'Hanlon's was quiet at 9:00 in the evening, a handful of unmarried or unhappily married businessmen lingering over their drinks, watching the television above the bar. I stepped inside and saw Brady and Michelle at the table farthest from the door. They were sitting side by side facing the door and already smiling when I came in, but it was Michelle on whom the light from the table's candle fell, her eyes and smile that claimed most of the room's muted glow, so that Brady appeared almost dark beside her and insubstantial.

He stood and came striding toward me, hand stretched out. "Damn it's good to see you, Mike. Damn it's good." There was something about the way he squeezed my hand, a feverish quality that put me on guard.

He threw an arm around my shoulder and steered me to the table. Michelle smiled up at me but said nothing. She was wearing a white flowered dress with a high collar, the dress peppered with primroses, and

Incident on Ten-Right Road

her short white gloves. I could smell her perfume and was already lightheaded from it.

By now Brady was rubbing his hand between my shoulders, briskly up and down, too nervous to stand still. "Sweetheart," he said to her, "this is the man himself, this is my old buddy Mike. My best damn friend in the whole damn world."

She held out a hand to me. I took it softly and felt the pull of it deep inside my chest, felt my breath snag on her smile. "I'm so glad to finally meet you," she said. "I'm Adrianna."

Brady missed my flinch of confusion but she did not. Her smile flickered at the corners. Her eyes laughed.

"Adrianna Morgan," Brady said. "My Addie. The most beautiful woman in the whole damn world."

"Damn is his favorite adjective," she said. "Especially when he's been drinking."

I did not know how to react to the name change, whether to consider it a harmless joke or something else. She kept smiling at me and did not look away.

I realized then that I was still holding her hand, and let go of it, and turned to Brady. "You mean to tell me you've been drinking? And in a bar, no less?"

He laughed, too loud, and slapped me on the back. "Damn right, and so are you. Sit, sit, I'll get us some drinks. Beer for you, right? You know they don't even have table service in this joint? You have to order at the freaking bar."

Jim O'Hanlon, son of the original owner, was watching Brady from behind the bar. I pushed Brady toward his chair. "It's on me." He started to protest but I shoved him down.

At the bar I said, "Whatever they're drinking plus a ginger ale for me, please."

O'Hanlon gave me a smile and went to work. In his late forties, not a big man but, like his father and three brothers, as dignified as a deacon. "So how's life this evening?" he asked me.

"Sorry about my friend over there."

"You might ask him to turn it down a notch or two."

"He's nervous is all. Introducing his fiancée to me."

O'Hanlon handed me a ginger ale. "Is she what's got him so nervous?"

"He wants us to like each other, I guess."

"But not too much?" He set two martini glasses in front of me and filled them from the shaker.

I didn't answer.

"Women that beautiful are more trouble than they're worth," he said.

"You think so?"

"I'd never go near a woman that beautiful."

"No?"

"Just don't ever tell my wife I said so."

I laid a couple of tens on the table and grinned at him and picked up the drinks.

I sat with Brady and Adrianna for a while and we laughed and everybody seemed to be relaxing a bit. Then Brady drained his glass. He pointed to mine, still half-full, as he stood.

"I can't. I have to go back to work."

"A quick one," he said, and went to the bar.

The moment he had his back to us she reached across the table and took my hand. "Are you angry?" she said. "Please don't be angry with me."

Incident on Ten-Right Road

"You caught me by surprise."

"It was just a little joke, spur of the moment. I didn't even think about it when I did it. It was almost as if—"

"It's all right. Let's just forget about it now."

"The thing is, when I first saw you and felt that connection, that... Michael, Michelle, it's just how I felt, it's... do you understand what I mean?"

I looked down at her hand gripping mine, the ridges of her knuckles through the thin glove, bones so fragile and small.

"I wanted us to have something in common right from the start."

"We have Brady in common," I said.

"Yes but that could work against us. Don't you see how it might?"

Off in the distance was Brady's voice booming. I turned to the bar and he was leaning over the counter, shouting at O'Hanlon, who stood there with both hands resting lightly on the edge of the counter, his face unreadable, eyes not even blinking.

Adrianna took my hand in both of hers. "I'll always tell you the truth about important things, Michael. I swear I will."

I felt mildly disoriented and drew away from her and pushed back my chair and went to the bar and put a hand on Brady's shoulder. "What's going on, pardner?" My voice sounded high and tight.

"I'm trying to teach this nimrod how to mix a proper martini. But he's either too stubborn or too stupid to learn."

I squeezed the tendon in Brady's shoulder until he winced. "Walk me across the street," I said.

"We're going to have another drink first."

"Walk me across the street, Brady."

Something wilted in him then and his body sagged beneath my hand. We turned back to the table and I said goodnight to Adrianna, then Brady and I went outside and stood at the corner and waited for the light to change. When it did, neither of us moved.

Finally I said, "Here's what you're going to do."

"I know," he said quickly. "I know."

"What?"

"I'm going to go inside and apologize to the bartender for being such an ass. Then I'll give him a huge tip. Then Addie and I will leave."

I turned to look at him. "What's going on here, Brady? This isn't like you at all. You don't behave like this."

He blinked and watched the traffic. He had something he wanted to say but could not express it. Only a part of it could be articulated. "You're the only real friend I've ever had," he said.

I tried to make a joke of it. "Christ, that's pathetic."

He didn't laugh. "You're the only guy who didn't hang out with me because of my money; who didn't expect me to pick up the check every time. You're the only guy who would tell me when I was being an asshole."

"You didn't used to be so good at it."

Finally, he smiled. He also looked as if he might cry. "Can we get together tomorrow? Just hang out a while and talk? Just you and me?"

"I'd be disappointed if we didn't."

He nodded but did not say anything.

"I gotta go, Brady. They'll be waiting for me in editing."

Incident on Ten-Right Road

He nodded again.

I crossed against the light and went to the station's front door and turned to look back. He was still there, standing where I had left him. He waved a hand at me.

I went upstairs then and before going to editing I got a coffee and went to the window and looked down on the street. Brady was still there on the corner, hands in his pockets now, his back to O'Hanlon's. He looked like a man who was trying to decide which way to run.

* * *

Next day I waited around my apartment until nearly 2:00, telephoning Brady's room every 15 minutes or so. Finally I left word with my doorman that I would be back by 4:30. I was going to tell Salandro today that this would be the last visit for a while, that I had to go out of town. I did not feel good about lying to the boy but he had to pull himself up out of his morass and he was not likely to do it if I kept climbing down there with him.

It was a warm gray day, quiet—one of those overcast days when the heat and dull light have either a mellowing or a depressing effect on people. Me, I just wanted an uneventful afternoon that did not get my stomach acids boiling.

At first I thought Salandro was not in the stadium that day; his usual box was empty. I did not know whether to be worried or relieved. Then I spotted him way up in the nose-bleed section in right field, sitting there with his skinny legs spread wide and his elbows on his knees, leaning forward like a man peering into the abyss.

He did not even say hello when I climbed up and sat beside him.

He said, "I worked all my life to get into this ballpark. And at the end of this season they'll start tearing it down. PNC Park. What kind of a name is that?"

"Your life is just beginning. I wish I had your possibilities."

He wasn't listening. "They say you'll be able to hit a homerun into the river. Four hundred seventy-nine feet from the plate to the water."

"More likely into somebody's boat."

"I could've been the first one to put a ball in the river from the new ballpark," he said. "I could've done it."

His tone was angry and he was challenging me to refute him. But all I wanted was to make my goodbyes without inciting a riot. He hadn't ruined baseball for me but in the future I was unlikely to hunger again for the same intimacy with a player, to ascribe to him virtues he was not likely to possess. I would enjoy the game from a distance, as a sport, nothing more.

We sat there without talking until the sound of voices floated toward us over the grass, voices broken and hollow off the stadium metal. I knew Brady was the cause of it before I even saw him striding through the gate near the third base line, Addie on his arm and a groundskeeper hurrying along behind them. Brady and the groundskeeper kept shouting at one another but Addie seemed unperturbed by the noise. She was wearing a pale blue sheath dress and her legs and arms were bare and the short white gloves appeared to glow against the backdrop of artificially greened grass. I did not like the way my breath caught in my chest at the sight of her.

Incident on Ten-Right Road

Salandro was smiling. "Some fans won't take no for an answer," he said.

"Those aren't fans," I told him.

But he was already on his feet and waving to them.

Brady turned to the groundskeeper and pointed up at us. The groundskeeper said something, then turned and went back through the nearest gate.

Salandro started down the stadium steps.

"It's just my drunken friend," I told him. "You don't need to go down there."

With his good hand he held his broken arm against his chest and galloped down the steps, over 300 pounds pummeling the metal stairs, every step like a cannon shot into an empty well. Finally I made myself get up and follow him.

On the last step above the grass Salandro paused. He pulled a baseball card and pen from inside the sling and scrawled his name across the card. He was probably carrying a whole pack of rookie cards and had been waiting for an opportunity to autograph one. Then he stepped down and handed the card to Addie. She looked at it and turned it over and then Brady took it from her hand and said something laughing and Salandro's good hand closed into a fist around the pen and I hurried to get down there to them.

They were standing nose to nose when I reached them. Brady was smirking and Salandro fuming and Addie was off to the side with a fingertip to her throat and a look of mild surprise on her face. The baseball card was on the ground at Brady's feet.

"But what the hell kind of a name is that?" Brady was saying. "Are you Cuban or Puerto Rican or what? Habla ingles, amigo?"

I grabbed Brady by the arm. "Knock it off. His family is from Texas."

Brady kept smiling at Salandro. It was the ugliest smile I had ever seen. "That explains it then."

"Explains what?" Salandro said.

"All those refried beans. It explains why you're such a big tub of guts."

Salandro lunged forward and swung his cast against Brady's chest and knocked him backward. Brady stumbled but did not fall and just before he charged into Salandro he cut a quick look at Addie. Then he lowered his head as if he meant to tackle Salandro, but the pitcher stepped neatly to the side and clubbed him once on the back of the head and Brady went down on his face in the grass.

Brady lay very still with one cheek to the turf. His eyes were open but he did not try to get up.

I turned to Addie. I thought I saw an apology in her smile, though it might have been something else. Then Salandro picked up the baseball card and dusted it off and without a word or a look in my direction he walked away toward the clubhouse.

I went to Brady and stood over him but did not bend down. He rolled onto his back then and, blinking, began to giggle.

"Christ," I said. "What the hell is wrong with you?"

He kept giggling and pointed a finger at Addie. "It's her fault, Mike."

I felt sick to my stomach. I turned away and headed for the parking lot.

"Michael?" Addie said.

I did not look back.

All the way to the exit I could hear Brady giggling.

* * *

I remember thinking after work that night that now my life could get back to normal. Now that I was through with both Brady and Salandro. I had a shower as usual and then sat on my bed and wondered if I should go upstairs to see Isabella. It was not my regular night but I wanted some company and whatever else it is that women like her provide. But I did not want to go upstairs and find her with someone else. In the end I decided it would be better to take a walk alone, even if it was nearly 2:00 in the morning.

Out in the hallway I had turned the corner toward the elevator when the bell dinged and the door slid open and Addie stepped out. Something sank inside of me as I waited for Brady to appear. But she was alone. She was smiling but her eyes were sad and she walked with her hands reaching out for me. The first scent of her reminded me somehow of Christmas. I felt as tremulous as a child.

"I am so sorry about this afternoon," she said.

She took both my hands in hers and held them together against her chest. "Are you on your way out?"

"No, I... I'm just getting in."

"Can I talk with you a minute? I won't stay long, I promise."

"How did you get up here?"

"One of the other tenants let me in. Jeannie, from the fourth floor? She was just coming in, so I told her you were expecting me but that you must have fallen asleep. She probably thought I was a prostitute. Please don't be angry with me, Michael. I really do need to talk with you."

We went back to my place. I switched on the living room light but remained by the door. She went to the window and looked out. I smelled the fragrance again and that was when I recognized it, apples and cinnamon, the scent of Christmases when I was a boy, the scent I woke up to every Christmas morning. The effect was disconcerting, even dizzying, of Christmas in July, the scent of this woman stealing my breath away.

Beyond her the city was a sea of white and yellow lights. Without turning she said, "Sometimes I wonder if the only reason I'm with him is to take care of him."

"The Brady I knew never required a caretaker."

She turned to me. "Nor the one I first met. But these last couple of weeks... I can't explain why he's acting this way."

"He's afraid of losing you. He's trying too hard."

"Trying what?"

I was too tired to think about it. I had lost a lot of sleep over Brady in the past 48 hours and some over Salandro and I was going to lose more tonight with the scent of apples and cinnamon in every breath I took.

She saw the weakness in me and she came across the room. She switched off the light and then stood against me and laid one gloved hand atop my chest. She said, "If you tell me to go back to him, Michael, I will."

"Will you?" I said. My voice was hoarse and dry, my chest was tight.

"If you tell me to, yes. Just please. Please don't tell me to."

The world beyond her was a sea of lights and all around us was a sea of darkness. I intended to tell her that Brady was my friend no matter how badly he

Incident on Ten-Right Road

behaved, but then she laid her other hand against me too, and I did not.

* * *

I awoke before sunrise, just as I used to the summer I was 18, when I would slap some water on my face and brush my teeth, and after gulping down a plate of sausage and eggs I would pile into an old Thunderbird and ride off to the steel mill with my father and three burly men, all strong, honest men in work boots and dungarees, men with a hard but simple day ahead of them, a lifetime of hard but simple days.

I awoke before sunrise but no longer 18 and consequently unrested, feeling worse than the night before. Because now there was guilt on top of everything else. I dressed and brushed my teeth and without waking her or even writing a note because I was afraid to let the words get started, I went out into the first sunrise I had faced in several years.

As I drove I thought of what my father had told me one morning while we waited at the end of the driveway for the Thunderbird to arrive. I had complained that I hated the steel mill, that I loathed the red dust in my ears and nose and mouth, and that after just two days on the labor gang I wanted desperately to quit.

Stick with it, son. The suffering will make you stronger, you'll see.

Stronger for what? I asked.

He thought about it while he stared, squinting and smiling, at the horizon. All I know, he said, is that it's impossible to see this beautiful sunrise with your eyes on the ground like that.

I answered that I couldn't care less about the sunrise.

You should, he said. You never know when you'll be looking at your last one.

But all summer long I never lifted my eyes to the rising sun.

Now as I drove into Pendleton County, West Virginia, the sun was already well above the trees. I stopped at a diner for a plate of sausage and eggs, then bought two ham and cheese sandwiches, two bottles of water and a daypack at the general store, then drove the last miles to the trailhead at the base of Seneca Rocks.

The granny trail corkscrews up a sandstone mountain a thousand feet high. The only people on the trail at that hour were a few hikers who wanted the same thing I did, solitude and sweat. We nodded to one other but did not say hello and were careful not to walk too closely. The path was damp with dew and still dark more than halfway up the mountain. My muscles felt old and stiff and I knew I would be sore the next day but even the tightness in my calves was somehow pleasant now. Maybe I enjoyed it because I was glad to be punishing myself. Maybe I imagined that the pain would make me stronger.

I made the summit before the sun reached its zenith. On the naked peak I sat atop a rounded boulder and felt the coolness of stone beneath me and without asking any questions I watched the valley below as if I had never been down there, never been one of those ants racing off to somewhere important only to race home again, one of those leaf-cutters day after day feeding slivers of weed to his fungus of ambition.

I drank one bottle of water and then hiked west

Incident on Ten-Right Road

along the lower ridge until I was 100 yards or so off the main trail. In the shade of hemlocks I lay with my daypack for a pillow and slept for two hours.

The sound of horses woke me, the soft nickering and clop, four horses and their riders coming up the south side of the mountain on the horse trail. I sat there and ate my sandwiches and drank half the water in the second bottle and wished I did not have to go back down. I had given myself a hard simple morning but unfortunately it was only a morning and not my life. Soon I would have to go back and clean up the mess I had helped to create. The clean-up itself was bound to be messy but I could not walk away from it. For 37 years my father awoke every morning at 5:00 a.m. and rode off to the red dust and heat of the steel mill not because he enjoyed it but because it was what he had to do for his family. I had no family but I had an old friend and he did not deserve betrayal.

I also thought about Salandro and that I had not been as patient with him as I should have been. He was just a kid and what was it I had expected from him anyway? He was not supernatural. If he had disappointed me it was because I had tried to make him into something other than a frightened young man. There were things I could do for him if I really wanted to. And now, finally, I did want to. I wanted to repay the favor he had done for me all summer.

I decided that as a discipline I would not let myself drink any more water until I reached the bottom of the mountain. But, once there, I still would not let myself drink anything until I crossed the border back into Pennsylvania. Then it seemed the natural thing to extend the discipline until I reached my apartment. I was under the illusion even then that deprivation and discomfort could cleanse me somehow, could set right what had been irrevocably polluted.

* * *

There were no messages on my machine and nobody answered the phone in Brady and Addie's hotel room. I spent the rest of the afternoon lying face-up on my bed, staring at the white ceiling, hearing the sound that had begun in my head halfway down the mountain, a high sharp whine more felt than heard, a fine filament of shriek stretched as tight as knotted fishing line.

That evening I went to work as usual though everything felt off-balance to me. There were the usual emergencies every 10 minutes, each one precipitated by the wounding of somebody's ego. My ego was numb and I conceded without argument to every demand. I found it to be a very pleasant way to work, so detached, though the high thin note in my head would not let me enjoy it with impunity. I had a strong feeling that Addie and Brady were waiting for me across the street at O'Hanlon's. Or probably it was just Brady waiting there.

After work I stood on the sidewalk outside the building. If Brady was at O'Hanlon's he would see me through the window. But no one came out of the bar.

All the way to the parking garage I had an uncomfortable feeling of being followed. But each time I turned around, nobody was there.

* * *

Incident on Ten-Right Road

At home I stayed in my shower for a very long time with the hot water drumming down on my head. When I finally stepped out I could smell her in the steam, the Christmas scent again, and it made my stomach twitch. Without drying off I pulled on my robe and went to the threshold. The reading lamp on the bedside table was lit but the ceiling light was not. I had left them the other way around. I did not even want to look around the corner to the bed.

"How did you get in?" I asked.

"Last time I was here I found your extra key. In the kitchen drawer. I knew you would want me to have it."

"I want you to leave."

"He's unconscious again, don't worry. He'll sleep until noon. And don't worry about my having been seen this time, I was very careful. Nobody saw me come up. Nobody knows I'm here."

I said, "I'm not doing this again."

"I'm not leaving. I won't."

I went back into the bathroom and put on my old clothes. Still not looking at her I came out of the bathroom and said, "When I come back I expect to find you gone."

She did nothing to stop me and for a while I was surprised by that. I went down to the lobby and thought about getting my car out of the garage but then I went outside and started running. I hadn't run except on a treadmill for a very long time and I was pleased with how good it felt even in street shoes. The movement made me think that I was getting away from something.

I jogged for maybe a mile before I came to a playground in a nice residential area. I sat there on a bench until I got my breath back, and then a satisfied kind of weariness seeped into me. The night was warm and a few stars were visible through the haze. I told myself that I was going to take a couple weeks off soon and plot out a new future, something satisfying and regular. I convinced myself that I could do it. And then I decided that I would stay there on the bench until first light, that I would watch the sun coming up on a new way of life for me.

Another hour or more must have passed before the fine mist woke me. I took it as a good sign, a cleansing. A fresh start. Then I got up from the bench and walked home.

The red strobing lights were visible from two blocks away, pale at first, like fluttering pink ghosts galloping over the sky. I thought it was a fire until I came within sight of my building and saw all the police cars and the ambulance out front. I stood across the street and could not make myself go closer.

Eventually a couple of policemen noticed me and came across the street and asked for my name. When I told them they took me inside and upstairs. Brady was lying just inside the door. Salandro's baseball bat was not far from his head.

One of the policemen said, "You want to tell us what happened here?"

I looked at him and said, "You need to call Addie."

"She's the one who called us. After she came and found her husband like this."

"They're not married," I told him.

"According to her they were married yesterday afternoon in Maryland."

Incident on Ten-Right Road

And in the sudden lucidity of the moment I understood everything. Addie would have told them by now that two nights earlier I had tricked her into coming alone to my apartment, and Jeannie from the fourth floor would confirm the visit and remember whatever story Addie had told her. Addie would have sobbed when she told the police what I had tried to do with her that night. Maybe I had been successful and maybe not, it did not matter which version she told. What mattered was Brady's outrage when she told him about it. What mattered was how worried she had been when he had rushed over here a couple of hours ago, and the sick feeling that had made her follow him some 20 or 30 minutes later, and the horrible disbelief when she had pulled open the unlocked door and found her husband on the floor. The police would assume that I had buzzed Brady in when he came, but they might wonder how Addie had gained entry into the building. If I explained that Addie had stolen my extra key two nights earlier, that she had come again tonight and I had told her to leave and then walked out but she had probably stayed and called Brady to meet her here and had buzzed him in when he arrived, the police would explain it all away. That would say that according to Addie I had telephoned the hotel room several times this evening, and after the last call she admitted to Brady the awful things I had done to her or the awful things I had said, and that was when he had come rushing over to confront me. The police would look in the kitchen drawer where I always kept the key and they would find it there. They would check the phone records and would learn that the final call from my apartment to the hotel room had occurred during the time I was allegedly out jogging or sitting in the park. But O'Hanlon to his great sadness would remember how I had looked at Addie in the bar. He would remember how I had squeezed Brady's shoulder and insisted that he go outside with me. My colleagues at the station would remember how oddly I had behaved the past few days. The police would find no fingerprints but my own on the key and the phone and the baseball bat because white gloves leave no fingerprints.

It was all very hard and simple and there was no way to refute any of it. I wanted to turn and walk away but a policeman was blocking the door. I turned toward the window. The sun was coming up finally, only my second full sunrise in a very long time. A lovely red wet light glowed far away outside the glass.

On the Verge

Two a.m. on the cruise ship *Grand Adventurer*, a day and a half out of Miami on its tour of the Bahamas and the eastern Caribbean. Rudy Fenton walked the lido deck and smoked a borrowed Lucky Strike. A clear, moonlit night, cool for July, more like an autumnal night, a fat autumnal moon, the air heavy with the chilly scent of deep ocean. The cigarette did not taste as good as Rudy had hoped it would. Nothing did.

Fifteen minutes earlier, after crawling out of bed in his inside cabin, the smallest and least expensive class of cabin on the ship, Rudy Fenton, unsated by sex, restless with a vague discontent, had left his girlfriend Amy to lie there frightened by his desires while he wandered the corridors, gradually working his way toward the uppermost deck. On deck four he encountered a steward and borrowed a cigarette.

"I quit two years ago," Rudy told him.

The steward held a lighter to the coffin nail. "Didn't we all."

Then the slow meander toward the top of the ship, blowing smoke ahead of him, pushing his face through it. On the lido deck he took his discontent to the aft rail and tried to blow it out to sea in smoke rings that would not hold together. The low throb of the ship's engines scratched at his skin, vibrated his nerve endings.

Every aspect of Rudy's surroundings added another facet to his discontent, became another mirror in which he saw himself reflected, his image cast back at him like a prick in the eye. This ship with its glittery lights and polished surfaces, this carefully packaged luxury that he could afford only through thievery. The vast black sea that frightened him, a poor swimmer, a mountain boy. The star-speckled sky forever out of reach. Worst of all that cramped little cabin, windowless, nearly all the floor space taken up by the bed.

After the first full afternoon on ship he had refused to accompany Amy to the fitness center, the sun deck with its pool and spa. Refused to explain why, except to himself. Because his body and hers were different from all the others there, that was why. Not out of shape, but shaped differently, marked differently by their jobs. He and Amy had blue-collar bodies. His arms were pale except below the biceps. Otherwise only his face and neck were tanned, his body pink or pale in all other places, not evenly browned on a tanning bed. He was hard and lean but stippled across the shoulders and buttocks with tiny red pimples. Amy's buttocks were soft, her thighs were soft, not long and sinewy from hours on an exercise bicycle. He was too hard, a wage-earning grunt. She was too soft, a meek little paper-shuffler.

The cruise had been his idea, he had had to talk her into it. Talked her into lying to her boss of only seven months, finagling a week's vacation five months before she was eligible for one. Rudy had made up the story for her, even contrived an old friend in Michigan to send a letter:

Incident on Ten-Right Road

Dear Amy, As you know, your Grandmother Idy's cancer has progressed

to the point where there is nothing left for the doctors to do....

Rudy had financed the cruise by liberating three laptops from the Walmart warehouse where he worked. Sold them to friends at 30% off retail. It had been the biggest heist of his life, of 20 years of shoplifting and penny ante thievery. The first at the age of five, a bubble gum cigar from the drugstore. Up until now they had all been impulsive acts, whims, spur of the moment. This one had been different.

"I can't go," Amy had argued. "How can I go? I'm not even eligible for vacation yet."

"You have to go," he told her.

"Well I can't."

"In that case I'll just have to take somebody else."

Tears welled up in her eyes. "Would you really do that?"

"Only if you force me to."

"But it's so expensive. I mean, a cruise. They're expensive, aren't they?"

"I'll pay for everything."

"How can you manage that?"

"I'll manage," he said.

In any case he had to get away from the loading dock for a while. He had to or something was going to explode in him. He felt on the verge of something, he told her, though he could not say what, or whether it might be good or bad. But he had felt something looming inside him, building to crescendo. It had started the morning Alex hadn't shown up for work.

Alex the college kid, barely 19 , summer worker between his freshman and sophomore years at Duke. Alex didn't show up one Friday, so Rudy telephoned the boy's home to chew him out for not calling in sick, for leaving them short-handed. The boy's mother said, "Oh didn't he tell you? Alex left for Seattle, he's accepted a job there. Computer graphics, web design, 120k a year to start, plus a 25k signing bonus. They'll even send him to school at night to finish his degree! Isn't that wonderful?"

Immediately a knot bloomed in Rudy's stomach, a lump the size of a grapefruit, twice as sour. It sent tentacles into his chest, scratched at his throat, pinched his testicles. *Nerdy little snot-nose*, he thought, and even muttered it out loud from time to time, like the phrase from a jingle he could not get out of his head.

And so, the cruise, the get-away, the laptops. Two days of figuring out how to fudge the paperwork. How to conceal the laptops in the warehouse. How to slip them into his truck.

The cruise was supposed to dissolve that knot in his stomach. And for the first few hours on the water, he had imagined it might work. He had still felt on the verge of something, but something promising, explosively good. Barely underway, he and Amy had stuffed themselves at the buffet table, dropped a few dollars in the casino, made noisy love on their bed.

That night they both drank too much, though for different reasons. Then, back in their little room, she had been unusually receptive to experimentation, allowed him a pleasure previously denied, and afterward she would not take her hands off him until he was ready to make love again. Then she straddled him and rode him furiously, oblivious to or maybe even excited by the noise she was making, and startling him when she began to talk out loud, something she had never done before, always the most silent of lovers, but this time adamant, unrestrained, vociferous.

Later, lying side by side, he had said, "You never talk like that. You never act like that. I should get you drunk on champagne more often."

"It's something about being here, surrounded by all this, I don't know, this luxury. It makes me feel dangerous."

It was only on the second day, after lunch, that the sense of promise soured in him. Amy had insisted that they go to the sun deck. In their Walmart swimsuits and rubber sandals. Her beach towel sporting a picture of Winnie the Pooh, his a bottle of Budweiser. He spent two hours neck-deep in the whirlpool, simmering with embarrassment while she paraded her soft pale body around the deck.

That same evening, after dinner, he liberated a bottle of champagne from the buffet counter, took it back to their cabin, tried to reverse the entropy. But that night she wanted only conventional lovemaking, no auditory accompaniments. Afterward she kept her hands to herself, rolled over to watch a movie on their TV. He stared at the ceiling. After a long while he eased up close against her back and maneuvered himself against her buttocks. She neither moved nor acknowledged him there. He pushed a little harder. She rolled over suddenly and looked at him with frightened eyes and shook her head no.

That was when he climbed out of bed, told her he needed a cigarette.

"But you quit," she said.

"I'll quit again tomorrow."

Up to the lido deck he went, smoking, staring at black water. The feeling was strong in him now. Something was imminent, something was coming. Maybe he was going to kill somebody. Maybe he was going to kill himself. Maybe he would return to his cabin and do whatever he wanted to Amy whether she liked it or not. He felt capable of anything that night. Every possibility existed. All he needed was a sign, something to point him in the right direction. Consequences were of no importance.

He started walking. Quietly, stealthily, because he understood somehow that he was sneaking up on something. Sneaking up on himself perhaps. The end of Rudy Fenton, Walmart employee, the boy from Hickory, North Carolina, the poor swimmer with the pimpled back. He seemed to be the only individual out there in the moonlight, everybody else holed up in the casino or the disco or locked away in their staterooms doing who knows what to each other.

He walked for 20 minutes, circumnavigating the lido deck twice, then finally, cigarette gone, smoked to the butt and tossed overboard, he went up the stairs to the sun deck, to the stars at the top of the stairs.

Two steps from the sun deck he heard them. A man and a woman, over by the whirlpool somewhere. He crept forward slowly, scrutinized the dark. There, that shadow on the darkness. Two people wrapped in a blanket on a chaise lounge, the chaise lounge rhythmically scraping, bucking atop the deck.

Had it not been for the woman's voice he might not have watched, might not have inched closer. But

Incident on Ten-Right Road

her voice was resonant and rich, the purr of a big cat, it growled at the man. "Not yet, damn you," she told him. "Don't you dare. Not yet."

Rudy pressed himself to a bulkhead, crept closer, just a little bit closer. He could smell her perfume now, the spiciness of it, a tropical breeze, something like cloves and lavender. She was atop the man and kept talking all the time and she did not limit herself to just one phrase as Amy had done. This woman's vocabulary was extensive. The more she talked, the more Rudy felt that he was getting some of what the man beneath her was getting.

By the time the man moaned and arched his back, she had thrown the blanket off her shoulders. She was standing up, straddling the chaise lounge, doing deep knee-bends as vigorously as she could.

But the man was finished and she was not happy about it. "Damn you anyway," she said. She swung one leg over him and stood for just a moment beside the chaise, looking in Rudy's direction just for an instant, so that his breath caught in his chest, snagged on something sharp. But apparently she had not noticed him. She turned back to the man and straddled his head and lowered herself atop him and started talking again.

Rudy had to meet this woman, that was all he knew. He wanted desperately to see her face so that he could recognize her in the daylight. She was what he had been waiting for and what had been building inside him.

He scrutinized the deck for an opportune place to conceal himself, a place from which to watch when, inevitably, she would rise and return to her room, with or without the man, walking through sufficient light that

Rudy could see her face illuminated. He required only a glimpse in order to memorize her face forever. He had already memorized her body, the silhouette of heavy but not ponderous breasts, the strong and tireless hips. He guessed that she was nearly as tall as him, feet 5'9 ½". Not a small woman certainly, not a girl timid and uncertain, not a girl too soft inside and out.

He identified what he thought would be the perfect hiding spot, and was on the verge of moving toward it when the woman cried out, one long sustained *Yesss!* so loud and uninhibited that Rudy almost giggled, but held his own noise in check, made his chest ache by trying not to laugh.

She shivered for a moment and shook herself, her head hanging limp. Then she stood and reached down for a glass on the deck and raised it up and drank deeply from it. She drew back her arm then and hurled the glass far out into the sea. Then she dragged a second chaise lounge up beside the man's and pulled the blanket off the deck and draped it over her body.

"You mind if I have some of that?" the man said.

"Yes I do."

He got up and walked over to a deck chair where there was a stack of folded towels, took two and returned to his own chair and covered himself. "You might try to hold it down a decibel or two," he told her. "Just a suggestion."

"You might try keeping your suggestions to yourself," she said.

Rudy was so focused on the woman now, leaning toward her, drawn to her like a needle compass to magnetic north, that he no longer heard the throb of the ship's engines, no longer heard the music from the

Incident on Ten-Right Road

disco three decks below. He was breathing her in with every breath and he could swear that her heat was washing over him in dizzying waves.

He saw every movement she made, every gesture, so keen was his attention. He saw when she raised her right leg, stuck her toes out beneath the end of the blanket, bent and cracked her big toe. He saw when she reached across to the man and took his hand in hers, laid his hand atop her breast.

And when she began to talk again, it was in softer tones than before, sweetly, seductively. With every suggestion by her and every agreement or counter-suggestion from the man, Rudy felt more certain of his own destiny, more certain that the vague something on whose verge he had been standing since leaving Hickory was now within his reach.

Finally he understood it all, understood every last flutter of anticipation he had been feeling. This man and woman were formulating a plan and Rudy was a part of it. It did not matter that they did not know he was a part of it. This was his call from Seattle. This was why he had been compelled to steal those laptops. It was not about sex at all. Sex, next to the things he overheard that night, was icing on the cake.

He waited until their conversation waned and the man and woman began to stir, to reach for their clothing. Then he backtracked, creeping backward on his heels. He went to the place he had picked out earlier, behind the corner of an equipment locker, and knelt like a shadow, and tried to calm his racing heart.

When the man and woman walked past five minutes later, she was so close that he could have reached out and brushed her cheek with his fingertips.

She trailed the scent of cloves and lavender and the dizzying musk of her flesh. In the glow of the lights along the rail, he saw that she was older than he had thought, maybe 10, even 15 years older than him. But her face was lovely and angular and she had the calmest, most confident eyes he had ever seen.

He waited another five minutes before returning to his own cabin. Amy was asleep. He undressed at the foot of the bed, not even attempting to be quiet. But still she would not awaken. Finally he drew the covers off her and slid in beside her and with his arm behind her back he pulled her against him.

"Mmm," she said, but she did not open her eyes.

"Get up on top," he told her.

Her eyes came open, but only for a moment. "I'm too sleepy."

Gently he rolled her onto her back and moved atop her. He was very noisy and maybe too rough but soon she was wide awake again and she did not seem to mind.

* * *

After that it all moved quickly. In the morning Rudy and Amy crowded into their snug, narrow shower and he recounted the conversation he had overheard on the sun deck.

"Did she actually say it?" Amy asked. Even under the hot spray, she had goosebumps. "Did she come right out and tell him to kill her husband?"

"She said shoot, not kill. 'That's when you shoot him,' she said. But I don't think she was talking about a flesh wound, do you?"

"They must have been joking."

Incident on Ten-Right Road

"Like hell they were. This woman is serious business, believe me."

The man had asked her, "Why don't I break into the house some night? I'll be a burglar. I'll shoot him in bed. Maybe I'll rape you, tie you up, wrap some duct tape around your mouth."

"You'd enjoy that, wouldn't you?" the woman had said.

"There's no chance of being seen if I do it at the house."

"Who's going to see you at the factory? It's out in the middle of nowhere."

"Somebody could drive by and see my car there."

"Nobody ever uses that road anymore, you know that. Teenagers maybe, after dark. But you'll be long gone by then."

"I could take a rental, I suppose. Could I get a rental by paying cash? That's the only way they couldn't trace it back to me. If I can even convince them to let me pay in cash."

"Stop worrying so much," she said.

"That's easy for you to say, isn't it?"

"Listen, it has to be done at the factory and that's the end of it. The money is in his office."

"That's another thing I don't understand. What's so important about the money? It's insignificant."

"Fifty thousand in cash is insignificant to you?"

"It's nothing compared to what you'll get afterward. The business is worth what—two, three million a year?"

"It has to be at the office," she said.

"So that you can be at the club with your friends. Playing tennis. Beyond suspicion."

"Listen, Caspar Milquetoast," she told him. "It will be months before I can start drawing anything from the business accounts. Plus he's got partners. They're going to wrangle for every penny. And in the meantime, what are we supposed to live on—your income? What do you make a year? Minus my tips, I mean."

"You're sure he'll be alone in his office?"

"What did I say already?"

"And the money will definitely be in the safe?"

"One last time," she had said. "Now pay attention. The last Friday of every July, and the last Friday of every January. Two packets of cash, $25,000 each. One for each driver. The factory closes at 5:00, everybody goes home except for Russ. The trucks show up right after dark. They load up all the barrels of old chemicals, Russ gives each driver his money, and off they go to dump the stuff who knows where. The entire operation takes less than two hours."

"And between the time the factory closes and the trucks get there. What's Russ doing all this time?"

"What would he be doing? He has his dinner, he watches TV—"

"How?"

"How what?"

"How does he get his dinner? Does he order in? Does he drive into town? Where's the food come from?"

"He picks it up at lunchtime. A Blimpie's and two glazed doughnuts."

"You know this for a fact?"

"I can even tell you what's on the damn sandwich. I've been married to him for 19 years, haven't I? Don't you think I know the man's habits?"

Incident on Ten-Right Road

"He just waits there alone in his office. Watching TV."

"He's not alone. He's got his Blimpie's and his doughnuts. He's in heaven."

"Okay then. From the time the factory closes, how long do you think before he starts to eat?"

She blew out a breath.

"I'm the one who's taking the risk," he'd told her.

"The suspicion always falls on the spouse."

"Except when she's playing doubles at the country club."

"There's no risk. I've taken all the risk out of it for you. I'm the one who's taking the risk."

"You?" he had said.

"Who stole his office key and had a duplicate made for you? Who drove to that idiotic gun show in West Virginia and bought you a handgun?"

"Try to keep your voice down," he said.

"You either want to do this or you don't. You either want to be with me or you don't."

"I do want to be with you, you know that. But this other, it's...."

"Then forget it. Don't do it. Forget we even discussed it."

"And then what?"

"Then nothing. Nothing changes. I keep living with a slug and playing tennis five nights a week. And for an hour every Wednesday, you keep trying to improve my backhand."

"You have a lovely backhand," he told her.

She said nothing to this.

"Did I ever tell you," he asked, "that I have a master's degree in psychology?"

185

"And?" she said.

"I wanted to be a therapist once. Wanted to help people."

Again she remained silent.

"Have you ever wondered—" he began.

She held up a hand. "Don't. Don't start wondering on me, please."

Half a minute passed. She said, "Just so you know. I despise weak people."

This was followed by a two full minutes of silence. Finally she spoke again, but very softly this time, so softly that Rudy could barely hear. "Do you want to change your life or don't you?"

The man in the chaise lounge did not answer. But Rudy, his spine hard against the bulkhead, had nodded in the darkness. His lips had mouthed the answer for all of them. *I do. I do. I do.*

* * *

For a while Rudy did not press Amy for any kind of decision, did not let her know that his own decision had been made. Instead he suggested that they simply observe the couple as closely as possible, eavesdrop, ingratiate, glean whatever useful information they could.

On the fourth evening of the cruise, when Amy returned to the ship after a shopping trip ashore, while Rudy had followed the man to a dive shop on the beach and then passed the rest of the afternoon alone on the sand, Amy came into the cabin and tossed her bag onto the bed and told him, too happily, "We can't do it."

Incident on Ten-Right Road

He, lying on his belly in his undershorts, his back flame red, said, though he already knew, "Do what?"

"They live in Pennsylvania! Halfway between Pittsburgh and Erie, she said."

Now he sat up. "You talked to her?"

"I was in a shop, looking at this sun dress." She pulled the dress from the shopping bag and held it up for him, a batik-patterned dress, deep blue and pale yellow.

"Nice," he said. Then, "So?"

"So she came into the shop. So I, you know, I remembered what you had said about observing them and all, so I just walked up to her and asked her what she thought of this dress."

"You didn't."

"Women do that all the time. We ask each other's opinion. It wasn't like I was doing something odd."

"Okay, okay. Let's get to the point."

"The point is, she said how nice the dress would look on me, and then I tried it on for her and it did look nice. And then we just kept talking and we ended up going to lunch together! She paid for everything. She even bought us a drink afterward. A Dubonnet, it was called. It looks like Doo-bonnet but it's pronounced Doo-bo-nay. It's dark and kind of sweet—"

"The point?" he said.

"The point is that she is really very very nice. Her name is Helen."

He tried the name out on his lips but not aloud, felt the way his tongue separated the syllables against the back of his teeth, the same movement of tongue he would use on her, the taste of her mouth in his....

"I don't want us to do this to her," Amy said.

"Look, she's the one who's going to have her husband whacked, remember? All I plan to do is to take the money from her boyfriend afterward."

"I know but... I just...."

He waited.

"I mean, they're in Pennsylvania, we're in North Carolina, it's just impossible, isn't it? I don't see how we can even think about it."

He sat at the foot of the bed and stared at the wall. The wall was only four inches from his kneecaps.

Very lightly, with almost no touch at all, she placed three fingers on his shoulder. "You really got burned today. I can feel the heat coming right off your skin."

"I'm doing it," he said.

She lifted her hand away.

"You can go back if you want," he told her. "Go back to being somebody's peon the rest of your life. But I can't. I'll be 25 years old in two months."

"Twenty-five is young."

He turned to her. "Ever since I was 10 I've been listening to my old man piss and moan about how fast his life is going by. He used to lecture me about not letting all my opportunities slip away, about how I should stop expecting a better opportunity tomorrow. Well, you know what? He doesn't lecture me anymore. Why do you think that is?"

She stood there blinking, her lower lip stuck out.

"Because he's given up on me, that's why."

She shook her head no. Tears welled up in her eyes.

"I'm getting that money, Amy. It's what I'm supposed to do."

Incident on Ten-Right Road

"Nobody is supposed to rob anybody."

"Nobody is supposed to kill anybody either. But they're the ones doing it, not me. Why do you think, out of all the hundreds of people on this ship, that I'm the one who happened to overhear their conversation?"

"I don't know why," she said.

"You don't know what fate is?"

"Fate's not about bad things. It's not about breaking the law, is it?"

"I'll tell you what it is about. It's about it being our turn."

He reached for her hands, covered them with his own, drew them close and held them pressed against his cheek. "*Our* turn," he repeated. "How can that be bad?"

* * *

While still aboard ship they emptied out their individual checking accounts. A little over $800 from hers, a little under $300 from his. He sent a fax to his boss at Walmart, informed him that Rudy Fenton had been offered a job in Seattle, please forward the last paycheck to my father. He e-mailed his friend in Michigan to send another bogus letter to Amy's employer, Grandma Idy is holding steady but still gravely ill. Consequently Amy will be staying on indefinitely to care for her; she does not expect her job to be held open.

"Now nobody, nobody will know when we go to Pennsylvania. We pay cash for everything, so they'll be absolutely no paper trail. This is foolproof," he told her.

He kept her from wavering too precipitously in her resolve by being generous with the champagne, doing a lot of window shopping, pointing out all the jewelry and clothing she could buy soon. Only once did she point out to him, "Fifty thousand dollars won't last all that long, you know."

"It's a hell of a beginning though. It's at least half of a house. You want us to have a house of our own, don't you?"

"You mean... we'll get married?"

"You don't expect us to live in sin forever, do you?"

After that she was more optimistic about the plan. As for Rudy, the very thought of possessing $50,000 in cash only whetted his appetite for more. He found himself watching the older woman, Helen, at every opportunity.

On the last evening of the cruise, he was watching her from across the dining room, watching the way she raised a fork or a champagne flute to her mouth, the way her lips opened and closed, such full, moist lips. Every time he looked at her, his gaze was sooner or later drawn to those lips.

"She's going to see you staring at her," Amy whispered.

Under the table, he slid his hand out of his crotch.

"You should lighten up on the shrimp," he told her. Her plate was piled high from her third trip to the buffet table.

"Hey, it's the last night," a man at their table said. He and all of his other dining companions, including Amy, were gorging themselves. Rudy felt something like revulsion for all of them.

Incident on Ten-Right Road

They have no discipline, he thought. *They're weak. And I despise weak people.*

He did not care if Helen caught him staring at her or not. In fact she had already done so, not once but several times. Most recently, she had held his gaze for a few seconds, and then, whether the gesture was accidental or deliberate, he didn't care, she slipped her tongue through her lips, moistened her lips from corner to corner. Rudy winked at her. And she—she made his heart turn over, she smiled at him. Maybe she was laughing at him, maybe she found him amusing, he didn't care. He continued to stare.

A few minutes later, both Helen and the tennis instructor said goodnight to their tablemates. They left the dining room arm-in-arm.

Rudy watched them exit. Then, "Excuse me," he said, and pushed back his chair.

Amy asked, "Where are you going?"

"Restroom. Have some more shrimp."

Out on the deck, Helen and the man were standing at the rail, 20 feet from the dining room entrance. Rudy waited in the doorway.

Helen and her companion talked for a while. At one point the man turned and walked off and then came quickly back to her, his face red. She jabbed a finger against his chest and said something that made him squeeze shut his eyes. Rudy found it all very entertaining. Especially when the man strode off and left her alone at the rail and she snapped open her purse and pulled out a new pack of cigarettes and tapped it—banged it, Rudy would have said—against the rail.

Rudy walked up to her. "Any chance you've got an extra one of those?"

She looked at him. Said nothing. Kept looking at him as she took a lighter from her purse and lit her own cigarette. Then slipped that cigarette from between her lips and handed it to him.

"Thanks," he said, and felt immediately light-headed, even before he raised the cigarette to his mouth, and more so afterward when he tasted the smudge of lipstick around the filter. He fought off the urge to lick it.

She lit a cigarette for herself.

"Not many smokers on this cruise," he offered.

"That's because it's restricted to only a couple of places. This isn't one of them."

"I like women who take chances," he said.

She seemed uninterested in that subject. "You're Rudy. Amy's boyfriend."

There was something of a challenge in the way she said this, something of an accusation. It felt like foreplay.

"How are you enjoying the cruise?" he asked, and made an effort not to drop his g's, to keep his hillbilly accent in check.

"Like everything else, it gets boring after a while."

He nodded. Then told himself to stop nodding, stop grinning, stop looking like an Alfred E. Newman dashboard doll with a bobbing head.

"And Amy?" the woman said.

"Huh? Excuse me?"

"Is she enjoying the cruise?"

"Sure, yes. She's having a grand time." As far as he could recall he had never before employed *grand* as an adjective. "Of course, this is her first time."

"Everybody has one," the woman said.

Incident on Ten-Right Road

Despite his best efforts, he nodded. "I don't believe I caught your name," he said, just because he wanted to hear her say it, wanted to see her mouth open, see her tongue flick against the back of her teeth.

He waited, but she did not answer. She watched the water. He had come up with a sentence he wanted to say—*It will be good to get back to my work on Monday*—hoping that it would incite her to inquire of his work, and he would answer, carelessly, *Computer graphics, web page design, that sort of thing.*

But she did not tell him her name, gave him no opening. Instead she asked, "How many computers did it take?"

He forced himself not to jerk away, to appear too startled. "Excuse me?"

"To pay for this cruise. How many computers did you have to steal?"

And now there was something in her voice that emboldened him. The mockery was gone. He sensed a conspiracy in bloom. "Only three," he said.

"Even so. It couldn't have been easy."

"Laptops," he told her.

"Laptops? Well that's a whole different matter, isn't it? Laptops wouldn't be difficult at all." She was smiling now, smiling very broadly, warmly, her body turned toward his.

"A walk in the park," he answered.

He noticed that she did not lean away from him after this exchange, did not face the rail again. He could almost feel her breast against his arm. He felt himself inclining toward her, in danger of falling. With his right hand he gripped the rail.

"I might suggest, however," the woman said,

"that Amy should be a bit more discreet with such confidences. She got lucky this time. I really have no interest in petty thievery."

"Actually it's classified as grand larceny," he said.

"Oh my, well, that's much more impressive, isn't it?"

He inhaled deeply with his smile, filled his lungs with her scent. "You're right about Amy though. She's such a child sometimes."

"I'm sure she'll grow out of it."

"Not soon enough for me."

She said nothing. He could feel her eyes on him, could literally feel her gaze moving across his face. And he heard himself thinking, *This is your chance. The only one you're going to get.*

Until that moment he had not admitted to himself that he was waiting for a chance, but there it was suddenly and he was not about to let it evaporate. "I much prefer older women," he told her. "Women who aren't afraid."

She smiled at this. "Afraid of what?"

"Of keeping up with me."

"Oh? Are you difficult to keep up with?"

"Always," he said. He could not bring himself to look at her. His face was warm, his ears burning.

"What I have discovered," she told him, "is the tendency in men to brag loudest about the qualities they least possess."

He was about to answer that he was the exception who proved the rule, when it dawned on him suddenly that if he argued her point, he would be proving it correct. He thought this a brilliant insight, the most

Incident on Ten-Right Road

profound idea he had ever conceived. There was something inspiring about this woman, something that brought out the best in him.

He tossed his cigarette over the rail, flicked it away as if nothing in the world had ever mattered to him, then, smiling, watched it fall until the tiny orange ember blinked out.

He then brought his gaze up slowly, up over the invisible horizon, high into the ebony sky. "It's going to be a good night to see the stars," he said.

"You're a stargazer, are you?"

"The sun deck is a good place to watch them from."

"Is it indeed?"

"At midnight. Midnight is a good time."

"How nice for you," she said.

Despite her words he believed that he had made himself clear. He understood what she wanted from a man, what intrigued her. That was why he turned to her now and with a calm and steady gaze looked her straight in the eye and smiled without the slightest trace of nervousness and said, "Goodnight, Helen."

He turned his back to her and walked away.

She said, "I can't imagine that it would be very difficult to keep up with a man who watches the stars."

"I'm sure you're right," he said, and he did not look back.

* * *

Eleven forty-five p.m. Amy was asleep, finally sleeping. He had done all he could to wear her out, had poured half a bottle of champagne on top of all that shrimp, and then had draped himself on top of her until she had had enough. Of course he had done the latter for himself as well, to quiet his nerves and increase his stamina for later, if it turned out that he needed it, and he was not at all confident that he would.

But there was nothing to be gained by not trying. To that end, he slipped out of bed and tiptoed into the bathroom and closed the door. A very quick shower, the spray turned low so that it would not patter loudly against the glass. He brushed his teeth and noiselessly gargled. Eased open the bathroom door but left the light on so that he could find his clothing.

Amy was sitting up in bed. "Hi," she said. "Did I fall asleep?"

He reached for his trousers. "A couple of minutes is all."

"Aren't you coming back to bed?"

"I'm feeling a little restless. Thought I'd take me a walk. Get some fresh air."

"Please come back to bed," she told him. "We can do some more of what you like."

He picked the remote off the bed and handed it to her. "See if you can find us a good movie. I'll be back before long."

He dressed quickly and slipped his shoes on and kissed her on the cheek so that she would not smell the mouthwash. Then out into the corridor and half-sprinting to the elevator. Up six decks to the top of the ship. It was already two minutes until midnight and he knew in his bones that Helen, if she came at all, was not the kind to wait for anybody.

He walked onto the sun deck and was surprised to see it so brightly lit. Somebody had turned on the lights in the pool and the whirlpool and the light over

Incident on Ten-Right Road

the open-air bar. She was standing at the port rail, her back to the ocean, hands shoved deep into the pockets of a trench coat, a man's long brown gabardine with epaulets on the shoulders, the coat held together by a belt tied around her waist. Her feet were bare.

He came up to her and stood facing her and smiled. She was not smiling. "I thought you said this was a good place for looking at the stars," she said.

"It's all these lights. Let me turn some of them off."

She grabbed the front of his shirt. "What else have you lied about?"

He opened his mouth to speak but he had no answer, no rebuttal. She gave him a last searing look and then ripped her hand down over his shirt, tearing off the buttons. She then laid one long fingernail atop his sternum, pushed in hard and dragged her fingernail down to his navel. He held his ground and tried not to grimace. The cool air stung his chest. He felt certain that he was bleeding but he would not let himself look down.

She turned her back to him then and leaned forward over the rail, laid her breasts on the outside of the rail as if she were trying to see something on one of the lower decks.

"Lift up my coat," she told him.

He heard the words but they confused him and made him dizzy and he wished she would say them again so that he could be certain of their meaning. But she said nothing and did nothing except to move her feet a little farther apart. He saw again that her feet were naked and though he had known it already it somehow seemed new to him, a revelation.

Gingerly then he took the tail of her coat in both hands and lifted it up like something dangerous and folded it over her back. Still she did nothing. He slipped his hands underneath the fabric and holding his breath leaned forward, alert for her protest, which did not come. Finally he smiled to himself and lay against her and pulled the front of the coat open. With one hand he cupped her breast, and with the other hand unbuckled his belt.

* * *

All the way to Pennsylvania on the Trailways bus, he felt himself wanting to be cruel to Amy, to say cruel things. So instead he was excessively polite. He allowed her to choose the motel where they would stay for the next two days, the Ramada on the outskirts of a little town called Tionesta, and the name under which they registered, Mr. and Mrs. Thomas Dubonnet of Seattle, Washington.

His only insistence was that they maintain a low profile at the motel, that they remain in their room like newlyweds, eating only take-out from the fast food restaurants across the highway.

"Can't I even use the pool?" she asked.

"It's more for your protection than mine."

There were two orders of business to attend to before the last Friday of the month. Both were easily accomplished. At a Walmart a half-mile from the motel, he purchased a paintball mask, a pair of black batting gloves and a small mallet with a blunt steel head. He would have preferred that the last item be a 9mm Glock but the paperwork could land him in prison. The man he intended to rob would no doubt be armed, else how to commit the murder? But he was

Incident on Ten-Right Road

after all a tennis instructor at the country club. How ferocious could he be?

The other order of business was to identify and locate the intended murder victim's factory. This Rudy accomplished with a page-by page perusal of the town's yellow pages.

"It can't be a big factory," he told Amy, who sat on the bed with her Biggie-sized french fries and watched Melissa McCarthy on TV. "She said it closes at 5:00 every day. That means one shift only. She also said that it's out in the country on an old road that nobody uses anymore."

"I guess," Amy said.

"This would be a lot easier if you could remember her last name."

"She didn't tell me her last name. I already told you that."

Rudy shrugged. "She also mentioned that there'd be chemicals. So, whatever the factory makes, it requires chemicals of some kind. Toxic chemicals. The kind it would cost more than 50 grand a year to deal with legally."

"Sounds right," Amy said.

"Here, listen to this. McManus Specialty Wood Products, 487 Old Pike Road. According to the county map," and he flipped to the front of the telephone book, "it's about two, almost three miles out of town. This could be it!"

Amy squeezed a glob of ketchup onto a french fry but her heart just wasn't in it. She sat staring at the french fry longer than any french fry deserved.

"It's either that or the Bisque Barn," Rudy told her. "But I wouldn't call a barn a factory, would you?"

Beside her right thigh lay a spicy chicken sandwich, Value Meal Combo #7, still in its wrapper. She had no appetite for it either, and the french fries were not doing a thing to quiet her stomach.

"It's just not worth it," she said. "You could get hurt."

"Just what is bisque anyway? Do you know?"

She sniffled and blinked at the TV.

"Nobody's going to get hurt," he said.

"Nobody?"

"It's $50,000, Amy. How long would you have to work to earn $50,000? After taxes—how long would you have to work?"

"I don't care," she said.

"Two years. Two fucking years, that's how long."

"Please don't swear at me." She had started to cry again, that sticky, whimpery kind of weepage that set his nerves on edge.

"I'm sorry, you're right. I apologize." He turned away from her and focused on the phone directory again.

A few minutes later she said, "It's pottery."

"Excuse me?"

"Bisque. That's what bisque is. It's pottery."

"You don't make that in a factory, do you?"

"I wouldn't call it a factory, no."

He closed the phone directory and climbed up beside her on the bed and snuggled against her. "This is why I love you," he said. "You are so damn smart. You're practically a genius."

* * *

Incident on Ten-Right Road

The last Friday of the month. Approximately 2:00 in the afternoon. Amy sat cross-legged on the bed, hugging a pillow, while Rudy hitched and hiked to McManus's Specialty Wood Products on Old Pike Road. His route was a deliberately circuitous one, more than twice the true mileage from the motel. The last leg of the trip took him through a stretch of woods and across a shallow creek, but eventually he emerged on the western side of Old Pike Road, directly across the highway from the gravel lane that led to the factory.

Old Pike Road might have once been a two-lane concrete thoroughfare but now its pavement was broken and pot-holed, irregularly patched, the shoulders overgrown with scrub grass encroaching from the woods. The factory, some 50 yards away down a wide gravel lane, consisted of three adjoining structures. A rectangular steel building at least 40 feet long; attached at its northern end, a lean-to that housed the planning board and a few other pieces of equipment; at the southern end, a cement-block office building, painted green, three rooms at the most. The entire structure sat in a spacious clearing surrounded on all four sides by woods, second growth maples and oaks and now and then the shiny white trunk of a statuesque birch.

Rudy hunkered down behind a thick black pin oak across the road from the factory. He counted nine cars in the parking lot. He glanced at his wristwatch. Four-ten. He set down the Walmart bag he had been carrying and then turned it over and dumped its contents onto the leaf-matted ground. Two roast beef sandwiches from Arby's, a paintball mask, steel mallet, four packets of horsey sauce, one paper napkin.

*\ate**

5:10 p.m. One vehicle remained in the parking lot. A red Cherokee, this year's model. Rudy crumpled up his sandwich wrappers, empty sauce packets, napkin, plastic bag. Crumpled them all into a tight ball, scooped a hole five inches deep from the soft earth, buried the ball and tamped down the dirt. From a hip pocket he pulled a pair of black batting gloves and laid them beside the mallet and mask. A squirrel chittered in the branches above him.

5:46 p.m. A vehicle approached from the south. Rudy checked his position behind the tree, adjusted to the north. The vehicle, a metallic gold Bonneville with its sunroof open, was not moving fast, maybe 40 miles per hour, but it slowed to half that speed as it passed the factory lane. Rudy slid around the tree, as smooth as a shadow, but not before he caught a glimpse of the Bonneville's driver sitting hunched forward over the steering wheel while eyeing the factory, black ski cap on his head, black turtleneck, black driving gloves clenched around the steering wheel.

Rudy chuckled to himself. "Amateur," he said.

5:49 p.m. The Bonneville returned from the north. Without slowing, it passed the gravel lane. For a moment Rudy thought the driver had chickened out and was turning tail for home. But then, suddenly braking, the car veered to the left, onto the shoulder, came to a stop. The brake lights did not go out. The driver remained inside the car, forehead against the steering wheel, building up his nerve. Finally the brake lights went out and the back-up lights came on and the Bonneville backed all the way past the gravel lane, then

Incident on Ten-Right Road

stopped, jerked forward, and progressed, as if trying for stealth, to park on the opposite side of the red Cherokee.

Rudy stood up behind the tree. Leaned as far around it as he dared.

The man in the Bonneville climbed out, dressed head to toe in black. Walking quickly toward the office door, he glanced over his shoulder toward the highway, faced the factory again, yanked the ski mask down over his face. Standing at the door, he fumbled for his key ring, couldn't find the right key. In the end he tried the door and found it unlocked. Stuck his right hand under his sweater, pulled out a small black handgun, looked toward the highway, opened the door and slid inside.

Rudy bent down behind the tree. Pulled the batting gloves on. Slipped the paintball mask over his head. Picked up the steel mallet at the hilt, glanced up and then down Old Pike Road. Stood up. Took a deep breath. Then sprinted in a half-crouch across the road and down the lane.

Rudy's intention was to stand just outside the factory door and then conk the tennis instructor when he exited. But his paintball mask fogged up and he was lucky to have the red blur of the Cherokee to guide him as he ran. He crouched at the rear bumper, yanked the mask off and attempted to wipe away the fog. But there was some kind of protective film over the clear plastic lens, and another strip over the vented area for his nose and mouth. He fumbled for a corner of the protective film but could not grasp it with his gloves on. He removed one batting glove and peeled the protective film off the lens and that was when he heard a gunshot, dull and muffled but echoing throughout the metal shell of the factory.

"Sonofabitch works fast," Rudy said.

He pulled the paintball mask on again and then yanked on the batting glove and with his first breath the lens fogged because he had not removed the protective film from the nose and mouth vents. He tore the mask off again and now the front door of the factory office swung open, banged back against the concrete wall. The quick crunch of footsteps on gravel. Rudy raised himself up a few inches, peeked through the Cherokee's tailgate window. The tennis instructor was coming quickly toward his car, brown attaché case in left hand, handgun dangling from his right.

At the Bonneville's door the tennis instructor reached for the door handle but the handgun banged against it. The tennis instructor jerked away suddenly and looked at the gun as if seeing it for the first time, an awful thing, abhorrent, seeing it apparently as something like a giant booger judging by the way he shook it off his hand and flicked it onto the gravel.

Rudy saw the handgun laying not far from his feet and he thought, *What the hell*. He stood up without his mask on and came out from behind the Cherokee. The tennis instructor had the car door open now, but at the sound of Rudy's approach he jerked his head around and saw Rudy and froze for a moment, his eyes, Rudy thought, like Al Jolson's behind the ski mask. Then the tennis instructor turned as if to run back to the factory but Rudy reached out with the mallet and swung with a short downstroke against the back of the man's head.

The tennis instructor went down on his knees. Rudy grabbed him underneath the arms, pulled him backward a few feet, shoved him through the open door of the Bonneville.

Incident on Ten-Right Road

Rudy went to where the handgun lay, put down his mallet, picked up the gun. A Glock. "Nice," Rudy said.

The tennis instructor was moaning a bit as he lay on his side across the front seat, his left arm jerking as if he meant to grab hold of something, pull himself up, time to rise and shine, sleepyhead. Rudy helped him to sit up behind the steering wheel, pushed both feet inside.

The man's eyes kept opening and falling shut, opening and falling shut. Rudy was leaning halfway inside the car now, his face so close to the tennis instructor's that he could hear the man's breath as it rustled through the fabric of the ski mask.

It was then that Rudy suddenly knew what he would do next, what he had always wanted to do anyway, what he had been singled out and chosen to do. In the next second all of his future became clear to him, how this one act would change everything, make everything possible.

With his left hand he lifted up the man's ski mask, folded it over the man's nose. Put the barrel of the Glock to the man's lips and wedged it in, pushing and twisting, until the tennis instructor began to cooperate and opened his mouth wider. Quickly Rudy calculated the proper trajectory for the bullet so that it would blow out the back of the skull where the mallet had struck, but then the tennis instructor ceased his cooperation and began to gag and pull away, so Rudy squeezed the trigger and hoped for the best.

The man's head flew back against the headrest but then snapped forward and fell heavily against Rudy's hand, still holding the Glock inside the man's mouth. Rudy did not like having his fingers nearly inside the tennis instructor's mouth. He jerked his hand away and left the gun to fall onto the man's lap.

Rudy had intended not to look into the rear of the Bonneville but he looked anyway. There was a lot of unattractive brain matter stuck to and dripping from the interior roof of the car. Some of it had splattered onto Rudy's face, little gobs of the man's former personality, sticky little globs of hopes and dreams and fears.

Rudy gagged and turned away. Horsey sauce burned in the back of his throat.

But afterward, everything was easy. Everything seemed crystal clear. Pick up the attaché case. Gather up the paintball mask and mallet. Stroll back across the road and into the woods, scrub your face with a handful of leaves, then stroll back toward the motel and the fast-food restaurants, depositing all unnecessary accoutrements in various trash receptacles along the way.

He kept reminding himself that Amy was the only person alive who knew he was in Pennsylvania. As for Alex the nerd, screw him and his job in Seattle. Screw his signing bonus. Rudy had made $50,000, tax free, for an afternoon's work. What could be better than that?

* * *

"There, read that," Rudy said, and he tossed the morning's newspaper onto the bed where, at 11:00 a.m., Amy still lay with the blankets pulled to her neck.

"What is it?" she asked.

"Read it and see if you don't feel a whole lot better." He was no longer working hard to be polite and patient with her. There was no future in it. Her timidity rankled him. Her dullness was holding him back.

Incident on Ten-Right Road

She sat up and read the Tionesta *Herald*. **MURDER/SUICIDE AT MCMANUS**, the headline read. The article described how the bodies of a local businessman and a local tennis instructor, both killed by the same weapon, recovered at the scene, had been found at approximately 1:20 a.m. that morning by a sawmill worker named Larry Deible. Acting on a telephone call from Mrs. McManus, who had tried and failed to reach her husband by phone at his office, Deible had driven to the factory from his home a mile and a half away. Local police theorized that the tennis instructor had shot McManus in his office, then returned to his vehicle in the parking lot, where, seized by a fever of guilt, had taken his own life. The motive for the murder was unknown.

"I'll bet tongues are wagging all over town," Amy said.

"Let them wag," said Rudy.

"Can we go home now?"

"You can," he said.

"Why not you too?"

"I need to hang around a while longer."

"What for?"

"Because I do. Because... it just makes sense this way. If we split up, I mean. You go back home and I'll meet you there in a couple of days."

"I'm not going anywhere without you," she said.

"Look, you get on the bus—"

"I'm not going! Everybody will right away want to know where you are, why you didn't come back with me. What am I supposed to tell them—he's up in Pennsylvania reading the newspapers?"

Rudy dropped down on his knees beside the bed and reached under the bed and pulled out the brown attaché case. He lifted out the two stacks of money, too big bricks held together with rubber bands, and tossed them onto the bed. Then he went to the closet alcove and returned to the bed with a suitcase in each hand, one of his and one of Amy's, still packed with their clothes. These he tossed onto the bed as well, side by side, and popped them open. He laid one brick of money in the corner of each suitcase, covered them with clothing, snapped the suitcases shut.

"I don't care if you give it all to me," she told him. "I'm not leaving here until you do."

He stared at her hard for a moment, wondered what would happen if he struck her. Would she scream? Would she leap out of bed, go running from the room? Well, that would be something, at least. That would be—no, that would be bad. Because she knew. Only she knew.

He picked up both suitcases and marched back to the closet and slammed the suitcases against the wall. "Two days," he told her. "Two days and we're outta here."

"Why can't we go now?" she whined.

"Two frigging days," he said.

* * *

The next day was Sunday. A good day to put on a jacket and tie. Besides, he really liked this jacket, this brown corduroy, shoplifted from Walmart in anticipation of the cruise. He felt good in it, rakish and clever. He felt like Magnum P.I.

"How do you think I'd look with a moustache?" he asked.

Amy was still in bed, still in the same pajamas she had been wearing for the past 72 hours. A maid

Incident on Ten-Right Road

came in and cleaned around her every day, yet still the room stank of cheeseburgers and pizza.

"I don't see why you have to get dressed up just to go out and buy a newspaper," she said.

"I'm going to walk around a little bit, listen in on a few conversations, try to hear what people are saying about this thing."

"You hate wearing ties."

"Look, it's Sunday afternoon, people are coming home from church. I'll look out of place if I'm not dressed up."

"But you hate wearing ties."

"I hate a lot of things!" He was facing the mirror when he said this, but she was behind him on the bed, and he hadn't been looking at his own reflection.

"You promised we'd leave tomorrow."

"If that's what I said then that's what we'll do."

"Just so you remember. You promised."

He cocked his head strangely then and closed his eyes. She could see the muscles in his jaw working. She hugged her blankets.

Finally he opened his eyes, considered his reflection a last time, nodded once to himself, and headed for the door. "Stay put," he told her.

The door had not yet fallen shut behind him when she said, "You'd look even sillier with a moustache."

* * *

He found the funeral home without any difficulty. There were only two of them in town, both on Main Street. He went in and signed the guest book as Thomas Dubonnet. Walked around in the front room for a few minutes, admiring the floral arrangements, reading the sympathy cards. Then into the adjoining room, crowded with mourners. And thought to himself, *McManus must've been a popular guy.*

He worked his way through the crowd until he could see into the viewing room, could see the black and chrome casket in its bank of flowers against the far wall. Seated on a blue sofa to the left of the casket was Mrs. McManus, the grieving widow. She sat alone in the center of the sofa. *Tongues are wagging*, he thought, and tried not to smile.

He approached the coffin then, its lid closed, and stood facing it for a few moments. When he turned she was looking up at him. He crossed to her and reached for her hand. "I'm so sorry for your loss," he said.

She put a hand to his elbow, pulled him closer, put her mouth to his ear. "Find the restroom," she whispered. "I'll tap three times."

He nodded and patted her hand and drew away from her and retreated through the crowd.

The restroom was down a narrow corridor off the foyer. He was a bit surprised to find that it looked like any other private restroom, not particularly funereal, just a sink and a toilet. He drank four Dixie cups of cold water before she tapped on the door.

He unlatched the safety bolt. She opened the door and slipped inside, quickly reshot the bolt, turned to face him. He stood there with the backs of his legs against the toilet bowl, the cold ceramic.

She turned the water on in the sink basin, let it run, a splash and gurgle. She moved closer, almost touched him. "Now I understand," she said very softly, almost smiling.

"Understand what?" he asked.

"You know damn well what."

Incident on Ten-Right Road

"Do I?"

"Yes you do. Because you're very clever, aren't you?"

"Why the money wasn't found."

"I was beginning to think that Larry must have taken it. Even though he's not the type."

"The guy from the sawmill."

She moved even closer. He inhaled her scent. Roses. No, that was the funeral home. She put a hand on his waist. "You did me a favor, you know."

"I was hoping you'd see it that way."

She hooked two fingers over his belt. "We had a nice night together, didn't we?"

"Why do you think I'm here? Seems to me we'd make a pretty good team."

"Is that what you think?"

"You need a man who isn't afraid of things. Isn't afraid to do what needs done."

"Is that what I need?"

He took her hand and placed it between his legs. "Believe me," he said.

She did not move her hand at all, did not move it in any way. "Can you come out to the house tonight?"

"I'll be there," he said.

"It's another four miles from the factory."

"I already know your address. I got it from the phone book."

"The gate will be locked, but you can climb over it, can't you?"

"Don't you worry about me," he said.

"Ten p.m. On the dot."

"Just call me Mr. Punctuality."

Now she moved her hand. She moved it several times. "Is Amy with you here?"

211

"Only technically," he said. "She's at the motel."
"Don't tell her where you're going tonight."
"I don't tell her anything."
"Don't let anybody see you."
"I'm invisible," he said.

She smiled then and backed away from him.

He reached for her. "I've been dreaming about your mouth," he said.

She smiled with that mouth. Kissed the air. Turned and unlocked the door. Peeked out. Slipped away.

He relocked the door and remained in the small room a while longer.

* * *

It was a large estate, at least 50 acres, all of it surrounded by a wrought-iron fence eight feet high. The pickets were spiked but blunt, no challenge at all. He strolled up the asphalt lane in the moonlight, walked a full 10 minutes before the lane veered left behind a row of arborvitaes and he finally saw the house, a huge house, colonnaded, bigger than the first school he had attended back in Hickory.

The house was dark but for one small light in a second-story window. He went to the front door and rang the bell, heard it echoing dully inside the house.

An upstairs window slid open. "Over here," she whispered.

He stepped back into the yard, crossed to stand beneath the window. "Hey, beautiful," he said.

"Are you sure nobody saw you coming here?"
"I was more than careful, don't worry about it."
"Where did you leave your car?"

Incident on Ten-Right Road

"I stole a bicycle in town. It's down the road in the weeds."

"How clever you are," she said.

"Didn't I tell you?"

She disappeared from the window then. He returned to stand waiting at the front door. But the front door did not open. Instead there was a noise at her window, a bang and a scrape, and he went into the yard and looked up again and saw an emergency escape ladder hanging against the wall. She leaned out the window and told him, "Come join me."

"Up that? Just come down and unlock the door, why don't you?"

"The security system," she said. "Everything's monitored. It's all computerized and recorded. Every time the front gate is unlocked, every time the door comes open."

"Impressive," he said.

He went to the ladder and pulled himself up. The first few rungs were the most difficult, learning how to stabilize his weight, to keep himself from swinging side to side against the building. He moved slowly and deliberately, did not want to appear clumsy now, but a very clever man, as graceful as a cat.

A few minutes later he put his hands on the windowsill, pulled himself up so that he could look inside, where he expected to see her waiting on the bed, red lips smiling.

But she was not on the bed. She was standing off to the side of the window. She held a black-barreled .45 revolver. And now she pressed that barrel cold and hard against his ear.

"Where is it?" she asked.

"What, the money? Are you talking about the money? Don't worry, it's safe."

"Where?"

"Back at the Ramada," he said. "We'll get it in the morning, don't worry."

"Give me your room key."

"You can't go there now—Amy's there! She'll freak if you so much as—"

She put the lovely long fingers of her lovely left hand against his face, fingers splayed, palm of her hand against his nose, and shoved him backward off the ladder. He turned in mid-air in an attempt to right himself, arms and legs flailing, but there was not enough time and he landed first on his right knee, felt the impact like a red flare of lightning all the way up his spine, a mushroom cloud of red pain expanding inside his head.

"Oh fuck," he moaned. He rolled onto his left side, felt his right leg flopping uselessly, a throbbing burning flap of pain. And now he was getting nauseated to boot, he was going to pass out, going to throw up on the grass and then pitch forward unconscious. Everything was red all around him, an oscillating red on black, red stars in a swirling black sky full of pain.

And in the midst of it all, the garage door started to rise. It ground slowly upward, grinding like his bones. He turned his head toward the sound, searched in the pulsing red night for the source of that sound, found it just 20 feet away, a three-stall garage, the center door rising. Beneath the door a golden light bled out, blessed light, he loved that light. He rolled toward it, he started to crawl.

The door was not yet halfway up before a dark

Incident on Ten-Right Road

shape emerged, a dark shape that then broke into four shapes ducking under the garage door. Four dogs, very large dogs, four very black dogs with very red eyes. The biggest of the four, named Gogo, was also the gentlest. He went for the stomach. Gogo's three younger sisters all went straight for the throat.

* * *

Amy was awakened by the light. She opened her eyes to find Helen McManus standing at the foot of her bed.

"Where is it?" the older woman said. She was wearing a long brown trench coat belted at the waist.

Amy blinked. She looked toward the window, saw darkness. She looked at the clock. Twelve-fifty-seven a.m. She looked toward the television, its volume turned low, picture still on. An old infomercial was playing, Suzanne Somers demonstrating a Torso Track. Amy squinted at Suzanne and blinked and tried to make some sense of it all.

"One more time," said Mrs. McManus very softly. "Where is it?"

Amy peeled back the covers and climbed out of bed, smelled her own musky scent as she did so, a sickroom scent, sweaty and stale. She moved slowly, uncertainly, feeling for the floor before she set her bare feet down on it.

She stood then and, her hand to the wall, went to the closet alcove near the bathroom. Looked down at the suitcases there. She felt too weak to lift both and so picked up only one for now, Rudy's, and carried it back to the bed. Laid it atop the foot of the bed, popped it open. Pushed his shirts and socks aside. Uncovered the money. Lifted it out. Laid it on the bed.

"Where's the rest?" Mrs. McManus asked.

And Amy said, not knowing she was going to, surprised to hear it from her own mouth, "What do you mean?"

"There's more than that. There should be more."

"That's all there is," Amy said.

Mrs. McManus flipped the suitcase over and dumped out its contents onto the bed, ran her hand through the clothing, scattered it, tossed it aside.

"Ask Rudy," Amy said. "That's all there is."

The older woman stared at the mess she had made on the bed. "That's all you know about?"

"That's all he told me," Amy said. And suddenly she felt sick again, that flutter in her stomach, that constriction in her throat. She began to stumble backward but was stopped by the wall, stood there uncertainly, both hands over her belly. She did not realize she was crying until she tasted the salt at the corners of her mouth.

Mrs. McManus studied her for a moment. "That boyfriend of yours is a lying sonofabitch," she said.

Amy said, "I think I'm beginning to realize that."

Nobody spoke for a while. Mrs. McManus sat on the edge of the bed. Amy allowed her own body to slide down the wall, to sit on the floor. She pulled her knees to her chest and hugged them.

Finally Mrs. McManus said, "How much do you know?"

"About what?" Amy said. Her voice was timid and weak, a whimper.

Mrs. McManus nodded toward the single brick of money.

Incident on Ten-Right Road

Amy said, "I've had the flu ever since we got here. I haven't been out of this room. All I know is that he said he was working on some kind of deal over at the Walmart. That's what he does down in Hickory, he works for Walmart there. In the distribution center."

"I hate Walmart," Mrs. McManus said. "They're driving everybody else out of business, you know."

"Tell me about it," Amy said.

Mrs. McManus shook her head. She was disgusted about something, but Amy could only speculate. Finally Mrs. McManus reached for the brick of money and held it on her lap. She looked at it for most of a minute. Then she removed the rubber bands, separated the brick by half, slipped one handful into the pocket of the brown gabardine trench coat, tossed the rest onto the bed.

"That's because he's not coming back," she said.

"He's not?" Amy asked.

"That's what he told me."

"You saw him tonight?"

Mrs. McManus gave her a look.

"What did he say he was going to do if he's not coming back?"

"I didn't ask."

Amy started to cry again. "What am I supposed to do now?"

Mrs. McManus stood up and headed for the door. "Thank your lucky stars."

Amy sniffed a couple of times. Then said, "You think?"

"Trust me," the woman said. She smiled at the girl and then opened the door and went out.

Amy sat there on the floor for quite a while. Eventually it dawned on her that her nausea had subsided. She stood, testing her legs, and was surprised to find them steady. Apparently it had done her a lot of good to get out of bed at last, to take that short walk to the closet and back again. Just look at all the good it had done her.

She went to the bed and sat at the foot of it and watched the television. Suzanne Somers was still extolling the life-changing benefits of the TorsoTrack.

"I'm going to get me one of those," Amy said. And this time she meant it. Considering the circumstances, she felt a whole lot more energetic than she had ever thought she would.

And Sometimes the Abyss Winks at You

Grayson Rath voice recording

I can't remember exactly when it was I first realized how good it feels to hurt somebody. There's not a lot I remember about the past. It's just not there in my head. I have a good memory for things that happened recently, right down to the tiniest of details sometimes, but the farther back I go in my life, the less I remember about it. I imagine that's more normal than odd. What's truly odd are the people who claim they remember every little thing the whole way back to birth. I don't believe that's even possible. Those people are lying, or else remembering what somebody told them. People will lie about anything, just to make themselves feel better about their miserable little lives. That's normal too.

I do remember playing basketball with my grandmother back when I was 11 or 12. Mom and I were staying with Al then. This was before the time she took off and said she wasn't coming back, so he became my legal guardian, even though they'd never married and he wasn't my real father. My grandmother would come stay with me while Al was at work. He put in long days, what with all the socializing he liked to do after he left the office. He called it schmoozing. Or networking. Either way, it reeked of booze.

Mom did come back eventually though, and after that she used to bring guys to Al's house too when I was at school. I could smell them when I got home. Not just a booze smell but also something different. Somebody different in the house. I never could figure out why Al couldn't smell them too. Even I knew how stupid it was to let guys come to the house like that. Didn't she realize she was going to get caught sooner or later? What really irritated me was that he didn't do anything about it. She's the one decided to leave after he caught her that time giving a blowjob on the back deck. If you ask me, she was just embarrassed is all. Embarrassed to have him catch her with some other guy's dick down her throat. Or maybe she wanted to be caught. Some people are impossible to figure out.

She left us lots of times. Sometimes just for weekends, sometimes for weeks or more. The longest time was for most of a year. And every time she came back, he acted like nothing had ever happened. I never got that either. Seemed to me on a par with watching your dog shit on the new carpet, and just cleaning it up without a word to the dog. That kind of behavior just isn't productive. Not for any of the parties concerned.

A little while after adopting me, Al adopted those three black labs that the shelter was planning to put down and he treated us all pretty much the same. Gave us a cage to live in, kept us fed and that was about as far as his parenting skills went. He liked to show us off to people too. These are my dogs. This is my Lainey. This is my boy. As long as he could do that, he seemed happy. I wander how happy he is now. And if he would take me back without a word after what I've done. I bet he would.

Incident on Ten-Right Road

But this day I remember when I first realized how good it feels to hurt somebody. It was in the fall, just like now, and there were red and yellow leaves all over the driveway where the basketball hoop was. Nobody else was there at the house except me and Grandma, so it must've been after school. I missed a shot and the ball rolled off toward the neighbor's yard. But this time instead of going after it, my grandmother said, You need to start getting your own ball. She was no bigger than me, maybe 4'10" or so, maybe 80 pounds, and I remember looking at her and actually thinking that, like I'd just then noticed it, thinking she's no bigger than I am. And I just walked over to her and socked her in the stomach. Don't ask me why. I wasn't angry or anything, I just wanted to do it. She doubled over and couldn't get her breath, and the way she was crying and gasping for air at the same time, I don't know, it just made me laugh.

I doubt that was the first time I hurt somebody, but it's the first one I remember well. Had lots of fights in school before and after that, and lots out of school. Kids calling me trailer trash and my mom a gold-digger and worse, and them just relocated rednecks themselves. Probably their sisters were their own mothers and they were just too brain deficient to figure it out. I'm guessing I hurt more people in the few years since socking my grandma in the gut than your normal person does in a whole lifetime. And that's not even counting the animals.

I remember sitting in the principal's office with Al and the guidance counselor, and her saying, this kind of aggression is serious, Mr. Murcko. It's not uncommon among boys his age but that doesn't make it any less serious. Al was sitting there with his arms crossed over his big chest, and the principal, he was doodling on a yellow tablet, I could see it from where I sat. He was making spirals that started out small like the tip of a funnel and then spread out wider toward the top. Little tornadoes is what they were. One after another all over that tablet. And the guidance counselor, she was the only person really into the conversation. I sat there looking back and forth from her breasts under that white sweater to those little tornadoes filling up the page. And she knew I was checking out her breasts, because pretty soon her nipples were standing up against the cloth. Al was giving them a good look too, but me, I was having a hard time not getting up and walking over there and sticking one of them in my mouth.

This was just a couple of years ago. I was 17. One big walking hormone.

Anyway, to make a long story short, she asked me into her office again the next day. Just me and her. So you can guess what I was thinking. But then she pulls open a drawer and brings out a little box and opens it up and shows me this recorder I'm talking into right now. Said I could always talk to her when I needed, but sometimes she wouldn't be available, so whenever I felt like smacking somebody, instead I should get my thoughts down on the tape recorder. It comes with earphones and a charger, she said, See? It's digital. You'll probably never fill it up, it has so much storage space. You can use it to record lectures if you want to. Just let your teacher know you're doing it. But mainly it's for your private thoughts. For whenever you're sad or feel angry or whatever. Just

Incident on Ten-Right Road

talk it out, she said. Nobody ever has to listen to it but you. Just take it and use it, okay? Talking into it will curb your negative urges, she said. Will you take it, she said, as a favor for me?

So I took it and shoved the whole box down into my pocket, which made her happy. Like she'd really accomplished something. Which, to be honest, made me a little pissed off for some reason. So out of nowhere I said, Should I use it every time I think about screwing your brains out? And her face turned the reddest red I've ever seen on a person's face. But she said, Yes then too, and reached past me and yanked open the door and sort of pushed me out into the secretary's office.

I used to get hard just thinking about her. I'd sit in class and be sending her telepathic thoughts to try to make her wet and come to the classroom and get me. I was so sure it was going to work. But come senior year, she was gone. Rumor was that she'd been banging Mr. Epps, the Driver's Ed teacher, and his wife found out and called every member of the school board. Whether it was true or not, I don't know, but old Eppsy did seem a lot quieter that year. Of course I already had my license by then, so there was no reason for me to care one way or the other.

* * *

from the blog And Sometimes the Abyss Winks at You *by Mia Swain*

Hello, my wonderful readers. I know you come to me for tips and chuckles about how my personal life is spiraling down the drain, but I am going to change gears here, and I hope you will stay with me. Allow me to answer one last reader question as a way of seguing into an abrupt detour that might come as a shock to you.

The reader question is this: *Keeping a blog fresh every week must be hard. Where do you get all your ideas?*

The way it works for me, dear Cynthia from Front Royal, Virginia, is this: First thing every morning (after a tinkle, of course), I take a book down off the shelf, any book at random, and then sit with my coffee and start to read. This will be around 5:00 or so in the a.m., with the windows still dark, and one small reading lamp on. Within a page or two, some word or phrase will hit me like a small, soft jolt, and in an instant a new idea will bloom. Anything by Anne Lamott is sure to get my creative juices flowing, but David Sedaris and Sylvia Plath are always reliable too.

This soft jolt of inspiration doesn't happen every day, of course. Usually not at all when I'm working on a long piece, but when I have no specific plan for that morning's work. When I am open to suggestion.

Yesterday morning, I was open to suggestion. A week earlier, my editor and I had finished the developmental edit of my very first novel (*Travels with Diazepam*, in case you've forgotten), so I was killing time until the copyedited manuscript arrives by email with its legion of traumatizing corrections. I started the day reading from Doris Lessing's *The Golden Notebook*. Within minutes I was at the laptop, ready to pound out a new short story. This had already happened six mornings in a row; six new short stories conceived and completed. *Very* unusual for me.

Incident on Ten-Right Road

Especially since I hadn't written a short story in at least a year prior to that blitz. I told a friend, jokingly, that it was like being in an odd type of manic phase. The mania would pass the moment I typed *The End* on that day's short story.

And there would have been a seventh short story too—although I lost all memory of it when I saw the news crawler headline about Grayson Rath on my start page. Something about his photo pulled me to it. He was just another scrawny kid with dirty brown hair and hooded eyes and an insolent, crooked smile. It was his senior picture from high school. I can't tell you how many dozens of boys just like him I have known in my life. (And yes, Ian, you duplicitous rat bastard, I am talking about you.) So there was that sense of familiarity that pulled at me. Plus the strangeness of his name. The too-fitting appropriateness of his name. I mean, who names their baby boy Grayson? Gray son. Especially with a surname like Rath, which immediately brought to mind both *wrath* and *wraith*. There is a theory that our names determine our fate, the person we become. If that is true, Grayson's parents, Alaina and Rodney Rath, damned him from the start.

That morning, I didn't even open up a blank Word.doc to begin the new short story. Instead I read everything I could find online about this 19 year-old boy who had slaughtered his own mother and her lover and was now on the run. The jolt I received from those accounts was far from soft. It kept vibrating in me, the wavelength tightening minute by minute until I admitted to myself that I had no choice but to write about him and try to understand him. And perhaps, in some way, to make a little sense not only of this whacked-out society from which he had sprung, but also—let's be honest here, folks—to make a little sense of my own unfocused, sometimes obsessive, possibly bipolar, hypersensitive self.

Tomorrow morning, to wit, I will be in my car on my way to Gilford, that little town outside Athens, Ohio where Grayson Rath stabbed and bludgeoned to death the woman who gave birth to him, and the man he caught in flagrante delicto with her in Grayson's father's bed. And oh yes, the three black labs. He killed them too.

* * *

Grayson Rath voice recording

The way it happened is, there was a break before my 2:00 class, and I had 140 minutes to kill. And I was starving. I can't stand the cafeterias, what with all the noise and lines and everybody jabbering about nothing important, so I figured I could blow 15 minutes driving home, make some mac and cheese or one of those frozen pot pies or both, and then decide if I wanted to blow off my afternoon classes or not.

But there's Mom's car in the driveway, when she's supposed to be doing an interview. There was a dentist in Athens looking to replace a hygienist about to go on maternity leave. Anyway that's what she told us the night before. But you could never tell about her.

The dogs have their noses pressed to the wire and are beating their tails back and forth. I'm the one that feeds and waters them, that's why they like me so much. With anybody else they act like they want to rip

Incident on Ten-Right Road

out your throat. I probably would have taken them out and let them run through the house while I was there except for the car in the driveway.

And the moment I go into the house, I know what's going on. I can feel it in the air. I think I might be a little psychic that way. Plus I smell the guy. Right Guard mixed with sweat. And that's when everything went gray on me. I'd describe it as walking into a room full of gray. That's how I get. Some people see red when they get mad, I see gray. With my head feeling like it's swelling up. Like my brain is pushing hard against the inside of my skull.

Things didn't really clear up after that until I was looking down at the guy on the floor. We're in the living room then. And I'm feeling pretty good. Feeling empty and light and a little bit sleepy. I mean I'm feeling right with the world. So I drop the ball bat and follow the blood upstairs, and that's when I see what I did to Mom. It doesn't really bother me much either. Like I knew she was going to end up that way sooner or later.

Then for some reason I think about the dogs, and what's going to happen to them now. Al never cared a damn about them, just took them in so the woman at the rescue center he was hustling didn't think he was a jerk, which he pretty much is, even though he promised he'd hire me on commission at the dealership come summer. He said I'd make a good salesman. Had the gift, he said.

Anyway, seeing as how that possibility was all shot to hell now, I went out to the garage and looked around for a peaceful way to take care of the dogs, because there was no way I could hang around that place anymore. Never did feel at home there. Or anywhere, to be honest about it. Even if I got rid of the baseball bat and bread knife, who knew how many people saw me drive up outside and park? Mr. Douglas next door is a busybody if there ever was one. Always coming out onto his porch and looking around because he heard a bird chirp or something.

Anyway, I saw the antifreeze and dumped out the whole bottle in a low spot on the kennel floor. They went after it right away, which made me feel good that I could leave them in peace.

I went back upstairs and peeled off my clothes and hopped into the shower, then dressed and threw stuff into a couple of leather satchels I always liked that belonged to Al, and grabbed whatever else I could find laying around, including his jewelry and a couple of her diamond rings, the cash she kept in her panty drawer, all the cash in the guy's wallet in his pants laying at the foot of the bed, the stash Al kept in old Bible, plus my own stash of cash and my laptop, some extra Metallica and Linkin Park CDs I liked plus a bag of food from the kitchen and what was left of a case of water. The back seat of the Camaro was piled pretty high by the time I was done. Didn't know where I was headed and didn't much care. If you want to know the truth of it, I was feeling free for the first time in my life. And figured I wouldn't be taking any more classes for a while, ha ha.

* * *

from the blog And Sometimes the Abyss Winks at You *by Mia Swain*

Yep, a new blog already. I can't help it; my head is spinning. So for now I am dumping the once-a-week

Incident on Ten-Right Road

schedule in favor of a whenever-I-feel-like-it schedule. But no worries, gentle readers; every blog will remain accessible in the archives.

And, if you were paying attention when you read the previous blog, you would have noticed that I have also jettisoned the 500-word limit I used to impose upon myself. How long will my new blog posts be? Don't know, don't care.

Here is what I do know today:

I spent my first morning in Gilford, Ohio reading the police report and talking to the officers who responded to the 911 call. According to that report, *eerie quiet* was how the mail delivery person, Amber Wright, 43, described the scene. I caught her along her route, and we talked for several minutes. Later I visited the Murcko home.

"Usually by the time I reach for the mailbox handle," Amber told me, "those three dogs are barking to beat the band. But this time they weren't making a sound. I couldn't even hear any birds singing. The whole neighborhood was eerie quiet."

The house, owned by Mr. Allen Murcko, owner of three Murcko Motors dealerships and Grayson Rath's legal guardian, is a 1996 two-story country-style home—one of 10 surrounding a small lake, with at least 100 feet of manicured yard between each home. A smooth macadam road loops around the rear of the houses, with second and third growth woods surrounding the other side of the road. The ten Balmoral mailboxes, all bronze with a powder-coated finish and golden flag, house number, and pull knob, rim the road, with the houses some 40 yards away facing the lakefront. A dog kennel made of chain-link fencing is attached to the side of the Murcko garage, with one of the narrow ends visible from the mailbox.

It was not uncommon for Ms. Wright to deliver a package too large for the mailbox, or one via airmail that required Mr. Murcko's signature. "Lainey was always buying stuff online, and Mr. Murcko got a lot of stuff from India or China or somewhere. In which case I'd drive up to the house and go knock on the door. Just so happened this was one of those days."

The silence as she approached the porch made her nervous. "Something just wasn't right, you know? Why weren't those dogs barking at me and going crazy up against the wire? And why was the back door standing open? It was a nice sunny afternoon but only about 48 degrees out."

The dogs, when discovered by police late in the day, were already suffering from acute renal failure. An empty gallon container of anti-freeze was found in the corner of the kennel, a wide stain on the concrete floor where the liquid had been poured out for the dogs to lap up. By the time they were taken to the local veterinary hospital, one animal had died. The other two were euthanized.

Earlier that afternoon, standing just outside the back door, which opens onto the kitchen, Ms. Wright had been able to see the upper half of a male body in the living room, with a conspicuous pool of blood beneath his head. "He was naked for as far as I could see, plus about half as wide as Mr. Murcko would've been if that was him laying there. But too big to be the boy. I was off that porch and back inside my Jeep in three seconds flat. Took me another 30 seconds or so to get my breath. And that's when I called 911."

Incident on Ten-Right Road

The murders took place on October 25th, a few days prior to my arrival in Athens. By the day of my visit, Mr. Allen Murcko had not yet moved back into the home, even though the scene had been processed and released to him again. I called Mr. Murcko's local car dealership from my hotel room that day, and asked for an interview. "I can meet you at the house if you want," he told me. "Give you a walk-through while you hear all the gory details."

Mr. Murcko is of medium height, 52 years old, with a head of shiny back hair. His deep chest and broad physique suggest a daily fitness regime. "I'm a gym rat and proud of it," he told me. "My workout puts a lot of those younger guys to shame." On the day he walked me through his home, he wore a tailored blue pinstriped suit, a crisp white shirt with the top two buttons loose, thick-soled brown dress shoes, gold cufflinks and a gold Rolex watch. He has a deep tan and reeked of cologne.

The house was immaculate, though the scent of cleaning solvents and air fresheners was as strong as his cologne, especially in the master bedroom. There were no mattresses on his king-size bed, and the oak plank floor was bare. "This is where it got started, apparently," he told me, and waved a hand over the bed frame. "Grayson was supposed to be at college that day, but the way things look, he came home early and caught his mother going at it with the guy who ended up downstairs."

"Blunt force trauma," I said, quoting from the police report.

"On him, yeah. Thirty-two inch Louisville Slugger. I bought it for the boy hoping he'd take to baseball, which he didn't. Anyway, before using it on his mother, he stuck a bread knife in the middle of her back. While she was riding the pony, apparently. Stuck it in and left it sticking in there. Then he whacked the guy across the head with his bat, then finished off his mother while the guy tried to drag himself down the stairs. The boy caught back up with him in the living room. The blood, I'll tell you, it was everywhere. Those cleaning people do good work. They should, for the money they get."

He seemed strangely removed from it all. I asked, "Were you surprised that she was having an affair?"

"Nothing people do surprises me. I've seen it all. As for Lainey, I caught her twice already before this. Different guys."

"Yet you stayed together?"

He shrugged. "I didn't appreciate her doing it right under my nose, but I felt sorry for her. Her and the boy both. I'm a generous person; ask anybody. Besides, she always had her problems."

"Such as?"

"Depression mostly. Starved for attention. Which she got plenty of, considering the way she looked. She was just weak is all. Needed somebody telling her all the time how beautiful she was. Like she couldn't look in a mirror and see for herself."

"She was, uh…"

"A babe? I certainly thought so. Me and every other man in town."

"What I meant to ask about was her age."

"About 30."

"If I recall correctly, the police report said 34."

"Go with that then."

Incident on Ten-Right Road

"So she had Grayson when she was...15?"

"Yep. She was one of those babymama's like you see on TV."

"And the male victim?" I asked.

"A little older than her, I'd say. Just another of life's losers. He picked the wrong house this time, that's for sure." He smiled to himself, then turned his gaze to me. "And how old are you, may I ask?"

"Thirty-one. Did you know the man? Before he was identified, I mean?"

"Didn't know him from Adam. Turns out he was a lawyer. Arguing a case over in Athens at the City Hall. Supposed to be on recess. How's that for poetic justice?"

"Married, three children," I added.

"Some people might say he got what he deserved."

"Would you say that?"

"Eh," he said. "I've never known a lawyer that wasn't a sleazeball. There might be some of them out there somewhere, but I've never met one. And I've met plenty."

"How long were you and Mrs. Rath together?"

"You look younger than 31, you know that? I bet you still get carded at bars, don't you?"

"I don't drink."

"That's why you have such beautiful skin."

He put a hand to my face, finger extended to touch my cheek, but I drew back. "How long were you and Mrs. Rath together?"

He smiled again. "Grayson was nine when I hired her to work for me."

That would make her 24 when she became employed by Mr. Murcko. "Doing what?" I asked.

"Cleaning person at the dealership. That's all she was qualified for. She never even finished high school."

"And then you started dating?"

"Dating?" he said. "Humping like rabbits is more like it. That doesn't offend you, does it?"

If he was hoping to make me blush, he failed. "Words are tools," I told him. "I believe in using the best tool for the job. So you hired her for the sex?"

He grinned at me and said, "Paying for sex is illegal, isn't it?"

He waited for me to respond, but I chose not to.

"I hired her to clean. The fact that we got down to it that first night, after everybody else had gone home, that was just a happy coincidence. Can't fight a mutual attraction. A week later, she and Grayson moved in and I had to hire another cleaning person."

"How old is she?" I asked.

He didn't like that question. For the first time all day, his smug little smile faded.

I asked, "How did you and Grayson get along?"

At this, he turned and pointed a finger at me. "Listen, I want to make it clear that I did everything I could for that boy. I was generous to a fault. To him and his mother both. I put her through dental hygiene school, did you know that? Associate of Applied Science. Shelled out for the boy's braces, new $100 sneakers every few months, whatever he needed. Her I dressed in the best clothes and jewelry on the market. Go ahead and look through her closet, if you want. Over there's her jewelry box. You look through it all and then tell me I didn't treat them right."

I cannot remember that conversation now without seeing superimposed upon it the image of another

Incident on Ten-Right Road

narcissist, one who also looked straight into the camera and made his own adamantine denial. *I want you to listen to me. I'm going to say this again: I did not have sexual relations with that woman, Ms. Lewinsky...."*

* * *

Grayson Rath voice recording

I knew the car was a problem. It was like driving a big red box with my name scrawled all over it. I had at best a four-hour start before Al came home. It strikes me as kind of funny that I don't even think about calling him Dad anymore. When did that stop? Sometime before my teens, I guess. He wanted me to call him that, like it was another accomplishment for his resume. CEO. Rotarian of the Year. Premier Dealer Award. That shit mattered to him. Me, I guess maybe I had no more respect for him than Mom did. He bought me stuff, so I was polite to him. That's about all there was to it.

If I have any regrets, it's for my grandmother. I always wished I could love her as much as she loved me. Though sometimes I felt sorry for her for being so easy to fool. She thought she knew me but she never did. Couldn't even begin to. Why would you love somebody you don't even know?

Anyway, back to the car. It was one of Al's, straight off the lot the day I finished high school. Al says, Pick anything you want. On that side only.

The used side, of course. What he called Certified Pre-Owned. I asked him once, how come somebody has to certify that it's not a new car? You can tell that just by checking the odometer. He laughed like I'd made a joke. Didn't even get what I was saying.

I took the red Camaro. 2013. Eighty-four thousand miles on it. And Al says, Alright, you're going straight for the pussy wagon. I can respect that.

Ha. The only thing Al ever respected was money and his own dick. I wish he'd been home when I got there. Wish I'd of caught them in a threesome. Al would probably be the one taking it up the ass.

Okay, enough reminiscing. I have to get rid of this car. That's what I'm telling myself all the way into West Virginia. I see this sign says Point Pleasant off to the right 16 miles, and I wonder where I've heard that name before, and then it comes to me, the Moth Man. That's the town the Moth Man made famous. I wouldn't mind seeing that town but not in this car, no way. So I drive on a little longer, another hour or so, and not far into Virginia there's this big Home Depot out along the road with a bunch of other businesses, and I figure that's a good place to start.

The parking lot is crammed full with people coming and going. Must be having a sale on doorknobs or something. So I drive around in the last couple of rows away from the building, waiting for a slot to open up. Then I just sit there with the windows down playing with my phone until I realize shit, this phone's a problem too. So right away I break it open and take out the battery and the sim card, and I toss them both as far as I can into the weeds out alongside the road.

It's probably a good 20 minutes before I see this woman coming my way dragging one of those rug shampooer machines, plus a couple of gallon bottles of the stuff you put in it. She's trying to hold onto it all and get her keys out of her pocket at the same time, but then she drops one of the bottles and my body just goes into

Incident on Ten-Right Road

action, like it was waiting for that sign or something. I'm going toward her and I say, You should have used a cart, and she looks up and sees me smiling at her and probably thinks I look like her brother or maybe one of her students or something, because she says I know, I wish I had. I thought the wheels on the rug cleaner would make it easy but they don't.

Too small for the job, I told her, and took both jugs of cleaner out of her arms. Plus they aren't made for rolling over pavement.

She says, I wish somebody had told me that inside. You'd think they'd tell you that.

Then she pulls out her keys and hits a button on the remote and the headlights blink on a silver SUV three down from mine, and I follow her to the back of it where she pops open the tailgate. I set both jugs into the corner, then pick up the machine and shove it inside and pull the tailgate down.

She says, That was so sweet of you to help. Thank you.

Have a good day, I tell her, and then I'm walking away like I'm headed to my car, but I'm timing my walk to hers so that just as she pops open her door and climbs inside, I pop open the passenger door and dive in and grab her by the back of her head and slam her face down onto the console as hard as I can.

I didn't even think about it first, just did it. That's what I find so interesting. It was like some part of me knew exactly what to do and just went ahead and did it. Like I had done it a hundred times before. It was amazing.

She wasn't dead though and started moaning right away, so I just put my hands around her neck and leaned on top of her and squeezed as hard as I could.

Her legs were trying to kick and her hands kept flying up and down like headless chickens but she had no room for any kind of effective movement, and in less time than I thought it would take, she was done. After that it was just a matter of moving all of my stuff into her SUV. The hardest part was getting her into the passenger side. I had to slide the seat all the way back, and after that she crumpled up into a snug little bundle on the passenger floor.

It was a nice vehicle. A lot roomier than mine. With one of those rearview cameras and a navigation screen and Sirius radio and everything. I got out onto the road and drove back to Point Pleasant and went to this little museum run by some really strange guy who said my best chance to see the Moth Man was down at the dynamite bunkers at night. But that I'd have to drive out there and hike through some woods or else wait around for a while and catch the shuttle bus, so I told him screw that, isn't there someplace else I can maybe see the Moth Man? He said maybe you'd like to see where the bridge collapsed and 46 people died, and I said did they all drown or get killed in the fall? And he said I don't know that that's ever been determined, which I thought was a lame answer if ever I'd heard one.

I ended up getting a Moth Man burger to go from a place there in town, then headed west, just following that little directional signal in the rear view mirror, until I swung south again for no reason in particular. When I got tired of driving I started looking for an inconspicuous little motel, of which there is no shortage of those in Kentucky, I'll tell you. I picked up some fries and a caramel sundae to eat back in my room while I watched the rest of *Two and a Half Men* on TV. It was

Incident on Ten-Right Road

an episode I'd already seen so I didn't pay it a lot of attention. But it's amazing how good food tastes when you buy it with somebody else's money.

* * *

from the blog And Sometimes the Abyss Winks at You
by Mia Swain

After interviewing Mr. Murcko, I spoke briefly with several of his neighbors. Most of them told the same story: Grayson Rath was a quiet boy, they didn't really know him very well, they never imagined he could do such a thing. Charlie Douglas, a widower and retired financial consultant who lives next door to the Murcko home, had more to share. He invited me into his living room, where he immediately went to a 5x7 photo of his wife on the mantel, took it down and handed it to me.

His wife was well-known in the area for her work in movies and community theater. "Everybody loved her," he said. "Adored her." In the picture she was a petite blonde beauty with her hair in ringlets. "She was barely out of her teens there," he told me, and tapped a gnarled finger to the glass. "This was around the time she was in that movie with Jack Nicholson and Dennis Hopper."

"*Easy Rider*?" I asked.

"Before that. One called *The Trip*. She played one of the waitresses. Slept with both of them."

"In the movie? I'll have to check it out."

"In real life. She had sex with both of them. And not just the once, either." His smile, as he gazed at her photo, was warm and nostalgic. "Of course I didn't know her then. But those were wild years for all of us. Summer of love and all that."

From there we moved the conversation to his front deck, where I inquired of his impression of Grayson Rath, whom he had watched growing up. The day was chilly, the trees bare, but he stood there coatless, gazing toward the lake, which was as still as a mirror. The late afternoon light threw the trees' reflections onto the water, so that the lake was colored a pale orange, and seemed to have a thick tangle of long black tendrils lying just below the surface.

"The picture I have in my head is of him standing out there in the lake of a summer's day. He used to do that quite frequently."

"He used to stand out there doing what?" I asked.

"He used to stand out there standing. He'd be maybe 30 yards out, the water up around his chest. And he just stood there looking back at his house. He would stand there like that for I don't know how long. Sometimes he'd sit on the dock, sometimes take the rowboat out and sit in it a while. But what stood out for me was him just standing out there like a statue, staring back at the house."

"And that seemed odd to you?"

"There's water snakes and snapping turtles in that lake. Carp as long as your leg. Of course the snakes aren't poisonous but that won't keep them from biting. And one of those turtles could snap a finger right off."

"What do you think he was doing out there? Just cooling off?"

"There's cooling off and there's cooling off," he said.

"What do you mean?"

"One way to cool off on a summer's day is to sit in an air-conditioned house. That's what most people do."

Incident on Ten-Right Road

"And the other way?"

"I'm only saying this because of what he ended up doing. Hindsight being 20/20, you know what I mean?"

"You think he was cooling off in a different way. Cooling off his anger?"

"You see, I take what happened in that house, and the mood he must've been in to do it. And I lay that on top of this picture I have of him standing out there chest-deep in the water and just staring back at the place."

"I understand," I told him. "How often did you see him out there like that?"

"Over the years? Dozens of times. Every summer he'd be a little taller and a little farther out into the lake."

"He didn't have friends over? This would be a great place for kids to party."

"Just him. I used to feel sorry for him, being left alone so much."

"How do you know he was alone?"

"Al never parked his car in the garage. If he was home, it was in the driveway. Most of us here have golf carts, just for tooling around the development. Al has one too. There's also an old Harley in there he never rides. I heard the boy trying to get it started a few years back, one of those times he was alone. He even pushed it out onto the driveway and tried to roll-start it. I just stood there on my porch watching, holding the phone in my hand, ready to call Al at work if the bike started up. Boy would've killed himself on that big thing. Fortunately for him he couldn't get more than a cough or two out of it. He finally gave up and pushed it back inside."

"Did you inform Mr. Murcko about this?"

"I mentioned it one day when I caught him out at the mailbox. He thanked me for telling him. And that was the end of it. As for the boy's mother... I have no idea what she was up to. It was a strange house, to be honest with you. Those people kept strange hours. And look where it got them."

The neighbors in the development keep an eye on each other's homes. It is one of the most affluent neighborhoods in Gilford, and several of the families have had canoes or kayaks or garden tools or bicycles disappear overnight. Some have installed security systems, though most have not. They want to believe that they are safe in their little enclave, and that the ugliness of poverty and violence will never invade their sanctuary, just as long as they all remain vigilant.

I imagine they will have a harder time maintaining that illusion now.

* * *

Grayson Rath voice recording

As of right this minute, that Home Depot woman is balled up in the cargo area of her SUV while I catch some winks in the back seat. It's warmer here than it was at home, so I've got the back windows down and the tailgate up to blow her stink outside. It's not that bad yet but noticeable. I could just dump her out here in the woods and it might be months before anybody finds her, but I don't know. She never did anything wrong to me.

The last couple of hours I've been wondering if there's any way in hell I'll get away with this. At first I was talking in the recorder just to keep my thoughts

Incident on Ten-Right Road

straight, but now I'm thinking there should be some kind of account of this adventure I'm on. It's not every day something like this happens. And let's say I do get away with it. There should still be a record of it. When I'm on my deathbed I could hand it over to my grandson and tell him, don't show this to anybody until I'm in my grave. He'll probably look at it and say, what the hell is it, Pops? And I'll say, it's what we used to use to record messages. He'll probably just have a chip in his ear for recording everything he hears. Won't even know what an iPhone or laptop was. That'll be something, won't it? I hope I live to see that day.

But just so you know, whoever might be listening to this 60 or 70 years from now, I didn't touch that woman's body sexually. Never once thought about doing so. I like sex the same as everybody else, but not that kind. I just want everybody to know that. I know the way people think.

So what else before I close my eyes?

Ha. Now I've got myself thinking about sex. People are probably going to want to know if I had a girlfriend. Well, I'll tell you the truth. I've been dipping my wick since I was 15 years old. You'd be surprised how many girls go for the bad boys. I've had girls walk right up to me and start a conversation, and ten minutes later we've got our jeans down around our ankles. This is not an exaggeration. Girls are aggressive these days. Their mothers would be horrified to know what their daughters are up to after school. And once those girls go off to college and are living in dorms where their parents can't see them? All bets are off.

So I never had just one girlfriend, no. Pretty soon they start acting like you're their property. Like you can't even look in the direction of another girl. I have no idea what makes them that way.

I remember this one class I had in sociology. The professor was a woman, and she wasn't all that bad looking either. Maybe a little bit scrawny, but who am I to complain about that? Anyway, she was talking about how women could rule the world if they'd just wise up about it. She claimed there was this place in Tibet or somewhere that was run entirely by women. They would let men from other villages visit, but only because some woman was horny and wanted to get laid. Afterward the man had to go home again. Then my professor talked about a kind of monkey, bobo something or other, where the females are in charge there too. And if two or three of the males start fighting over a piece of food or something, the female just has sex with all of them. Quiets them down in no time flat. And me, I'm sitting in the back of the room, and I spoke up and said, Sign me up for that place. Which got a good laugh out of everybody. And had a couple of girls following me down the hall after class.

It's not hard getting laid, that's all I'm saying. What's hard is dealing with the aftermath of it. Girls think sex means something. Maybe it does for them, but not for me. It feels good, there's no denying that. But so does a healthy sneeze when your head's all clogged up.

* * *

from the blog And Sometimes the Abyss Winks at You, *by Mia Swain*

Grayson's biological father, Rodney Rath, had a stunned look on his face when I called upon him at his

Incident on Ten-Right Road

place of employment, the Gilford Forge. His foreman allowed him a 10-minute hiatus to speak with me in the break room. We sat across from each other at a small round table; the metal chairs had blue vinyl seats and backs. The room, unlike the work space, was air-conditioned and chilly. At the end of our conversation, Mr. Rath was wearing the same slightly dazed expression on his face as when I had met him, so I can only assume that this is his normal countenance, or else the constant clamor of machine concussion and vibration, plus the low roar of the huge ventilation fans, has had a dulling effect on his thought processes. His speech was slow, and the pauses between each of my questions and his responses were long, sometimes of half a minute or more.

I said, "It must be at least 20 degrees cooler in here than out on the floor."

"You should come in summer," he said.

"It's really hot then?"

He nodded.

"Do you mind if we talk about Grayson a bit?"

He shook his head. "I never thought he'd do such a thing."

"What was he like as a child?"

He thought for a while. "Normal kid, seemed to me."

"Did you have a good relationship with him?"

Here a corner of his mouth turned up, and he waggled his head back and forth. "We was doing a lot of drinking back then. Weed too. Cocaine when somebody would share with us."

"You and Mrs. Rath?"

He chuckled. "It's funny to hear her called that. Mrs. Rath."

"You never divorced—is that correct?"

"Never got around to it. She had me sign those papers, though. Saying he wasn't my son anymore."

"You relinquished your parental rights."

Another nod. "I wasn't working then. Wasn't doing him any good. Him or anybody else."

"Have you seen much of him since then?"

"What for?"

"I don't know, just…to be sure he was getting along all right, handling things well?"

"You know," he said, and stared at the soft drink machine. "People want to blame me for what he done to his mother and that other guy."

"Do you blame yourself?"

He shrugged. "I could've done better." He turned his gaze to the wall. "But it wasn't me getting drunk and doing drugs while I was pregnant. She's the one should've known better."

"So are you saying that you share the blame with your wife?"

Here he turned to look at me. His eyes were blank. He pushed back his chair and said, "I need to get back to work."

"I think we have a few minutes yet. Can I get you a soda?"

He stood. "Naw, that's enough."

"Oh, by the way," I said. "I was wondering about your son's name. Grayson. It's an unusual name. Did you name him after someone you knew?"

"Tarzan," he said. "Lord Grayson. Because he screamed like Tarzan when he was born. But who'd name their kid Tarzan?"

"I believe that Tarzan was the Earl of Greystoke. Not Grayson."

Incident on Ten-Right Road

He cocked his head. "You sure about that?"

"I am."

"Huh. I guess we got that wrong. We were messed up a lot back then." He crossed to the door, opened it and strode away. He has a peculiar way of walking, so that each shoulder dips in synchronicity with the matching foot; it is a sad, resigned gait, as of someone who knows there is no escape from the past, and nothing but futility ahead.

The links between sociopathy and maternal drug and alcohol abuse are clear. But so are the links between sociopathy and early neglect/emotional rejection. Early exposure to violence. Abuse. Poor nutrition. There is also the possibility of biological dysfunction, a faulty wiring of the brain.

Not that any of that information is of much value now in regards to Grayson Rath. But thanks to all of the shootings and bombings going on these days, nearly everyone is hysterical about how to prevent such incidents, as if knowing what makes a person a sociopath or a psychopath would put an end to violence. I really do not believe that it will. Good people will do their best to do good, no matter what. Only in moments of true desperation will they resort to doing bad. Bad people will almost always do what's easiest, and what is easiest is often something bad. Does it help knowing what makes people bad? I suppose there is some value in it, but only in a *Minority Report* kind of way. In most cases a bad person cannot be stopped from doing bad. He can only be stopped from doing bad again.

That's called non-teleological thinking. It means dealing not with what might be or should be, but with what is. And in my honest opinion, that's what we have to deal with first: what *is*. Right now. Today. This minute.

In all likelihood, Grayson Rath was born with the potential to become a killer. The signs of sociopathic behavior began to show themselves at least by his teens, if not much earlier. Though his mother's promiscuity is the easy answer to what finally tripped Grayson's trigger on a sunny October afternoon when he was 19 years old, the definitive answer is far less clear, and will probably never be ascertained. The truth is, if that trigger hadn't been pulled when he was 19, it would have been pulled when he was 29, 49, or whatever—unless he had been locked up or lobotomized *before* he did anything wrong. Is that the kind of society we want? I'm not sure. Is it better to lock up ten percent of humanity so that the other ninety percent will feel safe?

In the meantime, I and a small army of law enforcement personnel continue to trace our way through the carnage left in Grayson Rath's wake, while praying, as I hope you are too, that he does not kill again.

* * *

Grayson Rath voice recording

What I miss about home is two things. No, make that three things. I might think of some more later on but for now let's settle on three. I never gave any of them much thought until just now, sitting here in another scummy hotel face-to-face with the fact of never going back home again, not even to get any more of my stuff. It's a situation that does make a person think.

Incident on Ten-Right Road

Most of all I guess I miss the food. Mom was never much of a cook, and stopped doing it at all back when I was still in grade school. Al didn't have the patience for cooking. Fact is, anything we ate that was home cooked, it was because I made it. Anything with pasta, I was good at. Primavera. Lasagna. Alfredo. Spaghetti with spinach and mushroom sauce was my favorite. I also made a mean pot of soup when I had the time and inclination. The trick is to always use broth, not water, and to reduce it down to half what you started with. Plus I liked to experiment with the ingredients. Add spinach and tomatoes to chicken noodle soup, for example. Use a pork loin instead of chicken. Add mushrooms to French onion. I miss food like that. And now I'm wondering if I'll ever have a nice kitchen to cook in again.

Second thing I miss is having my own room. You might say that the road is my room now, but if that isn't a depressing thought, I don't know what is. What I need to do is to find a big house out in the woods somewhere, with people living in it who don't go out much and wouldn't be missed. Maybe I could settle in for a while in a place like that if I can find one.

That would take care of the other thing I miss too, which is the quiet. I hate the noise people make. Which probably comes from spending my first few years with just Mom. Most times she was quiet as a corpse. That was because she never had much ambition. Was happy to sit around and wait for her life to get a little better. Even if it meant living on food stamps and welfare and whatever change she could find in Grandma's purse.

One of the few things I remember from being a kid was the day she met Al. First time I saw her take any initiative. I remember she and Grandma picked me up at school one afternoon when I was in third grade, and on the ride home we're passing the bank, and Al's standing out on the sidewalk laughing and talking with a couple other men. Those two men are both in jeans and work shirts but there's Al in one of those dark blue suits of his that sort of sparkles when the sun hits it. The men are all scruffy and dirty like they're construction workers or something, and Al's so slick and polished, it's hard not to notice him. And Mom, who's sitting on the passenger side in front of me, she says, who is that man? Grandma doesn't even ask which one, she just says, that's Mr. Allen Murcko. Owns the car dealership out across from the Agway plus two or three others. And Mom says, Looks to me like he thinks he owns the world. And Grandma says, He could probably buy a good piece of it if he wanted to. So Mom says, Take me out there to that dealership. And Grandma says, What for? You can't afford a car. You don't even know how to drive. And Mom says, I know how to do some things. Take me out there. I want to see it.

So that's where we go. Then she makes us sit there in that hot car for I don't know how long. Felt like forever. I even fell asleep a while. I'm pretty sure what woke me up was Mom saying, there he is, and then popping open the car door. I want to go inside with her since it's probably going to be air-conditioned, so she lets me tag along but sends me back to this lounge place where customers can get hot dogs and coffee and juice and cookies, all of it for free. Doesn't bother me a bit being left alone. A couple of hot dogs and a dozen or so cookies later, she comes to get me, and we go back to the car and wake up Grandma, and Grandma says, Well?

Incident on Ten-Right Road

Did you get what you came for? And Mom says, I start tonight. Right after closing. I say, Start what? And she says, I'm the new cleaning lady. Four hundred a week, tax free. And that's how we met the great Al Murcko, a legend in his own mind.

* * *

from the blog And Sometimes the Abyss Winks at You
by Mia Swain

Grayson Rath's grandmother lives in a small doublewide trailer a stone's throw from an old frame house that has no roof and only three remaining walls. The dismantled boards and trusses are stacked along the far side of the building, along with all the windows and doors. My knock on the door of the trailer was answered by a man in his late 60s or so. When I asked if he was Grayson's grandfather, he shook his head no and came down from the trailer, walked past me and grabbed a lawn chair from the yard and carried it over to where the old lumber was stacked. He sat there and took out a pack of cigarettes and began to smoke.

He had left the door to the mobile home open, so I went up the three metal steps and peered inside and saw a small white-haired woman seated at the kitchen table with her hands folded in her lap. She turned to look at me and said, "Who you with?"

I didn't think my blog would carry much weight with her, so I answered, "I'm an online journalist. I have almost 90,000 subscribers."

Her eyes widened just a bit. "That seems like a lot," she said.

I stepped inside. "And more every day."

"And they all know about us?"

"I won't mention you at all if you don't want me to."

She gave a little shrug, then said, "I'm not saying nothing about Grayson. Good or bad, it's not for me to say."

I crossed into the kitchen. "May I sit?"

A tiny nod. All of her movements were small and required close attention just to see them. I sat in the chair opposite her. "I wanted to ask you about Alaine. She was your daughter, correct?"

Another tiny nod. "She didn't deserve what was done to her. Nobody does."

"What was she like?" I asked.

She brought her hands up onto the table. Held her hands interlocked, all five fingers of her right hand cupped in her left. The thumb of her left hand kept rubbing back and forth over the knuckles of her right. "It's too easy for young people to get in trouble these days. It's all they see on TV is sex and drugs and destroying things. You can't stick them in a closet their entire lives, can you? That's no way to raise a child. So what's a person to do?"

We talked a while longer, but it was more of the same. As I was standing to leave, she asked, "Are these people you work for going to pay me anything for talking to you? She don't even have a headstone yet."

I took two twenties from my bag and laid them on the table. "I wish I could give you more. But I'm paying m own expenses."

She nodded and covered the bills with her hand.

As I drove away, the man outside stood and picked up his lawn chair and carried it back to the trailer.

Incident on Ten-Right Road

* * *

The man Grayson Rath discovered in bed with his mother was 46 years old. He was married to his second wife, with whom he had two children, aged nine and seven. He had a son, aged 16, with his first wife. I am not going to include any of their names here, even though other sources have already identified them. My first inclination is to label that man and all other men like him a philandering asshole, but we need to remember that for every cheating man there is a woman who lets him cheat, who enables his cheating, and who, as often as not, encourages him to cheat. It takes two to tango.

The truth is that women cheat just as frequently as men, and, according to some studies, more frequently. So maybe the problem here is not that both genders like to have sex out of wedlock; maybe the problem here is the way our society looks at sex, which is, after all—surprise! surprise!—the most basic and elemental urge on the planet. So thanks a bunch, Puritans. Thanks a bunch for spoiling a really good thing for all of us.

Driving gives a person a lot of time to think, you know? Especially if you turn off the radio. When I was younger and not nearly as wise as I am now ;) I used my car as a sanctuary more times than I like to remember. I did the same thing when I was living with good old Ian. Although I loved him madly back then, he could be a pain in the ass. When he wasn't singing or humming to himself, he was on the phone with one or more of his buds, chattering away about March Madness or the AFC North or the latest version of Halo or some other testosterone-soaked banality. He wasn't loud, but loudness is not a requisite of annoying. I couldn't hear myself think when he was around! Maybe it's just an introvert thing, but sometimes I wanted to hold a pillow over his face and smother him. I mean literally. I really wanted to smother him.

So yes, I sort of understand the attraction of violence. Thing is, I always suppressed the urge. That's what most of us do. I would grab my laptop and jump in the car and head for the nearest piece of quiet. And I would write. Writing, I think, is a kind of moveable therapist. We use ourselves to take the talking cure. I'm still doing it. Every day. Costs a hell of a lot less than a shrink, and, if you're lucky, you can find a way to monetize it.

Anyway, friends, what I'm wondering is this: Who did Grayson Rath have to talk to? I know it is *très grossier* of me to feel empathy for a murderer, but honestly, what if somebody had just *listened* to him once in a while?

Why can't we all just shut up, grow up and start listening to each other? Instead we curse and vilify and castigate everyone who says something we don't like. If somebody posts on Facebook, "I hate my life. I feel like offing somebody," where are the individuals close to that person? Why aren't they paying attention? Where are his friends and siblings and parents and grandparents? Did nobody ever say to Grayson Rath, "Hey, man, write a blog. Do like what's-her-name. Let it all out, brother."

Not that I am absolving Grayson Rath or anybody else of responsibility for their own behavior. But sometimes people are allowed to sink so deep into

Incident on Ten-Right Road

their own demented reality that they can no longer distinguish right from rite and wrong from won-ton. You know what I mean.

We make people get a driver's license to drive a car. We make them show an ID to get a beer. Most states require a background check before issuing a teaching certificate or gun permit. We require couples to obtain a license before getting married.

Would it be so terrible to make potential parents pass a basic competency test before they create another human being?

Unethical, you say? A violation of your civil liberties? Then how about this:

Hey, drug companies. You want to do something really useful for a change? Invent a contraceptive to be administered at birth that won't shut off until intentionally deactivated. By somebody with the mental competency to do so.

Eugenics! you scream? *Sexual totalitarianism!*

You'd rather we keep churning out killers and sexual predators and lonely, unwanted babies by the millions? No? Then you come up with a better idea. I'm all out.

* * *

Grayson Rath voice recording

Ever notice how dumb sportscasters are? I bet most people on television are below average intelligence, but sportscasters are outright dumb. I'm sitting here now talking to my little recorder, had every intention of talking about that rug cleaner woman, when what do I see on TV but that Troy guy wearing a blue checkered sport coat that looks like some kind of clown suit. I can't even describe the shade of blue it is. I've seen little girl's dresses that shade of blue, but never a man's jacket. The only thing I can compare it to is those little flowers on spindly stems that grow along the road sometimes. But with a shine to it. Neon almost. And the little guy beside him, he's wearing a gray checkered coat that isn't a whole lot better. I thought these people had other people who dress them for the camera. People who are supposed to know what they're doing.

And how come there's always the big stupid former athlete and the little guy who looks like the most athletic thing he ever did was to push a chess piece around? Are they supposed to balance each other out somehow? All they do is to make each other look even more ridiculous.

That ESPN channel, it was just about the only thing Al ever watched. That and the sports themselves, I mean. These sportscaster people get paid good money to say stuff the average person would get laughed at for saying. The team that gets the ball down the field, that's the team that's going to win today. The team that wants it the most. The team that makes the fewest mistakes. The team that puts the most points on the scoreboard. Idiotic shit like that.

I'm pretty sure that the only time Al cared enough to be disappointed in me was when I told him I didn't like sports. But you're a natural athlete, he said. Just like I was. I know an athlete when I see one.

What I didn't like was playing on a team. If my school had had just one sport that was for individuals and not teams, I would have kicked ass. In gym class I was the fastest kid in my class. But playing on a team is putting your fate in the hands of a lot of people who

Incident on Ten-Right Road

are at best mediocre. The more people on a team, the greater the chances of losing. That's a statistical fact.

Anyway, none of that is what I wanted to talk about. The only reason I turned on the TV was to see if anybody found that lady with the rug cleaner. I dumped both of them in a ditch along a gravel road about 10 miles from the Home Depot. I was thinking it shouldn't take long before somebody spots that rug cleaner handle I left sticking up in the weeds. People are always so freaking happy to get something for free. What do you want to bet that the first person to come along and spot that rug cleaning machine grabbed it and skedaddled? He'd be like, Sorry, lady, but you're not going to need this anymore. I'll just take it off your hands for you. Have a nice day.

Okay, nothing on the news. I guess what happens in Virginia stays in Virginia. What I need to do now is to get some Tennessee barbecue and switch out the SUV, which I'm going to miss. There's nothing like Sirius radio to make the miles fly by. That Howard Stern, man he makes me howl. And Joe Rogan, I like the way that guy thinks. That's a couple of guys I could see myself hanging out with. And oh yeah, I need to check out the spare tire space in the cargo area. I'm thinking there's probably something in there I can use. I'm hoping for a heavy-duty lug wrench. I mean, who drives around without one of those?

* * *

from the blog And Sometimes the Abyss Winks at You *by Mia Swain*

As you might already know, if you are following this case, the body of a woman who disappeared from a Home Depot in southwestern Virginia has been found. She is Katie Bohman, 37, mother of a boy and a girl, both under 10 years old. She had gone to Home Depot to rent a rug shampooer so that she could clean her carpets prior to her daughter's birthday party.

Initially, Virginia law enforcement did not tie Ms. Bohman's disappearance to the murders in Ohio. Unfortunately, the Home Depot lot's surveillance footage, because of her vehicle's distance from the nearest cameras, only showed the vehicle arriving and leaving the lot.

Two days later, Katie's body was discovered by a trucker along a side road south of Dunlow in the southwestern part of the state. Eighteen-wheelers usually don't run on that road, which is a narrow tar-and-chip lane leading to a scattering of modest homes, but the driver was headed home for the day. He slowed when he saw a group of four or five turkey buzzards standing alongside the road. He said they were reluctant to fly, even as his truck approached. Instead they moved closer to something in a drainage ditch, something they appeared to be guarding.

At first he didn't recognize the body of the woman who was to host a birthday party his own daughter was scheduled to attend—a birthday party that had been canceled because of Katie's disappearance.

There is more to the story, but I have no desire to relate it. You can find it easily enough online if you wish. I suggest that you don't.

A group of buzzards is called a wake. I like that term as a description of what they were doing beside the road, better than what they were really doing. That's how I choose to think of it: They were holding a wake for Katie.

Incident on Ten-Right Road

The turkey buzzard is a type of vulture, of course. The scientific name for vultures is *Cathartes aura*, which is Latin for "cleansing breeze." That's another nice way of thinking of a bunch of homely birds who do a very ugly job. And a job that was, in this case, wholly unwarranted.

The discovery of the body prompted closer examination of the Home Depot surveillance footage and parking lot, which resulted in the discovery of Grayson Rath's red Camaro parked three spaces from where Katie's SUV had been.

Katie had been strangled to death after being struck on the head.

All she wanted was to have clean rugs for her daughter's birthday party. Do you hear me, Grayson? You vile, contemptuous, despicable person. I hope you burn. I hope you sizzle and die.

* * *

Grayson Rath voice recording

I just now googled my name and came up with this dumbass blog some woman is writing about me! Before she started writing about me she wrote about some guy named Ian and how much she hated high heels and tampons and bras and other stupid stuff. She calls herself a neo-journalist. Called me despicable. Like she has the faintest idea who I am.

She seems to think she's hot on my trail. Ha. Even talked to my grandmother. Bitch. You better stay away from my people if you know what's good for you.

She's not bad looking though. Maybe I should invite her to ride along with me. A blowjob every hundred miles or so would sure help me stay awake.

Mia Swain. Swain. Swain swain, it's a funny name.

Seriously though. 89.5k followers. Now we're talking. Maybe I should send her a note. See how she likes having me following *her*.

* * *

It's funny how coming out of the gray room always changes things. It's like I said earlier, like a good healthy sneeze or shooting your wad. The day just seems brighter and clearer afterward. Everything you look at, and the way everything sounds. Smells, tastes, every little thing is better afterward.

Fact is, I didn't want to kill those two in the motel where I was staying, but I really didn't have a choice in the matter. They had an older vehicle, a black Silverado truck that looked fairly beat-up, which meant it almost certainly didn't have a tracking chip in it. And at the free breakfast in the morning, the guy said hello to me while I was waiting for my waffles, and asked if there was anybody else waiting to use the waffle maker after me. Then he invited me to sit at their table and they told me all about where they were going on their honeymoon. It was pretty pathetic, if you ask me. I mean Dollywood? Seriously? To them it was a big deal. She said this was the farthest either of them had ever been from home. I could almost smell the poverty on them, their miserable little lives. I actually felt sorry for them, and that's what made me pick them. That and their vehicle.

It's a 1999 Silverado truck. The guy, who called himself Richie by the way, said he and his brothers had put a new engine in it just a few days earlier, so it "should be good for another hundred thousand at least."

Incident on Ten-Right Road

Plus it had those big knobby wheels on it. Thirty-four inchers, he called them, with three-inch lifts. "It could probably climb a tree if I wanted it to," he said.

I was listening close to every word. He said they were packing a tent and two sleeping bags for when they got to Georgia, where his grandparents lived. He was carrying fishing gear and cooking stuff and everything they'd need for a week on Lake Lanier, which was a scant 11 miles from his grandparents' cottage. That's when the girl, Grace, leaned over and pretended to whisper to me. "He even brought his crossbow and two pistols, just in case I see me a better looking man and decide to cut this honeymoon short." He never batted an eyelash. Just said, "It's only one pistol. The nine millimeter. The .45 is a revolver." That's the kind of kids they were. They'd have told me anything. I probably could have asked him how long his pecker was, and he would have pulled it out and showed me.

So after breakfast we said goodbye, nice to meet you, and went back to our rooms. They still needed to get packed, they said, before checking out. I just needed to grab the lug wrench from the SUV. A couple of knocks and good old Richie opened the door right up and invited me in. He closed the door behind me, then turned around and said, "What are you carrying that lug wrench for?" And that's when I laid him out. Grace was still in the bathroom, so I just sat there on the bed and waited for her. For a while I was thinking about taking her with me, but in the end I knew she would just be trouble.

I washed up in their bathroom afterward, put on some of Richie's clean clothes and that was it. When I went back out onto the balcony afterward, it was such a pretty day. Everything was clean and bright. I don't think people understand how easy it is to kill somebody. In fact I'm sure they don't, or else there'd be a lot more people doing it.

* * *

from the blog And Sometimes the Abyss Winks at You, *by Mia Swain*

I can't believe it. I mean, I can, but I don't want to. He did it again. Grayson Rath has killed again. A couple on their honeymoon. Seems like every time I close my eyes to sleep, he kills somebody else.

I wonder how many people die every time a person blinks. I need to look that up. I'll be right back.

Turns out that the average person blinks approximately 28,800 times per day. And approximately 151,600 people die every day. That's just over five deaths per blink.

And that was before Grayson Rath went to work, along with all the other natural and unnatural forces of destruction on this planet.

It's a sobering statistic. Enough to make a compassionate woman want to never close her eyes again.

For those of you who aren't going blind reading every news account available online, as I am, here's the skinny on Rath's latest:

I'm sorry, that sounds cavalier and insensitive. *Here's the skinny.* How dare I?

I assure you that I am not feeling cavalier or insensitive in any way. I am appalled and sickened. So much so that I have chosen not to interview the

Incident on Ten-Right Road

couple's families. I don't think I could handle it. Plus, who am I to intrude upon their grief? Just writing this post makes me feel like something of a parasite. Journalism *is* parasitic, isn't it? I am a dung beetle rolling my little ball of poop back home for the evening meal. I used to feed on the spoiled fruit of my own foibles and failures, but at least I could console myself with the notion that confessional writing is not only cathartic for the writer but also for the reader. I even had the likes of Phillip Lopate on my side. His *The Art of the Personal Essay* has been my Bible. "Through sharing thoughts, memories, desires, complaints, and whimsies," he wrote, "the personal essayist sets up a relationship with the reader, a dialogue—a friendship, if you will," based on "as much honesty as possible."

So let me be 100% honest here: It was so safe and easy to write my blog back when all I wrote about was my own little life. I made such a big deal out of the petty annoyances of modern society. I feel like a fool for having been so self-absorbed as to believe that I was providing a service to other young women. Now I know that I was only stroking my own fragile ego. It took a monster like Grayson Rath to bring that fact into focus. Writing about him is so *hard*, so distasteful. So heartbreaking. I am not sure how long I can continue. I used to be funny. Now I just want to cry all the time.

But a promise is a promise, isn't it? I will not let myself be another Ian. No matter how much it hurts. Neither will I feed the prurient interests of others. And that includes Grayson Rath himself. So nothing graphic. I will not be one of those parasites who shoves a microphone at the grieving family and asks, "How did you feel when the police told you that the semen in your daughter's vagina was a DNA match with Grayson Rath?"

I might do a drive-by of the honeymooning couple's new home in Kentucky, but maybe I will skip that too. My aim is to have a look at the Tennessee hotel room where they died. God, that sounds ghoulish, doesn't it? I wish I could explain why I feel the need, the compulsion, to go there. Right now, I don't think I am in control of anything I do. I am being pulled on a leash, and I don't have the strength to resist.

So, with that said, here's what that monster did in Tennessee:

Somehow he tricked a young couple, the newlyweds Richie and Grace Stipes, into letting him into their hotel room. He then beat them to death with a blunt instrument, but not before having sex with Grace. Then he stole their money and their pickup truck. Grace's mother told the police that her daughter was carrying over $1,000 in cash from their wedding money, which they were using to pay for their honeymoon. They were planning to visit Dollywood, the Tuckaleechee Caverns, Gatlinburg, and several other popular attractions in eastern Tennessee. Richie was 20, and Grace was 18. Richie was excited about going indoor skydiving in Pigeon Forge. Grace only wanted to see Dolly Parton in person, and maybe get her autograph.

Grayson Rath, you make me want to puke.

* * *

Incident on Ten-Right Road

Grayson Rath voice recording

This pickup truck rides like a tank. Not that I've ever been in a tank or plan to be. I do like sitting up high like this though, looking down on everybody I pass. Except for the big rigs though; they get to look down on me. Or would if there were any of them on these boondock roads. All the twists and turns are making my neck stiff. I'm hoping to find a place to pull over soon, just some old logging road or ATV trail that hasn't been used in a while. A place to stop and get my head straight.

What I need to do is to figure out what I want. I mean exactly what I want. All of this aimless driving is getting me nowhere, even if it does serve a purpose. I mean how can the police know where a vehicle is going when the guy behind the wheel doesn't know? They might be able to know where I've been but they can't even guess where I'm going. That's all on purpose. I go west a while, then swing north, then for no reason at all cut south, and then maybe east a while. I just keep mixing it up. Right now I don't even know what state I'm in. Oh wait a minute, yes I do. The state of confusion, ha!

Can't last forever though, can it? They've got license plate readers all over the place. And not just in the cities and the major highways. They're in small towns too and on poles out in the country and on some police cars. That's how stolen cars get traced. So it doesn't matter how many times I change cars. If that car gets reported stolen, sooner or later the police can pretty much tell where it is. Sooner or later some hick deputy is going to call the FBI and say, hey, that vehicle you're looking for just went by here two minutes ago. And then what's going to happen? Roadblocks, that's what. Roadblocks in every possible direction.

The newer cars even have trackers inside them. Police can just shut a car engine down, just like that. So I'm still screwed to a certain degree. I need to find some way of moving around without a car. Which is going to be a pain in the ass but better than jail. And I need to be more careful about what I steal from people, cause you never know what has tracking software in it and what doesn't. Freaking NSA is a menace to society, if you ask me.

So okay, first things first. What do you want to do with the rest of your life, Grayson? That'll decide where you need to go. That's what Al would say. First you state your goal, your endgame. Then you lay out your moves. Except that Al would also say, Assuming you get away with what you've already done.

And I'd say, Don't you worry, I'll get away with it.

So said every killer sitting on death row right now.

They aren't me though, are they?

So said every killer sitting on death row right now.

You think you're awfully smart, don't you?

Smart enough to know that if you keep talking to yourself like you're two different people, you're going to end up in the loony bin.

Ha. Okay. Enough of that. So what do I want? I want to be left alone. That's it, simple as that.

So how do you make that happen? Sooner or later you're going to run out of money. How does a person live without money?

I need to be in a place where I can grow my own food. A place with good water. A place nobody would ever think of looking for me.

Incident on Ten-Right Road

I'm thinking Idaho. Or North Dakota maybe. Way out in the middle of nowhere.

Maybe if I can find the right place, and can get rid of the people who already live there, I'll just tell people I'm their nephew or cousin or whatever. And I'm watching the place for them while they're traveling in Europe.

I don't know but I think I could make that work. If I can find the right place. It has to be just the right place. Shouldn't be hard to find online. Places for sale, places for rent—

Wait a minute. Can a laptop be traced? Am I dropping breadcrumbs every time I go online?

Damn. I might be royally screwed this time.

* * *

Okay, I'm feeling better now. I had to risk going online again but found out I've got nothing to worry about. Well, not nothing but not what I thought anyway. According to the stuff I read, a laptop's exact location can't be traced unless it has a special kind of software on it. So whew! That's a relief.

I also need to pull over soon and catch a few winks. Also need to take inventory. Been spending a lot of cash on gas. I mean I know there's still a good bit left, what with all I brought with me plus what Richie and Grace had on them, but I have to plan for the future too, right? Can't get myself into a bad spot where I'm running out. It's not like I can just dip into Al's cookie jar anymore.

The family cookie jar, that's what Al called it. It was just an old Bible he keeps on his dresser, always had six or more fifties in it. Al said he never himself carries less than a grand in his pocket, probably just so he can flash it around to the check-out girls when he buys a pack of Tic Tacs. But the cookie jar was for me and Mom, he said, though we'd better not take advantage of his generosity, he said, because he would know from minute to minute how much money is in there. But if we found ourselves short or needed some groceries or something, we could take a fifty but never under any circumstances more than two at a time. And we'd better have a damn good reason for it and be able to account for every penny or he would shut off the tap. I don't know how many times I heard him say that. Once I said to him, I didn't know cookie jars have taps, especially a cookie jar that's a Bible, and he says, the problem with you is, you don't even know how much you don't know. And that got us into an argument with me saying nobody knows what they don't know, or else they would already know it. And on and on like that until he started laughing and said boy you got a mouth on you, just like your mother. You might want to consider being a politician someday. And that made me smile too and all the anger just sort of washed out of me. Like he could see into who I really was and liked what he saw.

I wonder what he's thinking of me now? I bet he's thinking, you got to be pretty smart to slip the fuzz the way he's doing. Got to give him credit for that.

* * *

So I'm just now getting ready to pull out from behind this little convenience store where I've been the last 30 minutes. Using their wi-fi. Apparently

Incident on Ten-Right Road

pretty little Mia Swain doesn't like me much. So I sent her a little love note. Just to help her sleep tonight. Ha ha ha.

She will call the police of course, and they will track down the IP, and this place will be swarming with feds in an hour. Wish I could hang around, fellas, but I feel like moving on. Enjoy your clusterfuck!

* * *

from the blog And Sometimes the Abyss Winks at You
by Mia Swain

OH. MY. GOD! Grayson Rath left a comment on my last post. *Grayson Rath!* He signed it *your friend and future lover, the Gray Man*, so who else could it be? And now what should I do?

Well, I will tell you what I did; I dialed 911. The dispatcher took my information and five minutes later I received a call from the FBI. I am not allowed to discuss our conversation with you, but they did say it was up to me whether I allowed the comment to stay posted or not. I decided to delete it. I simply don't think I want to ever read it again. I'm sorry; I know how much you want to know what he said. So I will tell you this much and your imagination can fill in the rest. He said that he enjoyed reading my blog and is sorry that he makes me want to puke, but that while I am on my knees puking into the toilet, he would be happy to violate me in a particular way.

I cannot believe what I have gotten myself into. This all happened a couple of hours ago, and my heart is still pounding. I haven't taken a full breath since I read the comment. I can't drive anymore today, and I don't want to write about Grayson Rath anymore. If I go silent for a while, please don't worry about me; I'm in a safe place. But this is way more than I bargained for. Please pray for the FBI to stop him soon. Pray for all of us. And maybe ask God why an abomination like Grayson Rath is allowed to exist.

* * *

Grayson Rath voice recording

I remember Al telling me that you've got to be none too bright to be poor in this country. That was one of his life lessons, he called them. None too bright or filthy lazy, he said. Or a good bit of both.

He said that Mom was the latter. That with her ass and face she could reel in a whale and be living on sushi if she'd put her mind to it. And I said, Isn't that what she did? He laughed at that and said, Guess you got me there, kid. But she's going to blow it one of these days if she doesn't mind her Ps and Qs. You don't need to worry about that though, he told me. Now that I'm your legal guardian, you have nothing to worry about. Then he cocked his head a little and thought about that for a few seconds, and then he said, that doesn't mean I won't throw you out on your skinny ass if you don't make something of yourself.

The worst thing for him was to be embarrassed. To have people whispering and chuckling at him behind his back. To me that was pretty pathetic. What does it matter what other people think? Then on the other hand he once told me, you can be the wolf or you can be one of the sheep. Eat grass and weeds all your life or stuff yourself every night on lamb chops.

That made more sense to me than anything else

Incident on Ten-Right Road

he ever said. That's why I enrolled in business administration at the college. He said I could work summers for him, starting at the bottom of course, which meant detailing the cars and keeping the lot clean and the lounge stocked and so forth, and then maybe by the second summer he'd give me a shot at selling. Said the sooner I proved myself to him, the sooner a college degree would be redundant and just a waste of time, which was why he never got one and had no desire to, he said, but figured I should at least get started so as to get some discipline. Whereas he got his from four years in the Army. Which was a shit show of mostly lost boys and power mongers, he said, but did him and lots of others some good nonetheless. He said as long as the economy kept chugging along like it was, none of his people would have anything to worry about.

I guess he didn't know who he was talking to. Ha ha.

* * *

I was watching this TV show one time, one of those cop shows in the big city, and there was a detective checking out a crime scene on the street. He got up real close to this one car and was looking at the bullet holes. Even put his pinkie finger in one of the holes; claimed he could tell the gauge that way. And maybe he could. I don't know about that. What I do know is that when a bullet goes through a painted surface, it wipes off a little circle of paint right down to the bare metal. Like a silver ring around the moon if the bullet hole is the moon. And there were none of those rings around the bullet holes the detective was looking at. So the show lost me right there. That's just being sloppy is what it is. How many hundreds of people do they have working on that TV show, and not one of them knows enough to say hey, there should be a little ring of bare metal around each of these bullet holes?

That's the kind of stuff that interests me. Little details like that. How I know about what bullet holes in metal look like, that's hard to say. I've seen plenty of bullet holes in road signs is probably why. Never made any of them myself, but they are all over the place out in the country. I don't know why people want to shoot up road signs. I mean, what do they get out of it? Especially since bullets aren't free. You've got to be pretty dumb to waste your money putting holes in a road sign.

A couple of years back I wanted a gun really bad, just to have one, you know? But Al says no guns in this house, no way. Why not, I asked, and even Mom said the same thing. Why can't he have one? And Al says, because he'll end up killing somebody with it. Maybe me.

It makes me laugh now to remember that. For a long time after that I was so mad I used to picture him walking around with bullet holes in his chest and the blood seeping through his shirt. He'd be walking around in the morning, slurping from a cup of coffee, talking to Mom about this or that. He's chattering away and she's half-asleep at the table and I'm sitting there spooning up my Cheerios and smiling to myself while watching blood seeping out through a half-dozen bullet holes in his chest.

Incident on Ten-Right Road

I wonder if Al remembers me asking for a gun. If he does I bet he's thinking, I should've said no to knives and baseball bats and lug wrenches too. God, that's funny. Good old Al. I bet he's shitting bricks right now.

* * *

Sometimes I wonder about being alone. I mean why I am? Why it's always been that way. Right from the start I always felt like an orphan, like I didn't come from nobody and had nobody to go to, even if I'd wanted to.

There are some people who just seem to attract people to them. My mother was like that. Al too. Me, it's like I have a force field around me. One of those invisible fences. It's nothing I do, not as far as I can tell. But something made me that way. What was it?

Back in that motel in Tennessee with the Stipes' girl I was almost ready to take her with me. Figured she'd have to get used to it sooner or later and stop bawling her eyes out. But then I just told myself, it's not worth the trouble. But now I wonder why I even had that thought. Do other people think the same way? If they do, how do they get past it so they can actually live with someone? With my mother, she seemed able to do it for a while, but then she'd always get the itch for somebody else, and we wouldn't see her for days or weeks at a time. Al on the other hand seemed to like having us around. Needed an audience, I guess. Somebody to preach to. The gospel according to Al.

Still, I keep thinking about that Grace. I could've taken better care of her, I guess. Shouldn't have left her the way I did. I can smell her on one of the sleeping bags. I don't sleep in that one because it will start to smell like me and not her. I just like to keep it close to me and lay it over my face sometimes.

I'm living in their tent now. Don't know if I already said that or not. I caught a tiny little fish yesterday in this stream I found, but by the time I cut off its head and tail and scraped out its guts, there was barely a bite. I used up all that survival food they'd packed. There was only six bags of it to begin with, and I finished them in the first three days. I do like it here, how quiet it is. And I've gotten pretty good at building fires. Richie packed one of those little fire guns for starting barbecues with, same as Al had back home. Plus those real guns of his are pretty cool. I spent some time figuring how to load and unload them but I haven't actually fired them yet. Dry fire, I think it's called. I've done that a lot. But from up here where I am, if I walk down this hill and up the next one, which is higher, I can see a house over on the far side of a little valley, maybe three or four miles away. Mostly just the red metal roof is visible and the chimney with a stream of white smoke coming out of it. It sets about halfway up the hill, with no other ones visible till closer to the bottom, where there are a couple of dozen or so. I keep scoping the place out with Richie's binoculars, hoping to catch sight of somebody around the house, but so far nothing.

I can't stay here forever, that's all I know. I finished my partial case of water a long time ago and am already halfway through Richie's. I drink a lot of water. Seems like I'm thirsty all the time. Thirsty and hungry both. And while this is nice it's not a good way to live, not having anything to do but to walk through the woods and lay in a tent and feed little sticks to the fire. I used to think it would be great to be so rich that I could just lay around all day and do nothing, but now I want just the opposite. A person's got to have something to do.

I wonder what Mia Swain is saying about me. I bet my little message turned her on and made her want to touch herself. If I could talk to her I'd ask her up here to go camping with me a while. Though I'm sure that would get stale in a while too. I've never yet met a girl I want to keep around after I shoot my load. Later, sure, I'll wish I hadn't chased them away so soon. It's like Chinese food. Or ice cream. Smoked almonds. Those little sugar cookies with raspberry filling in them Grandma used to make. It's good until you've had your fill, then you don't want any more, then four hours later you wish you had some again. I guess that's true about everything, isn't it? Even being alone. I need to keep reminding myself that every time I was with somebody more than 15 minutes or so, all I wanted was to be alone again.

* * *

from the blog And Sometimes the Abyss Winks at You
by Mia Swain

I know I said I was going *incommunicado*, but I am just so enraged by the message that little coward left on my blog. I hope you know that's what you are, Grayson Rath. Nothing but a weaselly, disgusting coward. Do you think it makes you a man to insult someone on social media? Does that make you feel important? You're pathetic.

Randall Silvis

Do you want to know who was a good man? A strong man? A brave man? Richie Stipes, that's who. He grew up in poverty, worked hard to get through high school, took a job in a furniture factory and never missed a day's work until he and Grace started their honeymoon. That is a man who will be missed. He was loved. He was appreciated. And you? You were given everything you wanted. Every opportunity. And what did you do with it? You flushed it down the toilet.

And now you're flushing yourself away. That's good, because you're nothing but a turd, Grayson Rath. A stinking piece of shit. Nobody cares about you. Nobody wants you around. And how do you feel about that, asswipe?

* * *

Grayson Rath voice recording

So you know that house I saw from where I was camping out? The one across the valley that I looked at through Richie's binoculars? Guess where I'm sitting right now. On a big brown leather sofa in the living room. Drinking a cold beer and watching out the window as the clouds roll by. It took me a while on those mountain roads to find this place, but I did it. And getting inside the house was touch and go. But here I am.

What I did was to drive up to the house and sit there in the truck at the end of the driveway. It wasn't long before some woman comes peeking around the back of the house. She looks about as old as my grandma but bigger, and instead of wearing jeans and a sweatshirt like grandma always did, she's wearing baggy pants and a jacket and a pair of work gloves and carrying a pair of

Incident on Ten-Right Road

pruning shears. She's just standing there squinting at me, so I give her a wave. And yep, she comes walking about halfway to me. I roll the window down and yell to her, "I think I missed a turn somewhere!"

She comes over and puts a hand up on the windowsill and looks in at me. That's when I shoved the 9mm in her face. She flinched some but then her face tightened up and she just glared at me. Then damn if she didn't turn around and start walking back to the house. When I jumped out, she started running, and just before I got to her the front door comes open and there's some old guy, probably her husband, aiming a rifle our way. But I'm right behind her so he can't take a shot, so I fire off three over her shoulder and she drops down on her knees and he falls backward into the house. I grab her by the hair and pull her up and she's trying to get turned to scratch my eyes out, but all I have to do is to give her hair a hard tug and that straightens her out again. And that was pretty much the highpoint of the day's festivities. As soon as I finish this beer I'm going to go see what other treats their refrigerator holds.

* * *

So it's my third day here and I'm bored stiff. They don't have cable or internet and I can't risk using one of their phones. And I am dying to know what Ms. Mia Swain had to say about my little love note to her. I'm thinking a quick trip to the bottom of the mountain might be justified.

There's got to be some place down there with wi-fi.

***

Whooee she was ticked. I couldn't stop laughing. I wish I'd had more time to sit and think before writing back to her, but I couldn't chance it. Some kid came out of the store carrying a bag of garbage for the dumpster, and when he looked in at me I just gave him a nod like I had every right to be sitting there sucking up the free wi-fi. And then I just hurried up and wrote, I bet you won't talk like that when you're laying underneath me. I bet you love every minute of it. See you soon. Stay wet for me. The Gray Man.

I didn't go back up the mountain right away but pulled over near the bottom to see if anybody from the store was following me. While sitting there I thought of lots of better things I should have written. Why is it all the good ideas come too late?

Anyway, I'm back in the house now. And I kind of wish I was back in the woods instead. I wonder how long I could live there with Richie's tent and sleeping bags? I don't remember ever feeling as peaceful as I did there before I got antsy. Let's say I loaded up the pickup, drove there and unloaded and set up camp again. Then I could drive back, fill the Rav4 with everything I wanted from the house and drive back to my camp. These old folks have all kinds of stuff I could use. And if anybody came there looking for me....

I don't know. Maybe I should just stay here. The nights are getting cold. I could maybe make a life for myself here. If anybody finds out I'm staying here, I'll just say I'm their grandson from Texas or somewhere, and that I'm watching the house for them while they're off somewhere taking the grand tour.

Incident on Ten-Right Road

That might be the better choice. I haven't shaved in weeks, and my hair's getting longer. Nobody's going to recognize me. I'll just be a different person. Whoever I want to be. After people get used to seeing me around, I could probably even get a job in town somewhere, something simple like washing dishes or driving a snowplow after somebody shows me how. That's what I'd really like to do anyway, is to become another person. See if I could make that work for me. I could even go to Alaska if I wanted to. Nobody would ever look for me there. I just might give it a try. What do I have to lose?

* * *

from And Sometimes the Abyss Winks at You, *by Mia Swain*

He's dead. Brain dead, anyway. Thank God for that.

And now I can tell you the whole truth.

No doubt many of you have been questioning my sanity. Maybe even my morality. Why would I ever walk away from my safe little life to go wading through the swamp and misery of a person like Grayson Rath? Hadn't I said I was giving it up? What made me keep going?

The men in black, that's what.

Yep. They called me. The same day the first comment from Grayson Rath appeared on my blog. The same day his comment brought me to a screeching halt in a diner south of Wytheville, Virginia. They said I could be of assistance. All I had to do was to be the cheese in the rat trap. Keep him talking, and maybe he would drop a clue as to his whereabouts. Just keep writing, that's all I had to do. And pray the cheese—me—didn't get eaten.

In the meantime they told me to go home. Two beautiful wonderful splendiferous agents stood guard outside my apartment. So I was never in any danger. They took very good care of me.

And I thought, Wow. So this is why I have been so obsessed with him. This is why I needed to write about him. This is why I'm still constipated and jittery from living on junior cheeseburgers and coffee from the place across the street—delivered, by the way, by those wonderful FBI agents, who kept admonishing me to *eat a salad once in a while, girl. Eat a salad.* Yes, this is why: had Grayson Rath not responded to my posts, nobody would have known where to find him.

What happened is this: Grayson kidnapped a retired couple at their remote home in the mountains of northwestern Georgia. Reed and Carole Ellsworth, both in their early 70s. What he didn't know was that the couple were regular visitors to the little village of Holmes at the bottom of the mountain. Every Friday afternoon before the post office closed, they would come down off the mountain to collect their mail. Then they would drive to the general store, enjoy a couple of bison burgers, coffee and pie a la mode, and load up on groceries for the week. When they didn't show up that Friday, the delivery boy, 17 year-old Pete Steiner, boxed up their usual grocery order in his dad's Wrangler and drove up the mountain.

But he knew right away that something wasn't right. First off, there was a beat-up old pickup truck parked near the back door. Not in the driveway, not in the garage, but pulled up close to the back deck. And Pete could hear heavy metal music playing inside the house. And, just two days earlier, on Wednesday, he had spotted the Ellsworth's Rav4 parked next to the store, but with "a scruffy young man" in the driver's seat. The Ellsworths were nowhere to be seen. So Petey had a bad feeling. He had a very bad feeling.

He memorized the truck's license plate number and got his butt back down the mountain as fast as he could. There he checked in at the local two-man police department. A deputy called the Ellsworth's home. Several times. No answer. Then he ran the plate. The owner of the pickup truck turned out to be a Richard Stipes of Tennessee. The deputy didn't recognize the name, so he did a database search. And bingo. He called the FBI.

The feds surrounded the place and ordered Grayson to come out. He promised to kill the Ellsworths if anybody so much as jiggled the doorknob. Then he refused to answer the phone, refused to speak to a negotiator or anybody else. The stand-off lasted for two and a half days. Then, in the middle of the night, a single gunshot sounded inside the house. The FBI fired gas and percussion bombs through the windows, then stormed inside. They found Grayson Rath in the back corner of the loft bedroom, with a self-inflicted gunshot to the head. But he managed to screw even that up, because he wasn't dead. He had blown half of his brain away, but his body was still alive. It still is. But it won't be going anywhere, or hurting anybody else, not ever again.

Sadly, the Ellsworths' bodies were discovered in the basement, pushed into a crawl space that was being used as a root cellar. The medical examiner estimated that they had been dead for three or more days, though the coolness of the root cellar had slowed decomposition.

But here's the ironic part of all this. When Grayson was finally taken into custody, he had a voice recorder in his pocket. He was keeping a kind of audio blog throughout the entire trip from Gilford, Ohio! From Day One of his rampage to the very end. That just blew my mind. (Whoops! Unintentional pun. Sorry, Grayson. No, I'm not. But I should be; I realize that. And I am determined to try harder.)

I don't believe that anger is inherently either good or bad. What matters is what we do with it. How we use our anger. It is normal to feel anger when we or someone else is hurt, but our reaction to that anger should be empathy and compassion, not violence. Violence gives anger a negative charge.

I am not saying that we should feel sorry for monsters like Rath. Or maybe I am. The whole thing is still very murky for me. They must be stopped, yes, and by whatever means necessary. More importantly, they must be stopped in their incipiency. We must be alert for the earliest signs of such behavior. We must not encourage or incite these people to act.

The fact that Grayson Rath was sort of blogging the whole time I was, that we shared that need to express our anger and frustration…it rattles me. I never wanted to believe that I had a single thing in common with a monster, but I did. Probably, we all do. It's scary. At first I told myself that all I'd wanted from my blog was some understanding and love, whereas all he wanted was to hurt and destroy, but I was being dishonest with myself. The truth is that every time I mentioned Ian, I wanted my words to stick another needle in him. Every time I insulted a politician or somebody or something that had offended me, I wanted revenge.

Incident on Ten-Right Road

Thank God my only weapons were words. Still, I wonder if hurtful words, or the lack of positive, life-affirming ones, were what eventually drove Grayson Rath to violence. What was it that made the difference in our lives? What tipped the balance? Was it really all the prenatal influences on him, none of which I suffered? Or was it a very simple lack of love in his life? I am always going to wonder about this and I will always be watchful from now on. You should too.

Anyway, that's it from me for a while. I am done with the abyss and all of its darkness. That includes you, Ian. This is my last goodbye. I will never mention you in print again. No more focusing on the negative. I am so hungry for the light.

I have no idea where this new path will lead me, but I'll be sure to let you know when I get there. Love and peace, my friends. Spread it around.

* * *

Grayson Rath voice recording

This message is for Ms. Mia Swain. I don't know where she lives or how to get in touch with her except that she writes a blog called *And Sometimes the Abyss Winks at You*. I thought that was a pretty weird title when I first read it, but I'm beginning to see what she means by it. The abyss is winking at me. Telling me it's coming. No getting away this time, it says.

Pretty soon, Mia, you're going to be saying to yourself, thank God it's all over. I am sorry to tell you, though, you will be wrong on two counts. First off, there is no God for you to be thanking. Not unless he's out there in those woods where I spent the best week of my life not long ago. I know for certain he's not where you are and not where I am or where any other human being is. Honestly, I don't believe he'd be caught dead hanging out anywhere near any of us.

As for the second count where you're wrong, it's not over. You think this kind of stuff will end with me? It didn't begin with me and it's sure as hell not going to end with me, sweetheart.

I remember my grandma telling me that back when she was young, people never got divorced. They might've wanted to, but they didn't, not most times anyway. They stuck it out and raised their kids, worked hard, were happy for what little they had. Grandma herself never once thought about getting divorced. Stayed with him through thick and thin until his heart quit on him. She never quit on him though. Not for a second.

She also said when she was a kid she hardly knew any other kids who were overweight. Maybe one or two in a class. And nobody talked about being depressed. Nobody took drugs for it. Nobody had celiac or crohn's or gluten allergies or anything like that. If you or your neighbors hadn't raised it or grew it, you didn't eat it, she said. And kids didn't sit in the house all day playing video games or watching TV or trying to make more "friends" on Facebook from strangers they'd never meet. They had chores or jobs to do. The biggest problems in school were fighting and being absent and not taking a bath often enough and now it's heroin and meth and pregnancy and kids with guns and knives. What I'm saying is, take a look around, Mia. Look at the people you know. Look at yourself. My, my how things have changed. And they're not ever going back to the way they were. They will only get worse.

Incident on Ten-Right Road

Coming up that long dirt road to this house the first time, I saw a hawk sitting in a tree. I've always liked hawks. They're always alone, you know? Sitting up high so noble and all, watching everything that moves. They can see for miles. Can spot a mouse twitching its tail in the tall grass. It always made me feel good to see a hawk. Made me feel like something good was going to happen. I used to think I was sort of like a hawk myself, just standing off away from everything and watching it happen. Above it all.

If those fellas outside ever let you listen to this, do me a favor and tell my grandmother I'm sorry. I know I'm nothing but another disappointment to her. If it makes her feel any better, tell her I'm disappointed too. And while you're at it, tell Al I said thanks. He was decent to me, even though it was mostly for himself.

Getting back to whether there's a God or not. If there is, it's kind of a waste, isn't it? A person like me, I mean. Have you ever thought about that, Mia Swain? Why would a God throw away a person after making him? Doesn't make a whole lot of sense, does it? Why would he let me do what I've done? There's only two possible answers to that. One, he likes to see us hurt each other. Or two, his intentions are good, but he screws up a lot.

Either way, I won't be the last, that's for sure. There's a million others just like me already. And a million more to come. If you don't believe me, just look into the abyss a while. Trust me, Mia Swain. Trust me. You'll see.

I guess that's it then. Screw it. I'm done with all this.

ABOUT THE AUTHOR

Photo © 2016 Maddison Hodge

Randall Silvis is the internationally acclaimed author of 20 books thus far. Also a prize-winning playwright, produced screenwriter, and prolific essayist, Silvis was the first Pennsylvanian to win the prestigious Drue Heinz Literature Prize. The recipient of two National Endowment for the Arts Literature Fellowships, a Fulbright Senior Scholar Research Award and six writing fellowships from the Pennsylvania Council on the Arts for his fiction, drama and screenwriting, he was awarded an honorary Doctor of Letters degree from Indiana University of Pennsylvania for "a sustained record of distinguished literary achievement."

Learn more about Silvis's work at
www.randallsilvis.com

He co-hosts the popular podcast *The Writers Hangout* at www.thewritershangout.com. You can follow him on Twitter @randallsilvis.

*Randall Silvis is an author's author. Those who write for a living (or aspire to do so)
could hardly do better than to study his significant body of work,
which has been critically acclaimed and recognized throughout the world—
an author who never disappoints.*
BOOKREPORTER.COM

Randall Silvis is a masterful storyteller.
THE NEW YORK TIMES BOOK REVIEW

ALSO BY RANDALL SILVIS

Ryan DeMarco Mysteries
Two Days Gone
Walking the Bones
A Long Way Down

Edgar Allan Poe Mysteries
On Night's Shore
Disquiet Heart (also published as *Doubly Dead*)

Other Novels
Excelsior
An Occasional Hell
Under the Rainbow
Dead Man Falling
Mysticus
Hangtime, a Confession
In a Town Called Mundomuerto
The Boy Who Shoots Crows
Flying Fish
Blood & Ink
Only the Rain
First the Thunder

Short Story Collection
The Luckiest Man in the World (winner of the Drue Heinz Literature Prize)

Creative Nonfiction
Heart So Hungry (also published as *North of Unknown*)

Other Mystery/Thriller Titles at Riverdale Avenue Books

Of White Snakes and Misshapen Owls:
The Charlotte Olmes Mystery Series
By Debra Hyde

The Tattered Heiress:
Book Two of the Charlotte Olmes Mystery Series
By Debra Hyde

Trashy Chic
Book One in the Bertie Mallowan Mystery Series
By Cathy Lubenski

Snarky Park
Book Two in the Bertie Mallowan Mystery Series
By Cathy Lubenski

Fifty Shades of Grey Fedora
By Robert J. Randisi

Sixers:
Volume One of the Macroglint Trilogy
By John Patrick Kavanagh

Weekend at Prism
Volume Two of the Macroglint Trilogy
By John Patrick Kavanagh

Sanctuary Creek
Volume Three of the Macroglint Trilogy
By John Patrick Kavanagh

The Ripper Letter: Book One in the Heart of Darkness series
By Katherine Ramsland

Track the Ripper: Book Two in the Heart of Darkness Series
By Katherine Ramsland

Made in the
USA
Lexington, KY